ALL THE DEAD YALE MEN

ALL THE DEAD YALE MEN

[CRAIG NOVA]

| COUNTERPOINT | BERKELEY, CALIFORNIA |

Library of Congress Cataloging-in-Publication Data

Nova, Craig.
All the dead Yale men : a novel / Craig Nova.
pages cm
ISBN 978-1-58243-828-3 (hardcover)
1. Lawyers—Massachusetts—Boston—Fiction. 2. Family secrets—Fiction.
3. Parenting—Fiction. I. Title.

PS3564.O86A79 2013
813'.54—dc23
2013001213

Cover design by Faceout Studios
Interior design by Elyse Strongin, Neuwirth & Associates, Inc.

COUNTERPOINT PRESS
1919 Fifth Street
Berkeley, CA 94710
www.counterpointpress.com

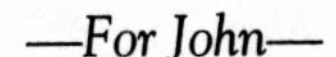

—For John—

THOU mastering me

God! giver of breath and bread;

World's strand, sway of the sea;

Lord of living and dead;

Thou hast bound bones and veins in me, fastened me flesh,

And after it almost unmade, what with dread,

Thy doing: and dost thou touch me afresh?

Over again I feel thy finger and find thee.

—GERARD MANLEY HOPKINS

ALL THE DEAD YALE MEN

[CHAPTER ONE]

THE ODD THING is that when I looked into how I was being cheated, not because of the money but because of the principle of the thing (fathers shouldn't cheat sons), I discovered things about my family, and my grandmother in particular, that I never dreamed possible. Dark indeed are the family secrets that never quite disappear.

Of course, everyone thought my father, Chip Mackinnon, was a spook. They confirmed this suspicion by the number of spooks who showed up at his funeral. I knew more definitely than that, since he was cheating me, and I wanted to find out not only why, but how, too. It wasn't hard to catch him at the spy part. He wasn't a very good spy, but then this ease of catching him explains why the CIA is such a bunch of fuck-ups and incompetents.

The cheating was another matter.

I was going to bring up the fact that he was cheating me on the day he died, which began with what would have been a high-speed chase and crash on Memorial Drive in Cambridge, Massachusetts. That is, it would have been a high-speed chase if the cops had been around to see it. I was going to mention the cheating as leverage, since I needed advice, and the kind of advice that only my father could give. He may have been a fuck-up, but he was good in a bad spot. And since I was in a bad spot, who else could help?

But he *was* a good man in a bad spot, and this was the trouble: he had been in so many bad spots that he couldn't take ordinary life too seriously.

And what is real trouble? Well, my father had been a pursuit pilot in the Second World War. He trained in Texas and was shipped across the Atlantic on an aircraft carrier, from which he took off and flew over Africa with the green canopy of the jungle below and the perfect circle made by the blur of the propeller. He ended up in North Africa, and there he was shot down as he tried to bomb Rommel's headquarters. Then it was three years in a prison camp in Poland, but when the war was ending, he and the other men in his camp were marched back to Germany. This was in the winter of 1945. It was snowing, and the men walked along the road, their jackets thin and worn, and often they had only rags tied to their feet for boots, which were black here and there where the bleeding sores from frostbite oozed through the cloth. The woods were mostly pine, dark trunks topped by an evergreen shimmer. The men walked toward Germany. They ate what they could: bark, leather from belts, anything that would give them the illusion of food. A good friend of my father's, a man named Bob Walters, sat down at the side of the road in a brown ditch the color of chocolate in the snow. A guard told him to get up, and when Bob Walters shook his head, too hungry to go on, the guard shot him in the head. The other men trudged toward the west, not even looking at that corpse in the ditch. Many others sat down and died, their eyes, my father said, looking at someplace infinitely far away, or not anyplace at all.

My father, who had learned German in the camp, took a guard by the sleeve and jerked him around.

"We're starving," said my father.

The guard shrugged.

"We know you are losing the war," he said. "And when it's over, there are going to be some trials. You understand? I'll make sure they know about you. That is, unless you get us some food and blankets. Right. Now."

The guard, in his long leather coat, which was lined with fleece, in his warm boots, his winter hat, reached to his belt and removed his pistol. After all, wasn't that the way to settle this? The snow began to fall again, big flakes like soap suds, and the cool tick of them on my father's face, he said, was like the most gentle touch, a reminder of all the delicacy of life, those moments that existed, I imagine, like the thrill of being in bed with a woman you loved, the surprise of some lovely moment, a kiss, say, when you least expected it. The feet of the marching men made that odd, almost muddy sound in the snow. The guard looked into my father's eyes and my father looked back. It might as well have been just the two of them, separate from everyone else in the world. So they hung there, feeling that snow, the gentle flakes of which fluttered down to touch them on the nose and cheeks. My father told me he was drawn to the bore of the guard's pistol, the intensity of it like the night sky, or the skin of the blackest snake imaginable: the emptiness of that small hole was the place that made him think of absolutely nothing, of a kind of exhausted entropy. This is what he had left after three years of being hungry and scared. And, my father said, the darkness was familiar, since the odor of gun oil, from the deer hunts he had been on as a kid, seemed familiar, too. The scent was almost reassuring. The guard nodded and put the pistol against my father's forehead. Black birds squawked in the woods. A soldier squatted in the snow with dysentery: the farting, gassy noise hung there like a cry of despair. The guard put the pistol away. The blankets and food appeared.

Of course, given what I faced, the threats, the possibility for disaster, I wanted advice from the man who could stand up to a German guard and who understood what it was like to be at the edge, where it was possible to vanish. He could stop on a snowy road in Poland and see the way things were and take action, too, and precise action at that. He told me he wasn't scared. The time for that was long since past.

And, as for his being a spy, well, you can make out of this what you want. My grandfather, a hard-drinking man with a love of mint juleps, and whose nose was covered with a web of veins the color of a radish, had set up a trust that paid me three hundred dollars a month. When my wife, Alexandra, and I began to have children after I had finished at Yale, just like my father, and Harvard Law, just like my father, and when I had become not a practicing lawyer but a district attorney, I needed a little extra money. So, I figured it was time to ask my father just what the hell he had been doing with the money. I had been paid three hundred a month for close to fifteen years, even though the stock market had increased a couple of thousand percent. As I say, it wasn't the money, but the principle.

The house where my father lived, alone then after his second wife had died, was off a small street in Cambridge: only four blocks long, but yet it still had a vista, or was long enough to suggest the road tapering off into the distance, and in the summertime it was shaded by trees that were so old they made an arch over the road.

In those days my father was a professor at the Fleishman School of International Relations, a breeding ground for spooks if there ever was one.

Even then, the hall of my father's house had a lingering scent of mold, as though a leak hadn't been fixed. The walls were a sort of sickly green, and the pictures on the wall had come from my grandfather's house: schmaltzy scenes, mostly, of huntsmen and hounds, water stained, too. So, I waited in the dowdy scent. I didn't think my father would take too long with his student. They were together in the living room.

My father wore a blazer and a blue shirt and a pair of gray pants, his bald head shining like a Christmas tree ornament, his hands on an open folder. He was far too intent on the paper and his conversation to notice me. On the other side of the table, Faro, one of his Latin American students, sat with the last of a Negroni in his hand, which had such short, soft fingers. This was my father's favorite drink. Vermouth and Campari. With some gin added for, as my father said, "wallop." Faro wore clothes that must have been bought in Argentina, knockoffs of American blue jeans and sneakers. A sweater that was ten years out of date. A cardigan.

"So," said my father. "The base you saw on your last visit home was one from Grupo de Caza or Grupo Técnico?"

"Grupo de Caza," said Faro. "A fighter group."

"Hmpf," said my father. "Good. Good. And I wonder if you could see the airplanes?"

"Yes," said Faro. "I saw them."

"You know there's a difference between the Mirage III interceptor and the IAI Dagger," said my father.

"I know the difference," said Faro. "I think these were Mirage IIIs. But maybe a couple of Daggers were there, too. They are transitioning, aren't they?"

I shifted my weight from one foot to another, and the floorboards squeaked, the sound like an animal in a trap.

"Let me take a note," my father said. "Hey, is that you, Frank? Well, go to the kitchen and get yourself a drink."

"Something smells funny," I said.

"A leak in the cellar," said my father. "Faro and I were just talking about his thesis. The movement of Argentinean capital in crisis years . . . "

"Oh," I said. "I'll get a drink. You want me to call a plumber?"

"That's OK," said my father. He closed the folder. "I'll do it."

In the kitchen, the voices sounded like a fly buzzing against a window, or two flies, one bigger than another. What kind of answer was I going to get about the money, given the nature of the discussion in the other room? The truth? Was I such a child as to expect that?

In the living room, Faro and my father sat back now, business done, Faro telling a story about a woman who was "cutting a swath" through Buenos Aires.

"I'll catch you another time," I said.

"It's best to call first," said my father. "You know. We have a lot of students writing a thesis at this time of the year."

"Sure, sure," I said. "Good to see you, Faro."

"It's always an honor, Frank," said Faro. He stood up and bowed. Or did he click his heels?

This, of course, took place years ago, as I said, when my daughter, Pia, was just a kid, but my father kept at it right along. Now she is graduating from Yale, and she came in to see me recently with a thick letter from Harvard Law. This part of the family seems hardwired, although, to be honest, that was where my trouble started. I tried to keep the hardwired part of it going.

Still, years ago, I had heard this conversation about conditions in South America, and in the modern age, my father thought it was a great idea to train and arm the Taliban to fight the Russians but couldn't see further down the road to what might happen after the Russians went home. Whenever my father and I talked about a politician in, say, Bolivia, who was causing trouble, my father always said, looking into the bottom of his Negroni, "You could always shoot him." Then he rattled the ice. "I don't mean we'd do it ourselves. You know, just encourage the right people."

"Right people?" I said.

"Well, Frank, I hate to be the one to break the news to you, but 'right' is one of those words like an eel."

"It means something to me," I said.

"No kidding?" he said. "Well, let's put the case, Frank, that you can save ten men by killing one. So, what's it going to be? Are you going to let ten men die for your sweet ideas about things? Isn't it time you grew up?"

"You mean growing up means killing people?"

"I wouldn't put it just like that," he said. "Not exactly. I'd include a little wiggle room in there. You'd be surprised how important wiggle room is."

"What if I'm not interested in something like that?"

He rattled his Negroni, as though it was a gourd in a primitive ceremony.

"When I was in prison camp, the best didn't make it. And you know what? They weren't interested in wiggle room, either."

"I'd like to think I would have made it," I said.

"Do you think so, Frank?" he said. "It comes at a price. And you pay interest on it. Every year."

On the night before the high-speed chase, I called my father and said, "Look. I need some advice."

"Jesus, Frank," said my father. "You must be in deep shit if you are going to ask Chip Mackinnon for advice. Have you put the

Mackinnon rules to work? Number one: never put someone in a position where they can say no to you; number two: if you are applying for a job, don't ask what the employer can do for you. Explain what you can do for him."

"It's more complicated than that," I said.

"No shit," he said. "Well, come on over tomorrow evening. My Latin American students are going to come over to my house for a piñata party."

He gargled on the phone. I guess he was having a big drink of his Negroni.

"I'll give you a little word of advice, Frank," he said. "It's Chip Mackinnon's third rule. I've never mentioned it before. But this is it: the truth is a dangerous substance."

[CHAPTER TWO]

SOMETIMES IT IS all a muddle. Or, maybe it is better to say that I have discovered some rules, too, and one of them is that events, particularly trouble, don't come with an even distribution, but in clumps, as though one large event has a gravity that attracts others. And so fifteen years ago, I didn't give up on how my father was cheating me. But this refusal to give up just proved out my own first law.

I am a lawyer, a prosecutor, and I used to think I was a good one. As I said, Harvard Law for me and my father, Chip Mackinnon, an apprenticeship in a law office in Michigan for my grandfather, Pop Mackinnon, which apprenticeship he never forgot and always wanted to disguise, as though his bourbon nose, his politics, his desperation to be loved, even when he was in his sixties, were signs of where he came from and how he was never going to escape it. If only he could have remade his history after he had turned forty, although I hesitate to imagine what a gaudy story that would have been.

My grandfather practiced customs law, and my father didn't do much at all except fritter away the money my grandfather had managed to get his hands on. I didn't want to use the law to avoid responsibility, as my father believed, but to use it to make a sort of order, which I thought of as a variety of beauty, at least in the beginning.

"Prosecutor?" said my father. "I paid for Harvard Law and you're going to be a prosecutor? What kind of money is there in that?"

"I thought you wanted me to do the right thing," I said.

"Yeah, yeah," he said. "It sounded like a good idea at the time. That's why I gave you every conceivable advantage. And now the birds have come home to roost."

Then he got tears in his eyes, told me he loved me, and began a story about the WWII prison camp he had been in: how he made liquor from Red Cross raisins.

So, fifteen years ago, I had started in. The first thing is that my grandfather, Pop Mackinnon, had a different idea of what a gentleman was. This, of course, just shows how antiquated he was and how much things have changed. Who, these days, talks about being a gentleman? Some of us don't use the word at all, and we try to do the right thing, but we keep our mouths shut.

My grandfather thought that a gentleman should have a farm, and so he bought a place on the Delaware River, about two hours from New York. The land was sixteen hundred acres with a farmhouse, two barns, a fish pond surrounded by a fieldstone edge in front of the house. My grandfather built a stone house there, too, down in the woods, and my father always sat in it, at the hunts he and I organized, with an expression that showed that the stone house had been built for my father's brother, a man my grandfather loved more than him, who had been killed in the war. So my father had inherited the farm and this stone house for the sole reason that he had survived. And sometimes I think this sense of not being loved is the key to it all.

His land also had a small greenhouse where Alexandra and I had gone when we were first going out together. A stream with brook trout ran in a ravine not far from the house, and around it the land supported deer, a bear or two, foxes, bats, wild turkeys, ruffed grouse, and copperheads. All of these creatures had been written about by my grandmother, Mrs. Catherine Mackinnon, in a series of notebooks. Of course, when I knew my father was cheating me, I thought these notebooks might give me a clue, a hint, something useful to use against him.

Well, the first thing is that Mackinnon's third law is damn right. The truth is a dangerous substance.

There weren't sixteen hundred acres anymore. My father had sold a thousand acres to the Girls Club of America, although, my father being the lawyer he was, he retained the rights to hunt the Girls Club's land and to use the original farmhouse, the one his father had owned, to store things he had no place for. From time to time recently the Girls Club complained about precisely where the property lines were, and other things, too, like a bear who spent most of his time on my father's land but who also liked to get into the Girls Club's garbage and to scare those girls from New York City and Philadelphia, who had always thought bears existed only on the Nature Channel.

So, when I was an assistant district attorney and wanted to find out how I was being cheated, I drove from Cambridge, where I lived, to the farmhouse, where my grandfather's things were stored in the attic. My grandmother's notebooks were a good place to start, particularly because of all the Classical Mackinnon's Laws, the most intense was this. My grandmother may have been secretive, but in her notebooks she never told a lie about anything. Ever.

At Hartford I got on 84 west and started the long drive to that piece of land that my grandfather had owned and left to my father, who more and more was oppressed by it, and even though he went there every year to hunt deer in the fall, and brought me along, and even though he felt it was his charge to hang on to the place, he was having trouble doing just that. The taxes were going up. People vandalized the buildings when he wasn't there. And so, I guess, that explained some of the motivation to keep money that should have been mine. As I say, it wasn't the three hundred dollars. It was the principal of something being violated between father and son, particularly when the cheating seems to be a sort of extension of some cheap CIA trick.

Close to Port Jervis, the Delaware Valley stretched out in a floodplain with five shades of green and that gunmetal mist beneath a sky that was a little pale, but still reassuring, as though all this was harsh but not unforgiving. Then the road went through Port Jervis, where the last business still thriving was a bathing suit factory. Even as you went by it you could feel the injustice, the wrongness of the fact that heavy, cold women sat in an enormous room to sew bathing suits all winter so that young, thin, and beautiful women could wear them to go to the beach.

The maples were in full leaf, full of moisture, shiny, the promise of them so keen as to make me think fall would never come. The lichen was copper-colored, green and flaky, on the stone walls that lined the fields. Here and there a deer flashed a white tail and disappeared, its coat that late spring gray. The turn to the gate was a hard left, and under the canopy of pines, the air smelled damp and ominous. The ponds came into view, and then the house with white siding and black shutters, the pond in front, surrounded by a stone lip, the water as still as fate (at least while it was hidden), the surface marked here and there by an insect that hatched with an anxious rush.

The house itself was of medium size, with white siding and black shutters, and had a porch that went around three sides. It was here that my grandfather Pop liked to sit and drink a mint julep and tell jokes that even today I would hesitate to tell to someone at work. I stopped in front of the house.

My shadow on the porch of my grandfather's farmhouse looked as if it were cut from a silky fabric dragged up the steps. Of course, we had the right to use the attic for storage. But still, I had qualms. Fathers shouldn't cheat a good son, but because someone is dead didn't make me free to dig into her most private secrets.

The farmhouse door opened with that sigh of recognition, as though it had been waiting, or so it seemed, all along. What had taken me so long? Of course, if you are frightened enough everything seems to revolve around you and to make you feel important. I guess it is this that saves you from panic.

The stairs creaked, too, just the way they did when my grandfather and grandmother lived here and when my father had grown up here, at least when he was home from school, and the way it did when I was here for vacations, too. Then I emerged into the hall upstairs, and off of it, here and there, were the doors to the bedrooms, which the Girls Club had made sterile and sad: all single beds, as though this place, so dedicated to young women, was training them to be alone.

The bulb in the attic made a stale light. And there, among the old bureaus and rugs that smelled of dogs, in with the rack of suits, all good tweed from Scotland, next to those lamps made of bamboo and the chairs that had come from a furniture designer's notion of what an Anglo-Indian outpost would look like (my grandfather loved this look: if he could have imported tigers for us to shoot instead of deer, he would have done it in a minute), was the chest. Made of canvas. Leather corners and straps. Old brass buckles, so tarnished as to look like time made visible. The top of the trunk had a little pouch for a card, and my grandmother had written on one that had been white but was the color of yellow teeth, "Catherine Mackinnon."

She had kept notebooks all her life, mostly devoted to the animals she had seen around the farmhouse and on this land. Here, in those leather-bound notebooks, were her descriptions of animals, written at the depths of her loneliness and despair, animals she had described so accurately and with such love. Her books were written in an ungraceful hand, although a neater, crisper script was there, too, just a page, but my grandmother had kept it.

Her discipline was obvious, her refusal to give into her despair as she wrote these things: it was a tensile strength that hung there in the dust of the attic, or in that zone where I now existed, in the musty stale light between the living and the dead.

I sat down on one of those phony Anglo-Indian bamboo and rattan chairs, and while I had only glanced at these years before, I now started in earnest and opened a notebook, which cracked at the spine, like a bone breaking in a violated grave:

> Human beings are the least natural of creatures. They always want what they can't have and are never happy with what they do have. Capable of such bravery and such cruelty, able to lie where they need to be truthful, truthful where they should keep their mouths shut. The female of the species is constantly available to mate, from the age of fourteen or so, when she will begin to search for a mate. The male of the

species does not understand her. When she looks for a mate, when she is enticing and revealing, when she wears a dress that shows the whiteness of her skin or hints at the shape of her breasts, when she walks in such a way that shows the movement of her hips, as though they were keeping time, or marked off the scale of life, as though it was a ruler, she is only having a little fun, just enjoying the power of life. The male of the species thinks she is connected to him, when she is not. She is only enjoying a little power, and still needs to be won over. After mating, birth comes in nine months, the young cared for depending on the deepest mysteries of all, the depth of love: this species is not different, in kind, from other creatures, aside from one critical fact: this love is known by the creatures involved. They know what it is, and either it makes them the best they can be, or the worst. They can be brave when confronted, or cowardly, and it is not known, in advance, how they will behave. The males tend to congregate to tell lies, and the females tend to congregate to tell partial truths. They are not a happy species, aside from particular moments, and these are the ones they live for. Their biggest flaw is when they try to do what is right, but dismiss the obvious objections to this, those things that will come back to haunt them. Tall, bipeds, beautiful, particularly since they know their time is limited.

So, I was at the habitat of family secrets that, of course, itched to escape. And what did she have to say about sacrifice and love?

She wrote, when my father had come home from Germany, "How changed Chip is. Wounded in a way that I will never be able to touch, let alone heal. This is the misery of being a mother of a man who has gone to war." And, as far as the brother who didn't come back was concerned, she wrote, "How do you live with the knowledge that the only way you could remember someone was by the grief of his absence?" To forget the grief was to forget the person, since that's all she had left.

This was dated fall 1950. The year I was born.

• • •

She continued:

> Of course, I have been writing about animals in this book, and they seem to me, of course, to be a glimpse, just the details of the glory of god, his delight in life and beauty. For instance, I wrote this about bears: "It is the bear's solitariness, his inability to be social, the prison-like quality of his life that interests me. A bear has no muscles in his face, nothing in cheeks or forehead to show anger, fear, or the desire to be friendly. He is confined behind that brownish skin and fur, in that lipped and thick expression he carries . . . . " But now that I am getting older, I want to say the truth to myself: I wasn't describing just the bears here, which, of course, are such mysterious creatures, but people, too, if only to make sense of them. For instance, I was thinking of Pop, my husband, when I wrote about bears, since he was so imprisoned by his lack of love and his attempt to obtain it. And, of course, he thought it could be bought, like anything else, and he often negotiated with Chip when what my husband wanted was not control but the lack of need for it. He really wanted the warmth of being loved. But Pop just didn't know how to do it. He was stuck with the details of financial deals; a worse way of getting love I can't imagine. Pop negotiated. Chip did, too. How much better it would have been if they could have done something else, especially when Chip took up with that Jean Cooper and almost destroyed us all.

• • •

So, I thought, that's something. My father had had an involvement, an affair. I always wondered why, after my mother died, my father chased certain kinds of women and married one who died of cirrhosis of the liver.

• • •

Then, in my grandmother's notebook, this:

> At a certain age, you begin to think about romantic moments, and while no one would have dreamed of the possibility, since I am the most discreet woman I have ever met, I think it is time to talk about a romance, if you can call it that, of my own . . . . Of course, I mean, after I was married. He was not an educated man, and, if I had to say what drew me to him, it was the color of his eyes, the texture of his skin, and an odor that was like paradise . . . and some other qualities that, from some perspectives, would have been difficulties, but which I found mysterious, as though he was in touch with the largest unknowns there are.
>
> Of course, when Pop found out, and he did (I am still ashamed at how much I hurt him), his reaction was to negotiate: how were his financial affairs going to be settled. For me, and for the next generation, Chip's children . . . . Could he control what I had felt with the promise of money? Could he hold my children as financial hostages, too?

• • •

My grandmother saw behind the surface of things, and this was too bald. She was hiding something, and more was embedded here than such a causal admission. If you want to hide something, you admit only part of it and leave the rest in the dark. And so that was how I was left. A little light. A lot of dark. But what was it? What did she want to hide? More to the point, too, was this: how did the hidden element affect me?

[CHAPTER THREE]

NOW, IN 2005, that I am in so much trouble, I often think of this line of lawyers, my grandfather, my father, me, and at least the possibility of my daughter becoming one, too, although that is part of the trouble I am in. It is as though the lawyers had some secret they passed down from generation to generation.

My father got into his car, an old Cadillac that he kept running in a sort of half-assed way, and drove along Storrow Drive, flipping other drivers the bone, honking the horn, and thinking how he was going to get away with pulling the wool over the eyes of his students at the Fleishman School of International Relations.

I've had plenty of time to think about how he used these drives to show his disapproval of the world. And when I think about this I wonder if somehow I passed this quality of fierce defiance from my father to my daughter and that she defied me in the same way my father defied me, as though I was caught in a vise of generations. Maybe my daughter just saw him in action and that was enough, although when she was young, she used to do imitations of him. "I'll just put a little gin in my wine," she'd say. "Who can tell? That's the beauty of gin. You want to see me walk a straight line?" Then she did just that, in the same way he did when drunk: with great precision and perfect balance produced by a monastic concentration. It had gotten him out of a lot of scrapes with the cops.

My father approached children with the same attitude as when he flew a mission as a pursuit pilot over North Africa in World War II: nothing to worry about. Piece of cake. Just come in low so they can't hear you coming. I translated this advice for me like this: Jesus, Frank, so you are having real trouble with your daughter, but daughters are going to drive you nuts. It's hard for them to tell you the truth, so you'll have to guess at what they really mean. It isn't a mean lie, just a sort of diplomatic maneuver. "Why can't you understand me?" they'll say if you miss the code. Mackinnon's Syndrome, he said.

But there is another matter between fathers and daughters. Not only do daughters have a mystical instinct that scares the father, the father has a fear of being diminished in his daughter's eyes. The last thing he wants is for her to sum him up and find him lacking. No matter what anyone says, it's a high-wire act right to the end: a daughter wants a father, and a father wants to be just that, and if he falls, if he shows that he is a moral klutz, it is a terror for all concerned.

• • •

My troubles began when my daughter Pia got involved with a young man who went by the name of Aurlon Miller. Sometimes he called himself the Wizard. His parents had conceived him on an acid trip in the mountains of Southeast Asia. Aurlon had, according to his mother, a blue aura. That's what he told my daughter. He wore a gray cape. And sometimes, I have to say, he appeared to have a sort of smoky haze around him, as though he emerged from some underworld where the smoke is the color of an iris and as cool as the mist of dry ice. He had the habit, too, of staring just over your head to make you think he was looking right through you.

You'd think this would be easy enough to handle. But, as in all disasters, the beginning is often disguised, and what initially seemed like ordinary foolishness was just hiding something else.

On that drive in his current death-trap Cadillac along the Charles River in Cambridge, after five or six Negronis and a half jug of Almaden wine that had been in the back of his refrigerator for a month, my father flipped the other drivers the finger and honked the horn. This time my father found himself behind one of those young men in Cambridge who ride their bikes with a devotion that verges on the pathological. This one, though, was in the middle of the road, just before the Harvard Boathouse. Maybe the biker was getting ready to make a left turn, and had just pulled out from the right-hand lane, bright in his spandex and reflector strips, all lit up for my father to come out of his boozy haze and to discover just what the Cadillac was about to run over.

The Cadillac, by the way, never had much in the way of brakes, and often when I had come for a visit to the house where I grew up in Cambridge (and where my father still lived, although I had moved to Brattle Street) I'd see a pinkish brake fluid on the apron, sort of like blood from a reptile or some creature that doesn't have a heart, not really, not a mammalian heart that is warm, but cold and more or less indifferent. That's what that pink stuff always reminded me of, although for my father it was just a matter of confronting that coldness, of showing that a devil-may-care attitude was the answer to everything. When he contemplated that brake fluid, he smiled, looked at me with a sort of challenge, and said, "Well, there's still an emergency brake. See you later."

My father came up behind the biker. I know these things because of the investigation that the police did, and, of course, because everyone in Cambridge knew my father and wanted to tell me about it, not to mention that I had enough experience with him myself to take a good guess. Usually, when he was driving along the river he liked to go about twenty miles over the speed limit and weave in and out of traffic, proving he still had the reactions and the skill of the pursuit pilot. The odd thing is that often he was able, through sheer physical ability, to get out of trouble that would have killed a man with lesser reactions. This time a car had just passed him on the right, and so when he jerked the wheel to avoid the biker, he found that he was about to rear-end the car in the right lane.

So, he was faced with a decision. And the more I think about it, the more it seems to me that this was a perfect expression of the difficulties he faced, almost always of his own making. Drinking, of course, has a lot to do with this.

My father was faced with the decision of whether or not to flatten the bicyclist or to drive over the curb and toward the river. And even this had some disadvantages, since the apron of grass between the river and the sidewalk was filled with men doing sit-ups, sunbathing women, Harvard undergraduates mostly, working on their tans, and then young men who were out there playing Frisbee.

My father turned toward the curb. I guess he was going about sixty at this point and so the car cleared the curb with a jolt that was moderated by the speed, since he was going so fast as to smooth out the bump as the car became airborne. Not for long, I guess, but ten feet or so. The women on the grass looked up, as though someone had called a name that they couldn't quite hear. One of the Frisbee players made a long jump, a dive for the toy, and he was suspended, like a still from a Coke commercial, as my father found that while having made the first decision to avoid both the car and the biker he now faced another choice, between the women on the grass and the man who hung in the air.

My father tried to avoid this decision for as long as he could, just the way he avoided everything else in his life. His reactions compensated, or so he thought, for all his failures of decisiveness. It made him think, when he got out of some physical mess, that he was still a pursuit pilot in World War II who had just done the impossible once again.

So, he turned toward the young women in their bikinis, their skin a little moist in the hot sun, their arms and breasts covered with light, their hair bright as only youth can make it, all filaments, the flash of promise itself. Then he turned toward the Frisbee player, who had now landed and who looked at the oncoming car with an idiotic acceptance of the facts: there he was, arm out, holding a pink toy while he was getting ready to die. He smiled a sort of apologetic smile and closed his eyes.

My father then jerked the wheel the other way, and the car slid sideways on the grass, the rear end coming around like a sling filled with a rock, and this sideways motion, actually the beginning of a spin, let him get around the kid with the Frisbee, between two young women in their bathing suits, who now sat up, holding their tops with a modest tug. My father went into the Charles River, where the first two tires hit the mud and then the rest of the car flipped right over, the water coming up in a silver spray.

The car sank.

A couple of sculling boats rowed over to where the car went in and the scullers sat there, oars trapped between chest and knees as they stared at the dark water, the rising bubbles, and an oil slick. The young women in their bikinis came down to the water and the Frisbee players did, too.

"Jesus," said one of the boys. "Did you see that?"

"A close one, all right," said another.

"All right," said one. "I'm going in."

The car was upside down under the water, and the door was about a foot into the mud of the bottom. The Frisbee player held onto the door handle and pulled, and while he was suspended in murk of the Charles River, the light came down in long, yellow, chemically tinted rays. My father hovered, his face in a bubble of air that was at the bottom of the car, although it came up as far as the window. The air bubble was getting smaller.

"Push," said the Frisbee player. "Push," although under water it came out as "Hooosh, hooosh." My father swung around and put his feet against the door, and then the player came up to the surface.

"I need help," he said.

One of the young women jumped in, too, and then she hovered in front of the window. She joined the young man, both outside the window where my father went up and down, into the bubble and then back to the window so he could look out, like a fish in an aquarium, with eyes that never really seemed to show concern about anything, not even dying. The young woman's hair floated around her head and she brushed it away with a sort of sultry, impatient gesture. My father took a deep breath in the bubble and dropped down so that his face was just opposite hers, only the thickness of the glass between him and pink, full lips on the other side. Then my father went back to pushing all the harder.

The bubbles rose to the surface with a steady quality and broke into the pale air with a constant *tick, tick, tick*. Then a tow truck that had been going along by the river stopped and a young woman waved it over. The truck driver backed up over the grass and unhitched the hook of the winch, which one of the young men attached under the Cadillac, to part of the frame, and the driver threw a lever. The winch made a shrill grinding, and for a while it looked as though the car wasn't going to be pulled out of the river but that the truck was going to be winched into the water. The oil slick was pretty big by now.

Then the car emerged from the water, dripping like some kind of monster, half machine and half animal that was climbing from the slime of the river onto dry land to give birth. My father kicked through the window and the last of the water rushed out, like amniotic fluid, and he slithered out onto the grass.

"Weren't you scared?" said one of the young women.

"Scared?" said my father. "I can hold my breath forever."

"Oh," said the young woman. She hitched up her top a little more.

"Come on," said my father. "Let's go up to the Wursthaus for a drink."

"I don't think so," said one of the young women.

"Why not?" said my father.

"I've got to study," she said.

"Oh," said my father. "That. I wouldn't worry about that."

"I don't think you need anything more to drink," said the young woman.

"That's where you're wrong," said my father. "Just look at this mess."

He walked over the grass, his sneakers filled with water, which made a steady *squish, squish* as he came up to the sidewalk, went up to the boathouse, crossed the street, and walked up to the Wursthaus in Harvard Square. He was still there when the Cambridge police came in. Both of them were in uniform, and while one was young and fit, as though he spent his off-hours biking along the river, the older one was heavy in the stomach and his skin seemed as pale and gray as an oyster. Their leather belts creaked, and their radios made some static that was interrupted every now and then by a dispatcher's uninflected voice.

"Jesus, Chip, you've got to stop doing things like this," said the older one.

"Come on, Billy," said my father. "Sit down."

"Jesus, Chip. You've got to listen."

"Not yet," said my father. "Not yet."

"When," said Billy Meerschaum, "just when is that going to be?"

"You'll see," said my father.

"We're going to have to cite you," said the other, younger cop.

"What for?" said my father.

"Leaving the scene of an accident," said the younger one. My father read the cop's name tag, white letters on black plastic.

"Drunk driving," said Billy Meerschaum.

"I've been here having a drink for a while now," my father said.

"You did that on purpose," said the young one.

"Prove when I had a drink," said my father. "I know the law."

"Yes, Chip," said Billy. "But there's more to life than that."

"You're kidding yourself," said my father.

The cops stood next to the table where my father sat. The Wursthaus had a sort of woody quality, and the dark wainscoting had a shine to it from the years of greasy food that had been cooked there. But now, according to what Billy Meerschaum told me at the funeral, the place seemed somehow frozen or suspended, as though this moment, which had come at the end of a lot of moments with my father in Cambridge, was a variety of milestone; that while my father had been stopped for drunk driving and had even attended a course for people who had been arrested this way, he had never run into the river before.

Meerschaum wrote out the ticket, just for leaving the scene of an accident. At the top, in his block printing, neat as an architect, he wrote, "May 25th." Then he passed it over.

"In the merry month of May . . . ," sang my father.

"We could arrest you," said the younger cop.

"Shitload of paperwork," said my father. "And what would it accomplish?"

"Not much," said Meerschaum.

"So, why don't you sit down and have a drink, like old friends?" said my father.

"I'm not your friend," said the younger cop.

"I'm going off duty," said Meerschaum.

The younger cop gave him a look and then said, "Fine."

Billy Meerschaum sat down. My father told Meerschaum a joke about a Russian gymnast and a French seagull, and it was so obscene that Meerschaum, a man of forty who had been a cop for fifteen years, couldn't tell it to me at the funeral without blushing.

Then my father got up and started walking home.

He went through Harvard Square, where the panhandlers sat here and there on the sidewalk, one with a sign that said, "Blind and with cerebral palsy, hit by fire engine . . . ," and where a man, known as the Raver, stood in the middle of the sidewalk and spoke, in a loud clear voice, about how he had been up in a flying saucer and that he had learned from the aliens, who were wearing uniforms of people who worked at Burger King, something called Zen and the Art of the Cosmic. He said, for instance, that life was just a breath, that it came and went. This is how, he said, one could appreciate the beauty of the stars. Here was the way, he said, the shortness of time is what makes for the possibility of beauty.

My father came along in sneakers that were almost dried out, but still making a little sound like a washing machine that won't drain completely.

The driveway of his house was filled with cars, and even from the street my father heard the students who had come into the house, at his forgotten invitation, to have a piñata party. They were used to his forgetting. My father taught diplomatic history and had made friends with his Latin American students (all the better to say, one afternoon, "Hey, Cedro, here's an old friend from Washington I'd like you to meet—a good guy"), and they came every year near the end of May to drink and celebrate the spring with a piñata, tequila, and food that came from the cuisines of Argentina (steaks, mostly), Central America (fried plantain), and Mexico (tacos with cilantro).

My father came into the house and then to the backyard, where the piñata was suspended from the frame for the awning of the porch. Ten or so students stood around, dancing to Mexican brass, and when my father came outside, they shouted, and one of them, a dark-haired Mexican woman, took him under the piñata where they danced and where the other students formed a circle around them. The students had made margaritas and now the pitchers were almost empty, covered with little rills of water where the mist on the glass had condensed. All of the students had been drinking on empty stomachs, and they had gone from nervous sobriety to outright hilarity, faces red, eyes bloodshot, shirts untucked, straps of dresses off shoulders. My father came in and drank the last of the margaritas. It was a May afternoon, warm, seductive, right at the end of the academic year.

The piñata was bright red, covered with small curls of shiny paper, and its legs were stiff. The head of the thing was like a small ironing board, and its eyes were as dark as a can of black shoe polish. One of the students pulled on a rope as the students blindfolded one and then another, making jokes about bondage and how it was done in Buenos Aries after dark. Then they went after the piñata with a baseball bat. The students couldn't have hit the piñata if it had been hanging there like a balloon, let alone being moved up and down on a clothesline through a pulley. But here is where my father's reflexes came in.

They blindfolded him and gave him the Louisville Slugger, and he stood there, in the middle of the circle of the men and women from Latin American, mostly short and overweight, some with bad skin, all of them swaying back and forth. He listened to the pulleys as the clothesline that controlled the piñata ran back and forth, the squeak of the pulleys mixed in with a little rumble, too. He waited until it was on its way down and then, anticipating where it would be, he took a good cut.

I often think that the explosion of the piñata was like that in the middle of his head, in the depths of his brain, which took place just then: the red piñata exploded, and the candy inside was wrapped in red foil, so that it appeared like drops of blood as it soared upward from the power of the swing, the bits of candy forming perfect arcs against that spring sky. The piñata broke, and the shreds of starched newspaper from which it had been constructed showered down too, the print, the bits of black and white photographs all appearing like memories that one could almost recall or that were in the midst of somehow being forgotten. The gray flak with red centers, the heat of the desert sand, a first kiss with a woman who wore red lipstick, who pressed herself against him so he could feel her heat. Then the red candies hit the patio with a light tinkling, a rain of shiny, moist-looking clots. Then the students ran to pick it up and my father fell.

My father used to love to do this, to fall down, and he often did it when he first came home or in the midst of a party like this, and so the students didn't think much of it until he began to wet his pants. He refused to answer when they asked if he was all right, his mouth moving in an awkward, fish-like way. The students dropped the candy and called an ambulance and they called me, too.

I got there just before the ambulance, and when I came onto the patio my father opened his eyes and stared at me for a moment. He strained against one dead hand, as though it was tied to the ground, and then he gestured slowly with the other. I leaned down. He still smelled of the Charles River, the drinks in the Wursthaus, the margaritas, too, but this was his usual scent. That is, his scent without the oil and piss of the river.

"Are you all right?" I said.

"No," he said. "This is it."

He strained against that one arm on the ground.

"Not much time, Frank. Too bad, since I know you're in trouble. Jesus, it must be something if you are coming to me."

"I was going to talk about it today."

He tried to swallow but had trouble and then gagged.

"It's getting buzzy, you know that? Your face looks like it was done as pointillism. I bet you didn't think I knew words like that."

The ambulance made its mechanical barking, not close yet, about a half mile away.

"So, do you want to tell me you love me?" he said.

"Yes," I said.

"Well, why don't you?"

"I love you."

My father cried, but tears appeared on just one side of his face.

"Here's the best I can say. Pick your spots. You think in Poland when I told you about that guard that I was brave? I know you think that. But it wasn't that way."

He drooled, and I wiped it with my handkerchief.

"Don't waste the time," he said. "Nothing but dots. Here's the way it was on that road in Poland. I knew I was going to die anyway if I didn't do something. And the guard thought he might buy a little goodwill. A chance for a deal. See? Pick your spots."

The ambulance arrived.

"Just dots now," he said. The men in white coats arrived and a woman, too, who pushed through the crowd to show that she was in charge. They brought in a sort of gurney and lifted him onto it with a rough, sudden gesture. The ambulance had its siren on as it went down the street, although everyone knew there was no reason to hurry.

The time of death was called at the hospital.

The world had been anchored by my father's existence, even down to its colors, the stink of the smoke in the air, the way women walked on the streets, the way light fell, the intensity of the shadows. In some subtle, pale way these things had changed, not so much in appearance, although there was a little of that, but in a more mysterious sense of not being so dependable. And, while the colors faded a little, and the stink of exhaust suggested the underworld, I turned into Christ Church in Cambridge and sat at the back.

A wooden bench, white walls, light coming in the windows, all at once ordinary and new, or at least different. The essential fact was the invisible wall between me and a man I wanted to talk to: maybe that is why the colors faded and the air seemed heavy. I opened the book in the shelf of the back of the pew ahead of me, and came to this:

1. How long wilt thou forget me, O LORD? For ever?
   How long wilt thou hide thy face from me?
2. How long shall I take counsel in my soul,

Having sorrow in my heart daily?
How long shall mine enemy be exalted over me?
3. Consider and hear me, O LORD my god:
Lighten mine eyes, lest I sleep the sleep of death;

In the light, in the musty silence, in the sound of the street, I found that while my beliefs were gone, that didn't stop my longing for a minute. All I had was that infinite desire for comfort, so unrequited, and the words printed on that onionskin paper that, for generations, had been so desperately handled.

[CHAPTER FOUR]

AROUND THE CORNER, in the Burger King, the young men and women moved back and forth from the counter to the kitchen where the sandwiches came out wrapped in wax paper or in those little boxes. The air smelled of french fries. I got a cup of coffee and then sat down by the window. A young woman, in one of those uniforms, came up to the table to wipe it down, since I had sat there, without thinking, after two junkies had been trying to eat a hamburger.

Still, the clatter and movement in the Burger King was at once reassuring and appalling: the sucking of the last Coke out of a cup through a straw (like a small death rattle), the crinkle of waxed paper, the laughter about a joke or comment, the shouts from the back of the kitchen, the alarm of a timer, as though the buns were on life support. And to make the collection perfect, my cell phone chirped, too, as insistent as a cricket on a hot night. I guessed word about my father traveled fast.

But, of course, I should have been thinking of my grandmother, Mrs. Mackinnon, who would have known that fate, that intricate machine of the gods, was just showing me an aspect of my own problems, which, of course, had at their heart the certainty of a scandal.

The caller ID showed Tim Marshall, a good friend, deputy inspector of the Boston police, hair the color of a silver dollar, face with a rose tint, blue eyes fatigued with one too many bodies found in the trunk of a car at Logan Airport, but still cheerful, in a way, and a man who would mean his condolences. He'd given enough of them.

"Your father?" he said. "Well, shit, Frank, I'm sorry about that. I really am."

"I know you are," I said.

"I wish this was a better time, Frank. I really do. You know that."

"There's never a better time . . . ," I said.

"I'm not talking about your father. I'm talking about a friend of yours."

"Someone else wants to call me?" I said.

"Cal Tolbert is getting ready to jump off the Tobin Bridge and he only wants to talk to you. Didn't he go to law school with you?"

"Yes," I said.

"I wish it were some other time," said Tim.

"OK," I said.

"The negotiator thinks Cal means it. So, when you get here, you're supposed to keep Cal talking. Tell him a joke. Do you know any jokes?"

"A couple," I said.

"Just get over here," said Marshall. "And Frank? Don't say anything about your father, all right? What good is that going to do?"

Maybe a lot, I thought.

"Do you know what's wrong?" I said.

"Who the fuck knows with a Dutch job? I'm a cop, not a shrink."

The cup of coffee went into the trash, and I hesitated at the door, trying to recall the small peace of the church.

• • •

The Tobin Bridge looks as if it were made with an Erector Set, and that the kid who built it liked V-shaped supports along the side and Xs on top. It is painted a sort of Boston green, the same color as the wall at Fenway Park, as though the city got a deal on some green paint. Mostly, I guess, if they thought they could have gotten away with it, they would have dumped it into the harbor and bought some more, to get another kickback. Boston. Not the cleanest place in the world, but it has a certain honest graft that keeps it on the up and up. Sort of.

• • •

So, the Vs and Xs were there, and even from a distance, Cal showed in his white shirt and dark pants, his tie flying like a flag of desperation as he sat in the pigeon shit on the rail of the upper level. Just there, like a white bird, a seagull, that had been blown in by a storm.

I waited back from the cop cars and from Marshall, who shifted his weight from one leg to another and stared in my general direction. Now, it seemed, was the time to cry, if I could, and so I sat at the steering wheel and thought of those times when my father and I had gone to that piece of land he had inherited from my grandfather and how he had made plans there for things he'd never do. How it was now mine. Or would be after probate. Or his advice about the facts of life: *You know, Frank, let it soak for a while. Women like that.* The steering wheel of my Audi was covered with black leather, and while I waited and hoped it would come (the crying) and that I would be over it, at least that part of it (not knowing it happened more than once and that grief, or tears, could begin when you saw beauty or horror, at a flower show, a museum, or at the scene of a murder), but for now nothing happened. Just that weight.

Cal was a bald man of medium height with the blue sky now showing in the sheen of his scalp. He owed me ten thousand dollars, and the first thing I wanted to say to him was that he didn't owe me anything.

Below the bridge were a row of houses, all made of brick, and in the spring light they seemed to harbor some chill, as though the winter had penetrated so deeply that it took months of heat to pull it out. Or maybe it was built into brick: constant winter.

The road was empty and in the distance the cops' lights flashed with a sort of patriotic display: red, white, and blue. Cal sat on the edge of the bridge, hands next to his thighs, head down, the empty air below studied and memorized. Or maybe it was just the fascination of the last thing you ever see. But that just showed how little I knew: at this stage, things like that don't matter at all.

"Nice day, huh?" I said.

"Little windy," he said.

"What do you expect, up in the air like this?"

"It could be a little more still," he said. "But you can't have everything."

"No," I said.

"Thanks for coming," he said. "Hope you weren't doing anything important."

"No," I said. "Same old. You know."

"Well, when we were in law school, I bet you never planned on meeting me at a place like this, did you?"

"I don't know," I said.

"What does that mean? You expected this?"

"No," I said. "I wasn't thinking about the future too much. Who had time for that?"

The new buildings in the skyline, all glass and aluminum, just squares and metal with jagged roofs, showed against the blue and smoky sky. Inside one of the windows, a man typed at a computer as though his life depended on it. Presentation, I guessed, an explanation of losses. Always a tough sell.

"How's your father?" he said.

"Fine," I said. "You can't kill a guy like that."

"You mean he has to do it himself?" said Cal.

"No," I said. "No."

"You know what's wrong with this bridge? I'm sitting in a layer of pigeon shit. Or maybe seagulls. Which do you think it is?"

"Cal," I said, "I really don't know. I'm not going to lie to you about that."

"Uh-huh," said Cal. "That's why I asked them to get you. You never told me any lies. You always knew what to say."

You poor son of a bitch, I thought. You're turning to *me*?

"So why are you sitting in the pigeon shit?" I said.

Down below, Burger King wrappers blew under the bridge, bits of colored paper in a wind tunnel. I guessed if Cal jumped, he'd be swept in the same direction: under the bridge, toward the houses.

"I'm having marital problems," said Cal. "At least I was having them. Now I've got something else."

"So what?" I said. "Everyone has trouble."

"Not like mine," he said.

"So, tell me about it," I said.

He moved his feet back and forth, a kid sitting on a pier.

He closed his eyes and started to cry, and I thought, no, no. It's catching. I bit my lip until my eyes watered.

Cal said, while sniffling, "What's wrong? Got a toothache?"

"Yeah, that's it," I said.

But I thought of those bits of memories, like newspaper becoming blank, as my father's head exploded. Was I one of those things that disappeared? Learning how to ride a bike or how to lick an ice cream cone? Did I exist a little less because he didn't think of me anymore? That's the horror of being on your own.

Cal's wife was an insurance administrator who had red hair, freckles, and a restrained air about her. You'd expect her to go around with kids on Halloween with a box for UNICEF. Wholesome, moral, distant.

"So, what's wrong between you and your wife?" I said.

"I wanted her to do something with me . . . ," said Cal.

"What was that?"

"Well, I don't know," he said.

The wind made his pants flap as though he were riding a motorcycle.

"Jesus," I said. "If you can't tell me . . . "

He nodded.

"That's why I wanted you to come over."

"OK," I said.

The layer of guano was a white-green, and as I put my hand in it, as though to steady myself, I slid through it to get a little closer to him. A little at a time. Like sneaking up on a mosquito that's sitting on the arm of a chair.

"I wanted my wife to sit on my face," said Cal. He still looked down, but he was absolutely still. "She didn't want to."

"So," I said. "Maybe we can work something out. There's got to be a woman on the planet who likes that. I bet I could find someone in a half hour. Come on. Let's go find one."

"I'm married. I can't have a scandal. I'm a prosecutor. Just like you."

The word "scandal" hung there, a kite in the breeze. So, what advice did I have about that?

"If that's all it is, let's go home," I said. "Come on."

"It's not that simple," he said.

"I guess not," I said.

"I bought this video clip, you know, a woman doing what I asked my wife to do, and I played it in my office. I thought I had disabled the software that keeps an eye on things like that . . . "

Cal's pants flapped in the wind and made a little shudder.

"But it wasn't the software. It was Jimmy Blaine. He comes in and sees it."

"You should have locked the door," I said.

"You're telling me," he said.

"So," I said. "Why don't we go over to a bar I know? You can see it from here. See. Over there."

"Listen," said Cal. "Blaine wants my job. You know that."

"Yeah," I said. "But he went to Essex and hasn't got a chance."

"That's not the way it's playing out. I said, 'Please, Jimmy, Please, this is just between us. Right? You don't have to do anything? You can just be quiet. I even have a little money tucked away . . . ' Of course, Frank, I was thinking of borrowing more from you."

"I'll give it to you," I said. "How much does that asshole want? Ten thousand? Twenty? I can get it. This afternoon."

"It's not that way."

"We'll buy him off. He's got to have a price, right?"

"Blaine looks at me, like he's adding things up, and then he goes down the hall to Martha Bingham and tells her and she gets the IT guy involved and the next thing you know everyone knows, and Martha calls Mary Coffin, you know, the PR type, and she says we should be proactive . . . "

"Proactive?" I said.

"Yeah, cut the DA's office losses."

"And what does that mean? Calling *The Boston Globe*?" I said.

"Bingo," said Cal. "And some other papers. And Martha Bingham wants them to know that she is running a clean ship and that a prosecutor was looking at porn but she is going to take care of it."

The constant pressure of the wind had a whiff of oil from the smokestack of a ship, the scent romantic and suggesting Bangkok, Singapore, Saigon. A bird flew over the bridge and the cop cars. Jimmy Blaine emerged from the line of parked cruisers and started walking, his tie blowing, too, in our direction. He came along as if he were just out for a stroll, calm and cool. Above him the helicopters hovered with that beating, whacking noise, as though they stayed aloft by a variety of cruelty.

"He's coming," Cal said.

"Yeah," I said.

"Can you beat that?" he said. "Maybe I can grab him and take him along."

I made a sign, with both hands. Back up. Stop. Stop. Blaine waves. Smiles. Keeps walking.

Cal looked down. The birds streamed by as though they were coming out of a hose, all going to the same place, all in a tight formation, one behind the other.

"Is he still coming?" said Cal.

"Yeah," I said.

I waved to Tim Marshall, who stared at me and then at Blaine. I pointed at Blaine and then made a quick movement under my chin, as though I was cutting my throat.

"If I went over there and hit Blaine in the mouth, would it be all right? Can I leave you?"

"Sure, Frank," said Cal.

I slid my hand closer to Cal's hand with its golden hair and the thin wedding band that probably won't come off, since he'd gained some weight. Tim Marshall walked out of that line of flashing red and blue lights. Blaine kept coming.

So, I was left with the choice. Should I stay there in the pigeon shit and paper, or should I stand up and leave Cal alone? To stop Blaine from coming any closer.

"You know why he's here?" said Cal.

"Blaine?" I said. "I don't know. Who cares? You want to hear a joke about some women who are taking steroids?"

"He wants to seem sympathetic, see?" said Cal. "Then Blaine can have it both ways. He fucks me and then shows what a sweetheart he is by coming here to stop me from . . . " He gestured with his chin to the empty space below.

The birds hovered on the wind, wings out, static: maybe it was their lack of movement, which suggested the serene, but I stood up.

"I never meant anything like this," said Blaine.

"Get back," I said. "Turn around. Walk away. Don't say a thing. Not a word."

"I just wanted to apologize," he said.

"Didn't Cal beg you to be quiet?" I said.

"He might have said something about that," Blaine said. "It was one of those confusing moments, you know?"

"Get out of here," I said.

Cal concentrated on those stationary birds, the squawking they made, so at odds with that scent of oil, of smoke that came from a funnel, from the stink of bilge that ships pumped into the harbor. Then Cal turned, his head moving as though Blaine had a sort of magnetism.

"So," said Cal.

"I didn't mean anything," said Blaine. "You know. Office politics. Nothing important."

The houses down below seemed brutal in their arrangement, more like teeth than a row of houses. And that coldness from the brick, the glitter in the street from the glassphalt. Like something that would always cut.

"Have you got the job yet?" said Cal.

Marshall ran along the side of the bridge, his jacket open, his tie over his shoulder. He took Blaine's tie and jerked him back, like a dog on a leash.

"What the fuck are you doing here?" said Marshall.

"I wanted to apologize," said Blaine. "It's all a misunderstanding. Don't you see? I didn't do anything . . . "

"Come on," said Marshall.

My hand sat in that green-and-white guano.

"You've ruined your pants," said Cal.

"So what?" I said.

"That fucking Blaine," said Cal. "And my wife. She's just shy, I guess."

The slimy guano made it easier to move my hand closer to his fingers, to his wrist. I was going to tell a joke, too, about the two Russian women who were athletes . . . Would that give me enough time, between the punch line and the laughter?

"And what are my kids going to say? You know my daughter is fourteen. DA watching porn at work, you know, that's how it's going to play in the *Herald*? How about that at school? At

Buckingham, Brown, and Nichols. What is she going to say? And my wife? She's already talking about divorce. I called before coming over here. What chance do I have with the kids? With getting to see them?"

I put my hand on his.

"Please," I said.

"It's thirty-two feet per second per second," said Cal. "Isn't that the acceleration of gravity?"

"That's what they taught us at school . . . ," I said.

"Thirty-two feet . . . ," he said.

"You remember Coulomb's law?"

"I'm hurt pretty bad," he said.

"I'll stick with you," I said.

"Sorry."

The bird shit was so slick that he slipped through my fingers: it was as familiar as dropping a chicken greased for the oven. His hand went through my fingers with a little sound, a kind of intimate squish. He fell at an angle, like a skydiver, arms out, tie over his shoulder like that flag of condemnation now, flapping in a trembling shudder, and as he fell, it seemed that the layers of smoke, the movement of birds, the bits of trash that blew in the air, were a sediment of trouble, a kind of airy strata, like you see where a road has been cut through a hill. He turned halfway around, arms out, and then hit a white bird that folded its wings and went down, too, like a pilot fish in front of a shark.

Even from the bridge, a hundred yards in the air, he hit the pavement with the sound of a ham dropped from a loading dock. A slap and a crunch, breaking bones and a fleshy explosion.

My hands left smears on my pants. Marshall and some of the others stood around, eyes over the bridge, as though if they just followed the path through the air accurately enough they could bring him back.

Then Tim said, "Well, there's a Dutch job for the books. Bird shit, porno, and office politics. Frank, I think I'm going to take an early retirement." He turned to a cop in uniform and said, "Well, what's to look at. Get the fucking traffic moving."

My handkerchief got off some more of the guano.

"I should have told you how slippery that stuff is. Like grease."

"Worse," I said. "Grease doesn't come out of an asshole."

"No," said Tim. "I guess not."

The wind was still constant, indifferent, but the birds funneled down on the place below.

• • •

In Cambridge, I found a place to park in front of the Burger King, and I sat at the same table and same young woman came back, her hair a little sweatier than before, and when she did she brought a coffee.

"I didn't think you'd come back."

"Well," I said. I shrugged.

"Yeah," she said. "I know what you mean. What's all that shit on your pants?"

"A mistake," I said.

"Well, sure," she said. "Sure. Who doesn't make mistakes?"

She took an index card out of the pocket of her uniform, where she kept her cell phone and a tube of lipstick. The front had a drawing of a nude woman who rode a spiral galaxy like a horse, and she shot thunder bolts, or maybe they were horse nebulae, from each hand. Hair in a ponytail. The waitress passed the card over.

"Here," she said. "The Raver brought that in just yesterday. That's a twenty-celon note."

On the back, the Raver had written in his script: *Be content to seem what you really are.*

"You sure you don't want it?"

"Oh, I've got a shitload at home. One whole wall is covered. The guy leaves tips in celons. Take it."

After an hour, the Raver came along, his coat covered with mirrors, each tinted a different color, and the effect was one of being scaled, like a new lizard. His skin was marked with acne scars and he wore his hair in a ponytail and he wore shoes made from tire treads, but he stopped a woman here and there, and said something that made them smile.

When he came up to the window, he stopped and looked in and said, his voice making the glass vibrate, "Observe constantly that all things take place by change, and accustom thyself to consider that the nature of the universe loves nothing so much as to change the things which are and to make new things like them." Then he picked out some french fries from the Burger King trash basket and had dinner. He came back and mouthed to me, through the glass, "You should be crying. Why can't you do that?"

"Habit," I said.

"It will come," he said. "Yes, my friend, it will come."

[CHAPTER FIVE]

THE BURGER KING at Harvard Square doesn't seem to be the place to try to come to terms with memory, desire, and amazement, but then where is a good place for that?

So, I considered my grandmother's notebooks and what I had read years ago in the attic of her house. A sign of how much I missed my father was that I was almost attached to if not affectionate for his goofy spy routine and the fact that he was cheating me, but, with that guano still on my hands, and the risk of desire so obvious in Cal's fall, spread-eagle, from the bridge, I thought of the first detail of my grandmother's own longing. It was the desire of another age and of another sensibility in the buzzing of timers for the hamburgers and the appearance of junkies who came in to drool at the tables.

I read this in my grandmother's notebooks when I was trying to discover the details of my father's financial arrangements. Of course, it would have taken a court order for me to get the terms of the trust. That is one of the laws of families, at least those who deal with each other before going to court. But families have far larger secrets than the financial, the scale of these hidden items so enormous as to leave me with nothing but the mystery of being human.

The notebook said:

> Chip, of course, almost destroyed us all when he took off with a young woman I had hired to copy these books, to get them ready, I thought, to show to a publisher, at least the sections about animals. She came into the house with her perfect carriage, her gray eyes, her smoldering quality that would have scared anyone with half a brain or anyone who knew just how powerful such a quality is. It has started wars. Destroyed empires. It is a flaw, it seems, in the godhead, in what makes things continue, since the attraction is so strong that it will strike anything that dares get in the way. A trial of gods and men was needed to atone for the crimes of the house of Atreus. Well, I don't want to overstate the case, but it is a miracle no one was killed when Chip, already engaged, ran off with a young woman in a way that had the air of erotic disaster so strong that most people recoil in horror, not from the obvious attraction, but from their own inability to entertain such a feeling. Or to act on it. This inability made them feel reduced, just human, rather than those fleeting moments of being in love when one feels like half a god.
>
> Of course, Pop negotiated, but fell in love with Jean Cooper too, although I think she let him have it in a way that suits an old fool. Chip was properly chastised. He married as he should, although to show the power we are speaking of, the farm was burned to the ground and had to be rebuilt.

Still, during the time when Chip was with Jean Cooper, he knew I was sympathetic, and I was, but not for any reason that Chip could have guessed. As his mother, I was concerned for him, didn't want him hurt, especially after those years I had spent worrying when he had been in a camp in Poland and Germany for prisoners of war. No. I surely didn't want to lose him to that erotic haze, and the trouble it can cause, violence and death. And, as I said, we came close. About as close as you can come.

But there was this other matter of my own, too, that had taken place some years before and which made me empathetic, as though Chip and I were charged elements, atomic particles that vibrated at the same frequency. In those days, women were quiet about the things that happened to them, or that they did, at least if they were American.

Pop and I had an apartment on Park Avenue, with, since Pop loved South America so much, a genuine Argentinian garden, with a false skylight. And, of course, we had the land on the Delaware River. Pop was a customs lawyer and spent a lot of time in Buenos Ares, Rio, Santiago, Lima, and other places. When he traveled, in those days mostly by ship and train, I preferred to live at the farm where I could wait to see a hawk, a deer, a bear, a snake, a grouse, and to write something about them, if only to understand what was happening to me, to my husband, and to my boys. This, of course, was before the war, but not much, when the boys were at Saint Paul's School.

When Pop had arranged to represent a meat-packing company in Argentina, a furrier in Patagonia, a mine in Bolivia, and was going to see them one after another, that is, he would be gone for some time, we started the barn I had planned for the lambs I wanted to keep. This was one of the buildings to burn when Chip began to flirt with those old attractions,

> more than just sex or love, but that passion that mostly just scares people.
>
> I should have known that a woman in her late thirties was flirting with danger, as definite as a tiger in the jungle. And the man had no sense, no sense at all. He thought that he could just sleep with me, just like that.

When I read this in the notebook, the dust settled around me in the attic, each small bit like a moment, a sparkling instant of time long gone. Then my grandmother breaks away for a moment from this man, whoever he was, and speculated about pain. She described emotional pain as though it was a creature, too, like her grouse, deer, and brook trout. Is pain a living creature, a thing that has evolved, too, and learned precisely how much it can exist before the host decides it is time to bring both of them, host and parasite, to an end?

The notebook continued:

> I plan, of course, to burn this before I die. And I hope that I have the time to do so, since I imagine, given my history, that mine will be a slow, continually approaching death, like a snake, a constrictor taking his time over its prey, but then I think sometimes I should burn it right now, so that no one will discover my sad secrets, which, I guess, should simply disappear . . .
>
> When I was young, I was not beautiful, but when I was in my thirties, something happened: not beauty, but a kind of glow, something like that air that Jean Cooper carried with her: not only attractive but dangerous. How could I deny it when all my life I had looked away from mirrors and now found that something had snuck into the frame while I had been looking away? This thing, this presence, was the tug of life, the scent of it, the allure of a new perfume, unlike any

other in the world, that hung about me, for a short time, I thought, like a cloud of desire.

So, I sat upstairs and looked out the window at this man, this McGill, tall, home from the First World War with a limp, in his thirties, too, and when I see him I feel more myself (a sure sign of foolishness).

And, I thought, what does that have to do with anything, with duty, with obligations, with what one feels at three in the morning when a child won't sleep and when you are so tired you can't remember if you are alive or dead? Then you remember the sense of being bigger and wonder at the seduction of it.

• • •

The dust in the attic was infinitely golden, infinitely fine.

• • •

Now I have times when I am alone with McGill. I go out to the barn, since sometimes he has trouble measuring and figuring and getting the most out of the lumber Pop has bought. McGill, who has had trouble since the war, was a bargain, and Pop loves a bargain. But McGill needs help. Sometimes he can't plan on the number of pegs he will need, or how to drive a piece of hardwood through a hole in the post and beam construction. I read, at night, about how barns are built this way. It makes me feel close to him.

• • •

You must do what's right, my grandmother wrote to herself, as though she was both the prosecutor and the defendant. And, in fact, I could sense this growing division between her objections and her desires. They made a sort of crackle that could almost be heard in that dusty attic. She told herself to go to the river and to sit by the water: it is eternal, she wrote, it goes on forever, and that is what you must concentrate on. The long term, the forever, since you are flirting with something that is far too intense to last and that, by its nature, the shortness and intensity, can't be anything but dangerous.

She knew she was going to have to pick up the pieces when this was over and she was good at that, although this, to be sure, was cold comfort.

She sat with McGill in the kitchen, her hand on his. And, of course, her feet were bare on the kitchen floor against that polished pine, yellow as an intimate stain. Upstairs, he sat on the edge of the bed. She said she knew better than this, that her husband was a decent man, and she had tried to learn to write so beautifully, but it had come to nothing. When they were done, when they had touched each other and were sweaty, they took a bath together in her tub with lions' feet.

The light came down all buttery when I sat with my grandmother's diaries, although it seemed to have a different color, still yellow, still weak, and in the sweetness of it I recognized my grandmother's profound sympathy: she wanted to leave a moment of delight, of love, of romance for her nosey grandchildren. That was why she hadn't burned this book. If she had burned it, those moments of tingling delight, when pleasure had been like the gold flecks of a sparkler, so surprising and complete as to leave people speechless with dismay. How could such intensity exist for ordinary human beings? It was like being close to a godhead, wasn't it? If my grandmother had burned this book, the smell of the sweat and wood chips and the bare floor under her feet, the touch of those sheets, the smell of that soap she used to wash him in the enormous tub with lions' feet all would have disappeared. In particular, my grandmother had made a note of that: the tub had lions' feet.

The notebook continued:

The new world caught us. Or, I should say a new airline, Pan Am, did it. Pop was in South America on business, and while he usually took a ship, he now took a plane home. McGill and I were in bed upstairs, and the dark Buick, driven by Pop's chauffeur, Wade, a tall man with tea-colored eyes, stopped in front of the house.

I recorded this, made notes, was precise, since it was a transformation. McGill pulled on his clothes and went out the front door, past Pop and Wade.

"Wade, put the bags inside the door," said Pop.

"Yes, sir," said Wade. "Mr. Mackinnon, I think I am going to put the car away."

Pop and I sat in the kitchen. Light came in the window and lay in squares on the yellow oilcloth on the table. I made tea and poured Pop a cup, the trickle of it into the porcelain at once cheerful and ominous.

In the yard, McGill cut some short planks to fit those places that hadn't been filled in the side of the barn. Pop put down his tea and stood, his shadow falling across me like a sheet.

"McGill," said Pop from the door. "Come in here."

McGill's boots came up the steps to the kitchen as though he was walking across the top of a hollow log. Then the squeak of the hinges of the door, that sigh and squeak. He stood in front of it, the door left open just a bit, as though that would make it easier to run away. I bowed my head on the other side of the table, not for shame exactly but because I didn't want to see McGill's face. Then he sat down.

"Yes, sir," said McGill.

I cringed at that "sir" as though this diminished him, and me, too. As though the "sir" was an indication of how desperate I had become or how silly, or how the two were so perfectly intertwined as to make no sense at all.

"Don't call me that," said Pop. "You know my name. Say it."

McGill said, "Mis, Mis, Mister Mackinnon."

"Would you like tea?" said Pop. "It's good, dark tea. We should drink something if we are going to negotiate, to decide things. It is very good tea."

"I know what kind of tea you have in this house," said McGill.

"Do you?" said Pop.

Pop poured a cup, his hands absolutely steady, the dark tea coming out of the spout of the pot, which looked like the neck of a bird, like a small goose.

"Sugar?" said Pop.

"Yes," said McGill. "I like sugar."

"Do you?" said Pop. "Life is hard without something sweet."

"I've noticed," said McGill without the least guile or without any understanding of the meaning of the word "sweet."

"One spoon or two?" said Pop.

"Two."

Pop put two neatly measured spoonfuls into McGill's tea, swirled the dark fluid.

We sipped the tea. The kitchen was bright. A silver spoon made a slight note against a cup. Overhead the geese honked with that steady, strained, alarmed sound. Pop nodded to himself, up and down, over and over. McGill held his cloth cap in his hand and reached out for the teacup and took a large sip.

"It's good sweet tea," he said.

"Do you have anything to say?" said Pop.

McGill bit his lip, and looked down. Then he glanced up at

me. The entire room was suspended in some invisible thing, like love or the impulse toward revenge.

"I have to say I'm sorry," said McGill. "I meant no harm."

"And you?" said Pop me.

"No," I said. "I meant no harm."

Pop went back to nodding, yes, yes, yes.

"There are two things we can do," said Pop.

Pop closed his eyes. The geese honked.

"You can go with him," said Pop to me. "There's a house vacant in town. You'll need some money. I'll give you some to get started. You'll need furniture, household things. I'll provide them."

"And the other?" I said.

"He goes someplace else," said Pop. "I'll give him something to get started."

"You mean money?" said McGill.

Pop held up a hand, as though directing traffic: stop. Don't speak.

"Talk it over with her," Pop said. "Don't be stu—" Then he stopped and bit his lip. "I'll be outside."

He stood up and he went out the door.

McGill and I finished our tea, although we didn't speak then. Gathering courage or admitting despair.

"Do you think I could keep you?" he said.

I shook my head.

"I could try," he said.

"Yes," I said. "You could."

I cleared the tea things and then McGill sat with his hat in his hands, his face sad, and when Pop came into the kitchen he took one look and then removed his wallet from his pants and took out a hundred dollars and pushed the bills across the table.

"It's better this way," said Pop.

"For you?" said McGill.

"For everyone," said Pop. "To eliminate complications."

McGill stood up and opened the door, letting the cool air in, and the smell of dirt and sawdust, and walked straight through the yard and then up the road, on both sides of which there were stone walls that had been built one heavy piece of rock at a time, over a hundred years. He put the money in his hat and put the hat on his head. He didn't even look back at me.

"All right," said Pop. "That's done. But let us finish."

"Finish?" I said. McGill had now vanished. "I thought we were finished."

"No," he said.

"So," I said. "We are going to negotiate?"

"What else is there? God? Church? No. None of that lasts. The law prevails, endures."

"So you want a divorce," I said.

"No," he said.

"What then?" I said.

"I am not getting younger. It is time to make a will, to set up a trust, to make arrangements for the money. Don't you see?"

"Have you forgiven me?" I said.

"Yes," he said. "But I want to make sure no more mistakes are made after I am gone."

• • •

In the attic I looked around the leavings of his time, the leather trunks, the fly rods in cases, the blankets, and chairs, the plaid cushions. All suspended now in the dust stirred up by an intruder, one of the living.

In a week, Pop had brought the papers, perfectly executed: when he died, my grandmother would have access to the income from the money he had acquired, and on her death the income would go to her sons (or only one, Chip, since his brother never made it back from the war), and then Chip would serve as executor for the next generation, that's me, and there, in the end of the notebook, was a copy of the trust. Ink like dried blood. And, of course, the details were there. Right there.

I read this fifteen years ago; the page of the last book turned with a little sound, like a creak in an old house. "Life is ninety-nine percent anxiety and one percent fear. The trick is to know which is which."

The diary ended. Just like that. The last entry had to do with a case of pears that were overripe and had to be returned. Pears.

The end paper at the front of the book had a small number "1" in my grandmother's dark, furious penmanship. If she had a 1, then she had to have a 2 or a 3 or 4. Isn't that the way it works? Were there more?

The trunk had piles of other books filled with plates of animals, of Audubon's drawings, of lovely drawings of moths and butterflies, and in particular a drawing of a moth that, when resting, had wings that were brown, but when they were spread for flight, triangles of pink that had been folded into the closed wing suddenly appeared: a pink like hope, like a raspberry, like a ribbon on lingerie.

So, there was more, but what? My grandmother had left the light, but not the darkness, and it is the darkness that teaches hard lessons. The bloom enthralls. The frost informs.

Still, I had the paperwork, and this is what I was going to use with my father on that day of the high-speed chase. I guess I had waited so long because if I had this, then I had information about my father's desperate affair, and, where decency was concerned, letting him know that I was aware of this secret was not worth three hundred a month. After all, I loved him.

But then my troubles began, and I was desperate enough to bring up the past, the toxic periods in his own life to get help with mine.

[CHAPTER SIX]

MY WIFE WAS waiting, of course, and one of the beauties of her knowledge, of her understanding, was that she had a way of discovering things before I had to tell them, and I was pretty sure she already knew about my father and about Cal. Still, the idea of not telling her directly, as I did about most things, was so far from the realm of possibility as to be nonexistent. And yet, who wants to walk into a room and say, "I've got some bad news."

I drove an Audi, which my father had called in his prison camp German, Der Grauer Geist, the Gray Ghost. I drove down Brattle Street, in Cambridge, after Cal had jumped from that bridge, and as I went by those squat, large New England houses, I tried to let their suggestion of time, of the weight of it, of the long-lastingness of it, like a geological formation, make that sense of my father's paralysis and the lingering slipperiness of

Cal's hand seem more remote or more natural or more ordinary, but instead it worked the other way: the old houses reminded me that this was the only time I was ever going to have.

The house Alexandra and I lived in and where our daughter Pia had grown up and still came to visit when she was home from New Haven was a New England saltbox, in a cul-de-sac not far from that daffodil color of the Longfellow House. Sometimes the color of the Longfellow House looked cheerful, like spring, but at other times like jaundiced eyes. You can guess how it appeared when I passed it and turned into our cul-de-sac. I parked just in front of the window in the study that was at the front of the house.

Alexandra stood just behind the glass of the window. She had blond hair and full lips, her presence edged by light, like a cloud at dawn. She waited, face near the glass, her eyes on the Audi. When we faced a tough time we played a game: she'd guess what had gone wrong, and I'd score it, one to ten. Now her breath made a small balloon on the glass of my study, like the place in a cartoon where someone speaks, and she beckoned with her fingers: come in, she seemed to say. Play the game. That's how we'll start.

The car sighed as it cooled, and the power steering pump drained under the hood. Maybe, I thought, with the celon in my hand, with the naked woman who threw thunderbolts and sat on the galaxy's face, maybe, instead of Cal falling through the strata of misery, as though it was measured in feet, or instead of considering my father's death, I'd pass the twenty-celon note over and say, in the voice we used for the game, "So, what's this?"

In the backyard we had beds of snapdragons, delphinium, lupine, and pink astilbe. When they bloomed the flowers screened a small graveyard. Or maybe you could say that half of the backyard is a graveyard. Often I went outside and stood among the fifteen stones that were there, surrounded by a metal fence with spikes on each bar.

The man who had built this house had been buried there, in the 1700s, along with this wife and children. Juduthan and Polly Wainwright. I used to stand there in an attempt to make difficulties less intense. After all, Juduthan and Polly must have stood out here, too, two hundred and fifty years ago, with difficulties of their own. Three children, twelve, nine, and seven, had been buried in a two-week period. Typhus? Cholera? You'd think that it would make the place gloomy, but it was oddly reassuring, at times, to sit there and think with a little luck I'd get through a mess. Or I used to think that. Now the place suggested something else: that I might get ensnared after all.

A wall of books was on one side of my study, Thucydides, Marcus Aurelius, Tacitus, Xenophon, which I read from time to time, and then my desk, which had been my grandfather's, a rolltop that still had some of his pens and pencils. A sort of lawyer-like odor: ashes and ink. A dark purple rug was on the floor, a sofa, a comfortable leather chair, an impressionist painting, a real one, not by Monet but by a pal who had been in Paris. A small bar in the corner.

And yet, if things worked out the wrong way, I'd lose Alexandra, too. What is like the feeling of lost love? Far worse and more complete, I think, than the itch of a missing limb. And the horror of lost love is that sometimes even the best memories are toxic, or tainted, and so I thought I'd better use a good memory now, as a sort of inoculation. Maybe that was the way to have the strength to grieve for my father and a friend.

On the weekends, before Alexandra and I had a child, we went to a small green house that was on the land that my grandfather had owned, and which was going to be mine, soon. The house was one big room downstairs and two bedrooms upstairs, and it sat in a field surrounded by stone walls on which copperheads sunned themselves. Alexandra put out broken crockery to discourage the snakes.

On those weekends, we arrived at this small house late on a Friday night, a basket filled with a picnic, ratatouille that she bought from a Frenchified delicatessen, french bread, a bottle of white wine in a chiller, pâté, cheese, olives, a pear tart, which we ate and then got into bed. One morning I woke up and found her in the upstairs bedroom of the house, which was white and had gauzy curtains. She stood in front of the window, which was a dormer, and there with the light coming in and marking the highlights of her hair, the pale shortbread of her skin, the luminescence surrounding her like a caress. She said, "Frank, is this what people mean when they are in love and happy? Just this? A moment like this when you are so glad you feel you could disappear, as though by magic?"

I opened the door to our house in Cambridge.

"What's that on your pants?"

"There was bird shit on the bridge."

"That's what it looked like on TV. They followed him all the way down."

"Even at the end?" I said.

"No," she said. "They chickened out about that."

"So they didn't show the hit?"

"No. Just before the commercial break."

She bit her lip and looked down, as though to say, *You don't have to describe that part.* That shape and a sound like a watermelon dropped from the fifth floor.

"What good would it do for me to cry anyway?" I said. "So, I sit here and blubber? Great."

She just nodded. What can you do? Patience.

A pair of sweats I wore in the evenings were on the sofa, and I stripped off the shit-stained pants, put on the sweats and a clean shirt she had left out, too, then took the dirty things and put them in a hamper for the dry cleaning that was at the back of the kitchen.

We had a drink and sat side by side. The warmth rose between us, just from the touch of one thigh against another, and it seemed to me that this was just as good as words, or maybe even better: warmth, touch, understanding.

Guano was still under my nails, and in the bathroom downstairs, I used the lavender-scented soap, but it didn't work. The stink lingered like some bad memory. My fingers had little green-white new moons at the tip.

"We need some Lava soap," I said.

We let the warmth build between us.

"Cal and I had some good times together," I said. "We were going to change the world."

"That's the best kind of friend," she said.

"I don't know," I said. "They get disappointed."

"So," she said. This was the opening for the game. That's the way we were going to handle this. "He did it because of money?"

"One," I said. "That's a one. The bottom."

"He was cross-dressing and got caught," she said.

"One," I said. "Not even close."

"His wife was sleeping with someone else," she said.

"Warmer. Say three."

"Ah, so it's the wife."

"Sort of," I said. "Or, at least, that's where it began. He wanted her to do something with him. She didn't want to. He was watching a clip at the office . . . "

"A clip of what?" she said.

"What he wanted the wife to do . . . ," I said.

"Her name is Ginny, right? Pretty uptight if you ask me," she said. "But what did he want?"

I whispered in her ear.

"Uh-oh," she said.

"Well, the thing is, he was watching the clip, you know, a woman doing what he wanted, and Blaine came in and saw it, too."

"Oh, Jesus," she said. "He went to see Martha Bingham. I'd bet anything. Why . . . "

"Cal asked him not to," I said.

"Well, sure," said Alexandra. "That probably made it better for Blaine. Don't you think?"

"That's a nine," I said. "Then Lady Martha, on the advice of the publicity director, to stay ahead of the wave, called the *Globe*. Next thing you know I was sitting with my best friend in pigeon shit. Then he slipped through my fingers." I swallowed. Almost. At least I had that first ache, down there beneath the larynx. But it didn't come to anything.

I gave her the index card with the drawing of the naked woman on it.

"What do you think this is?"

"This?" she said. "Why you poor mutt. This is a twenty-celon note. The Raver gives them out when he quotes Marcus Aurelius."

"That's ten," I said.

I closed my eyes. Cal turned in the air, the birds around him, the scent of the harbor and those layers of smoke.

"But listen," she said. "We don't have to worry about you doing anything like that, do we? I mean for the trouble you're in. For our troubles?"

"It's nice that you think of them as our troubles," I said.

"Well, let me tell you," she said. "Those people are going to have to deal with me, too. If they try anything."

"They'll try," I said.

"That's what I'm afraid of. Maybe I'll buy a gun."

"We've got a case, right over there," I said. In the corner of the room sat a small closet of Mannlichers and L.C. Smith shotguns, firearms I had inherited from my father and grandfather.

"I meant a handgun," she said.

"Well, my father's .45, his service sidearm, is going to be ours soon."

"That's more what I had in mind," she said.

Beyond the kitchen window the first spikes of snapdragons and delphinium grew, no flowers yet, just the green promise, like enormous asparagus.

"What are we going to do?" she said.

"I was going to talk to my father for advice," I said.

"Yeah," she said. "That was your father's greatest charm. Trouble."

"So, we'll just have to see how it works out."

"And how bad could that be? For you? For us?" she said.

"I wish I knew," I said.

She thumbed the edge of the celon.

"I'm sorry about Cal," she said.

"You know what the cops call it?" I said. "A Dutch job. Doing the Dutch. Or they call it a kervork. There's all kinds of kervorks. Water. Air. Parking."

"Parking?"

"When you start the engine of the car and close the garage door. That's a parking kervork."

"So for Cal it was just a dumb scandal," she said.

"Scandals aren't dumb anymore," I said. "Indiscretions aren't dumb. Sex is dangerous."

"Sure," she said. "But it isn't sex where you're concerned. At least I don't think so. You haven't withheld anything like that, have you?"

"No," I said.

"But, Frank, you're not going to go out on a bridge or something."

"No," I said. I picked at the green-white guano under my fingernails. "No. I guess not."

"I guess I better call Ginny. That was Cal's wife's name, right?" said Alexandra. "Make a ham and take it over. Maybe pick up the kids from school."

"You can tell her not to worry about the money Cal owed me," I said.

"I'll let you do that," she said. "And of course if he didn't leave a note, and if she asks why he did it, you can tell her. That's above my pay scale."

"I'll tell her," I said.

Alexandra took my hand.

"I know you miss your father," she said.

Her hand was like warm lotion that penetrated the skin.

"He had to be such a son of a bitch," I said.

"But that didn't stop you from loving him, did it?" she said.

"No," I said. "I loved him for the trouble he'd gotten through or the way he did, but I loved him for the way he fucked up, too."

"Well, he certainly didn't short you on that," she said.

[CHAPTER SEVEN]

MY FATHER'S WILL was in the finished cellar of his house in Cambridge, the room filled with the scent of mold from the condensation on the walls and from the constant leaks, which my father was always slow to repair. Two days after he died I sat at the card table he used, the one with the green top and the gimpy leg, and started looking through what he had left. I always thought he had been lazy or too devil-may-care to call a plumber right away, but the moisture had only made the papers harder to read. The ink on them, the long lines of figures, the notes about which banks he had used and even the canceled checks, were smeared like a woman's mascara after she has been crying.

No surprises in the will. Everything was left to me. Then I went through the rest of the papers, those moldy sheets and file folders my father kept in cardboard file boxes he had bought from Kmart then from Wal-Mart, the decline of the stores perfectly matching the increasing corruption of his efforts to manage the last of the money that his father had left. And, of course, the records showed what he had taken from my inheritance. It had a certain beauty to it. The most interesting items were in a file marked "Records for Frank. Open after death." "Death" had been put in quotes. The mold here was greenish and speckled, the ink harder to read. I guess he had left it under a place where the water condensed from an overhead pipe and dripped, one drop at a time, season after season, onto this file in particular. As a good spook, he had let nature take its course. If the papers were hard enough to read, he could appear to have done one thing while actually having done something else. And, of course, right there on top was a copy of the trust deed that I had found, years before, in my grandmother's notebooks.

Still, I had practical matters to face. The body had to be cremated. And so, a week after Cal had jumped off the bridge, I picked up my father's ashes.

This was the first week in June, my father's favorite time of the year. (*In June, Frank,* he used to say, *you have the feeling all is forgiven.*) The funeral was going to be held the next day in the town close to the land my grandfather had owned and which would be mine after probate.

The funeral parlor where I picked up my father's ashes was just beyond a prison on Route 2. The walls of the prison were gray and looked as though time had been made into a hard substance. Rolls of razor wire were at the top, and every fifty yards or so a guard tower protruded from the wall, and in each one a man stood, his face inscrutable from the distance of the road but yet, for me, as I drove to get my father's ashes, the inscrutable guards seemed to be an accusation. I supposed this was part of the feeling of picking up my father's ashes, but it could have been fear, too, of ending up in this place.

The funeral parlor was in Concord, a sad, pretentious town of such gloom as to seem that this atmosphere was the main product of the place. It was on a residential street, although a dry cleaner, a lunch counter, and a fast food outlet were mixed in with the single-story houses. The overall impression of the block was one of being washed out, dimmed somehow, as though the smoke from the crematorium obliterated all the colors on the street. A woman in a housedress pushed a cart from the Stop and Shop down the block, the basket filled with what looked like rags, but which was her dry cleaning.

The records in the cellar told a sort of story, really, although it was in running ink, indecipherable checks, the names of banks I guessed at more than actually knew. They were kept in my father's slanting handwriting, which was usually easy to read. The first pages were a summary of how much had been left, and a copy of the trust agreement, some parts of which were underlined. It had never been much money, although I was curious that while the stock market had increased, the three hundred dollars a month, which I had gotten as an undergraduate, never did. But even after his spy deviousness, when I had gone to see him years before, and maybe in spite of it, I thought that not talking about the cheating was a way, silent to be sure, of saying how much I loved him. As everyone knows, though, love can get tough, and I had saved what I knew until the time when I was in trouble and wanted to get his attention. To get him to take me seriously. And nothing would have done that like showing him how he was cheating. I was left with a particular emptiness, since I realized I had thought of this as a secret weapon, and what did I have now?

The path to the door of Michael and Green, the morticians, was like the path to any suburban house: shrubs of a dusty green, walkway made of brick, white aluminum door with dusty glass.

Inside, before the reception desk, a brown carpet, stained here and there, as though fluid had leaked out of one of the containers for the chemicals they needed. Mr. Green, a man in a tie and a short-sleeved shirt, waited at the counter, his eyes set on mine, his entire air one of reduced humanity. The ashes were in a wooden box, which he had politely put into a foil bag the color of a red piñata and as shiny, too. The oak box was held shut with a little hook. It smelled like an ashtray where my grandfather had been flicking the tip of a cigar, a good one from Cuba rolled by blind men, as he used to say.

"Would you like to take care of the balance now?" said Mr. Green.

"Yes," I said. "I would."

Mr. Green's fingers took the check with a respectful pinch, waved it back and forth while the ink dried, and then said, "Hot today, isn't it."

"A little smoky," I said.

"We always get that at this time of the year. Prevailing winds. Why we get all kinds of things from the Midwest. Coal dust. You name it."

"I guess that's right," I said.

"I'm glad you came to me for this service," said Mr. Green. "It's so easy to get cheated these days."

"Well, yes. It's seems very reasonable."

Mr. Green showed his bad teeth when he smiled. I thought the odor of the place was like that cellar in Cambridge. It was as though my father had been willing to let me see what he had done, sort of, since some of the papers were missing, and then he had waited to give me a glimpse after he was safely out of the way. Even as I flipped the pages, turned over the canceled checks made out to himself on the account that was for me, I knew that he had been struggling to come up with a legally defendable position that allowed him to do this, to take the money that was mine and still be on the right side of the law. About midway through the green-tinted paper, the running ink, the speckled mold that was so much like the black dust you see on an apple in an abandoned orchard, he had written "Eureka!" I guess he was so happy to have found a legal way to cheat me that he wanted to make a note, or to share it with himself, since the only other person he could share it with was me, and he knew, at least, that I wasn't going to be overjoyed at the discovery.

The box sat on the counter. Mr. Green gave it a little shove.

"That takes care of it," he said.

"Not quite," I said. "There's the funeral."

"Yes," he said. "There's always that. But it comes to an end, too."

He held the front door for me and then stepped into the hazy air behind me, a man who was tinted gray. I carried the festive bag. And when I was in the car, stabbing the key into the ignition, he waited, stooped, small and oddly defiant, too, as though he knew a secret that no one else had the guts to face. The cigar stink of the ashes hung in the car.

Perhaps I could put them in the trunk, but that seemed wrong. Somehow, we were going to make this trip together: me at the wheel, my father in the front seat. We used to go for a drive that way when I was first practicing law and then when I was an assistant prosecutor. He always wanted to celebrate at what he called the "farm."

So, after the "Eureka!" I knew I was getting close. The next page of the ledger also had a note clipped to it, too, and there, along with a moldy Xerox of the original trust, he had come back to the kill. The underlined section of the trust said that the trustee's fiduciary duty was to maintain the monthly stipend. Well, sure, that's right, I thought, but as I turned the pages, as the papers became more wrinkled where they had been wet, the shape of the strategy emerged. It had a sort of beauty, when you got down to it. He didn't have to produce more than the original monthly stipend, no matter what percentage of the original trust this was. Pop had been specific, I guess, because he didn't want any doubts about the amount, never dreaming that the market could go up two thousand percent.

Well, at least I didn't have to ask him about it, or to sit with him, at that card table, where we looked each other in the eyes and realized that the money was only part of the secrets that were hidden, not only by my grandmother, but him, too—that is his seduction or madness of the erotic over a young woman, years ago. What had been behind that? The years in a prison camp? The moment when he had looked down that hole in the barrel of the guard's pistol in Poland? Had it all snapped right then, in that smoldering, sultry look of a woman who just appeared and seemed, if my grandmother is to be trusted, to exist in a haze that so perfectly engulfed him?

Here, I think, is the time to add another one of those things from the dark. When my mother was dying and when my father sat next to her, she said to him, "Chip. Promise me one thing. You won't chase any cheap blonds, all right?"

Of course, he gave his promise, and within a month after her death that is exactly what he was doing, to the extent of finding one and even marrying her, although she died of cirrhosis within two years. Then my father lived alone. I feared I would end up the same.

[CHAPTER EIGHT]

I SHOULD SAY that my own trouble started eighteen months before my father died.

The first part was the Citron Modèle case. My father knew some of the trouble, but only a little on the surface. The trouble was deeper, far deeper than what my father knew.

Citron Modèle wasn't the man's real name, which was Jason Slivotviz. He was about six feet tall in his cowboy boots, and his hair was bleached "rock singer blond," as he put it. He wore a pair of black jeans, a sheer shirt, and a gold necklace. At least he dressed this way when he worked at the Citron Modèle Beauty and Nail Salon, which was in a failed auto parts store in Braintree. Perms, trims, bikini wax, full sphinx, nails, and piercings. Three chairs, a cabinet for lotions, dyes, conditioners, creams, mousse, and wigs on plastic heads. The place smelled like a cotton candy machine in a hot chemical factory. Discount prices. Coupons. A little card he'd punch if you were a member of the Citron Modèle Fashion Club. Ten trims or perms gave you a free one. A pile of *In Style* magazines, next to some back issues of *People* mixed in with *Extreme Sports* and *Cosmetic Surgery Monthly*. Citron Modèle was making money, although to get his salon started he had borrowed from some men who weren't regular bankers.

Sometimes Citron wore his hair in a ponytail, held there with a rubber band, so as to look like a sort of hippie transgendered cheerleader.

Citron was falling behind in his loan payments, at least as nearly as we could tell from the books he kept, the numbers and words written in a hand that he must have copied from a nineteenth-century manual of calligraphy for young women. Scrolls and swirls: two cases Condo Conditioner @ $56.95 per case, plus tax. And then an entry that said, "Need new girl for other chair. I skim her fifty percent and the rest is pure profit."

He put an ad in *Cosmetics Journal* and hired a woman who was in her twenties. She was thin with very pale skin, and she had short blond hair, no tattoos, no identifying marks of any kind (which caused us trouble later). In the salon she called herself Sally Sunshine, but her real name was Martha Franklin. She had grown up in Lodi, New Jersey, where she had been a cheerleader in a secondhand uniform with losing football teams, and yet she had been a good student but without money to go to college. She fled Lodi as soon as she could, on a Peter Pan bus to Boston, where she went to the Braintree School of Cosmetology. A certificate in a frame she bought at Target. During the trial, I went down to Lodi. The main road ran by the wetlands, where ducks floated in the back channels on the reflections of smokestacks from the oil refineries. Giants Stadium sat like a crater made by a meteorite.

Citron had a house in Braintree, which was a sort of second- or even third-tier suburb at the end of the Boston subway line. The house had one story with some dead grass in the front yard and a tree that produced some apples every year that fell onto the hard earth and which the kids in the neighborhood used in their Wham-O slingshots to hit cars that went down the street. Of course, the people who got hit, some of them with broken windows, called the cops, and the cops went to Citron's house.

The pit bull Citron bought to take care of the problem was called Blackie, and the dog weighed about ninety pounds, and every now and then the scent of a woman's perfume, the gait of a teenager who sulked in the street, the sound of a car that wouldn't start set him off. For instance, a woman with the wrong perfume came along and Blackie, after a silent but fast brooding, made a run for her. He hit the end of his chain and was lifted into the air like a pig being thrown into a vat. Citron didn't care about the women so much, but he took this as a demonstration of what Blackie could do if those kids showed up with their Wham-Os. Of course, when Citron wasn't around the kids did show up, and they peppered Blackie with the other stunted fruit they found in the neighborhood. It just made Blackie even meaner than before.

Still, when Blackie took a flying, rear-end-first leap at someone, Citron brought out a ball of raw hamburger and fed it to the dog and said, "Good dog. Yeah. Good dog." Blackie bit Citron in the eyebrow once when he was doing this, but this only made Citron fonder of the dog, since the scar in his brow made him look, as he told Sally Sunshine, "more cool."

Citron owned the house next door to his, and it was a smaller, more dreary version of his own: the dirt was a little harder in the summer, the mud deeper in the spring, and a couple of the windows were cracked and fixed with Scotch tape, not to mention the hardwood floor had come loose and been fixed with toothpaste.

Citron let Sally have the house at a somewhat reduced rate. This way, he got her to work for less, and he didn't do that badly on the rent. When she complained about the plumbing or the floor, he'd say, "Bitch, bitch, bitch. Why, that's all I ever hear. How about the taxes I pay? How about the furnace repairman? Jesus." Then he knocked on Sally's head and said, "Is anyone home?"

Sally said, "If you touch me, I'll kill you."

So, Sally began to work for Citron. She put in long hours, trimmed and cut and remade hairstyles, and she did the other things that Citron pushed her way, like the wax jobs, which Sally did with a sound like tape being torn from a cardboard box, although every now and then Citron, just to keep the upper hand, would say that Sally had done a lousy "full sphinx," and that he had had to "clean it up."

Sally looked at him at these times and said, "It was a good, slick job. Are you saying I don't give good wax? I give great wax."

"I'm talking about the crevices," he said.

"I get all the crevices. Some you don't even know about," she said.

"I know all about crevices," he said. "Front and back. You've got to think about the back."

"I think about it," said Sally.

Still, Sally was good with her scissors, and her layer cuts were known as far away as Boston. Women came in and waited for her, more than for Citron, and they liked her advice about romantic problems. And if a woman considered getting a tattoo, Sally said, "Listen, kiddo, life forces you to make so many irrevocable decisions, you want to keep them down to a minimum."

Citron cashed out on Saturday nights.

At the end of the first month, Sally stayed then, even when

Citron had told her to leave. She did the arithmetic, which she knew anyway, since she had been keeping track of just how much money she was bringing in.

"I think I'd like a bigger cut," said Sally.

"Not yet," said Citron. "You're still on trial."

"Me?" said Sally. "I'm more than doubling what you're making. They come to see me, not you. That's a fact."

"What about the house?" said Citron. "I give you a break there, don't I?"

"I want a bigger cut," said Sally. "Twenty percent more. No, make that twenty-five percent more."

"Oh," said Citron. "A regular teamster I've got here."

"I could start a place of my own," said Sally.

Citron put a rubber band around the cash with a deposit slip.

"Don't even think about it," said Citron. "I've got friends. You know that? No-teeth, tattooed ex-cons. You want to talk to them?"

"I'm thinking about it right now," said Sally.

Sally's diary said she got a mutt from the pound. I am guessing that the dog was her only luxury, since as nearly as anyone could tell, she lived alone, saved her money, although she used some for cocaine and painkillers, which she took with a shot of brandy. At least that's the impression her diary left. She liked to go to the movies, and I am sure she had a desire to go to Hollywood, but she was smart enough to know what she would get if she tried. Her friends, mostly women who worked at other hair salons or who folded clothes at department stores, said that she loved her dog, that she even bought steak for the creature. She sat in the kitchen, after a couple of Vicodin and a slug of brandy, and watched him eat with tears in her eyes.

The mutt got out every now and then and went next door. It strained, trembling with the effort, crapping just beyond Blackie's reach.

One afternoon, a Monday when the Citron Modèle Beauty and Nail Salon was closed, the mutt got out the back door.

Old women lived in this neighborhood, transplanted, I guess, from Sicily or Portugal, and they dressed in black and wore shawls when they came out of their houses, emerging from the shadows of their sad interiors to do their shopping, which they brought home in small carts with wheels, the squeaking of which haunted the neighborhood. They came out and stood together, in a group, having no need to talk, since they all knew what they were waiting for, just as their mothers had in those shadows of small towns in Sicily: trouble of the usual kind, violence, retribution, which all added up to a kind of restrained relief.

Sally's dog came up to the property line and, on this morning, it went into Blackie's realm. Blackie picked up his ears, his eyes a little rheumy. Sally's dog turned and strained, its rear end toward Blackie. Blackie caught Sally's dog in his jaws and shook his head from side to side, then opened his mouth to get a better killing grip, but Sally's dog ran back for the property line, one leg dragging a little. Blackie hit the end of his chain. Sally's dog whined at the back door.

Citron's door opened with an angry smash and then he crossed that urine-scented, hard-packed earth.

Sally slept nude, but she woke and went to the kitchen window. Blackie was on his back, feet in the air as he gasped, and her dog bled from its back. Citron put his hands on his hips and lifted his head so that his chin pointed at Sally's house, daring her to come out. Sally went through the door and picked up her dog. She carried it up to the property line and offered it to Citron, as though the dog were evidence of Citron's cruelty, his exploitation of her, his cheating her out of the profits, the skimming of the money from her tips, the surcharge on the lotions and creams, the dyes and bleaches. The false accusations about the wax jobs.

One of the women in black said, "*Guarda*. Look. She shaves."

"Get some clothes on," said Citron. "I am a respectable citizen."

"What?" said Sally. "A man who charges more than he should? Who won't be fair?"

"What did you say?" said Citron.

"You heard me," said Sally. "You and that ghastly dog."

"Get some clothes on," said Citron.

"What are you going to do about my dog?" she said.

"You heard me," said Citron.

Sally went into the house, where she put on a pair of blue jeans and a tee shirt, took some money from the jar on the kitchen counter where she kept her tips, went outside into the smoky air, and waited for the cab she had called.

The vet stitched up the wound, put on a bandage, gave the dog a shot, and then Sally brought the dog home. She took the bill and walked across the yard. She stopped in front of Blackie, who looked up with that ominous silence, as he always had before making that lunge.

Sally knocked on Citron's door. Citron answered and she said, "Here. This is yours." He looked at the bill, crumpled it up, and stuck it into the top of Sally's tee shirt.

"I told you if you touched me I'd kill you," said Sally.

Then he went inside and closed the door.

Of course, it wasn't just the dog, but the money, too. Each Saturday night, Sally said with a growing sense of certainty (now far beyond a threat) that she could open a place of her own. Citron knew that she'd take the new customers she brought in and probably half of his, too. Then he'd have to face those guys who came on a weekly basis to pick up the interest.

Sally continued to work at Citron's and then came home to feed her dog. Sometimes when she looked out the window, where Blackie waited at the property line, or as close as he could get to it, his enormous pink tongue hanging out in the sultry heat of a fall afternoon.

Sally had a regular cab driver who drove her from Citron's salon, and one night she asked the cab driver to come into her house. He put his hand down in front of Sally's dog, as though to make friends, and when the dog got up and limped and showed its bandage with a bloodstain in the middle, the cab driver said, "What's wrong with it?"

She just shrugged.

"Do you like dogs?" she said.

"They're OK," he said. "I've got a python. Its name is Dilly. Eats like you wouldn't believe. One gulp."

The cab driver swallowed. It was a good imitation of a python, eyes bulging to get something down rather than choking. At least that's the way we thought it happened after we talked to Sally's friends, the other women who worked in salons in Boston, and after we read her diary. After we talked to the cab driver, too.

Sally asked the cab driver if he would give her some help, and the cab driver, a man of about fifty, overweight, covered with tattoos, said, "Sure, what's your pleasure?"

"Can you read?" she said.

"As well as the next guy," he said.

Sally wrote a script right there, and then she got out her tape recorder and sat the cab driver down, gave him a drink of brandy, and asked him to read it. He did so, in a halting, bumbling way, but she kept after him until he got it right. Then she gave him fifty dollars, thanked him, and put him out the door.

At night, she sat with her dog in her lap, the stiff bandage under her fingers, her mood increasing with the warmth of the painkiller perfectly enhanced by the brandy. She turned on the tape. Outside, on the other side of the yard in a purplish light from the street lamp, Blackie went back and forth, always a little less than the absolute limit of his chain, as though inviting Sally to come a little closer. The cab driver's voice came into the room, seeming friendlier, more intense, more like the voice of Antonio Banderas than anyone else. He said, "Look, I know how much you are bringing in. I admit I am skimming you thirty to forty percent. Not counting the dyes and lotions. So, we've got to put this right. I owe you ten or fifteen thousand, but we'll have to figure that out later. I can't do much about that. But things can change from now on. We'll split everything fifty-fifty, after expenses, and each year I'll give you ten percent of the business. How about that? Shake on it?"

So, she sat, in that glow of warmth, imbued with that heat of perfect justice, or what seemed like perfect justice to her, and while suspended in this miasma, this cloud of sensation, which was just as warm as flesh under the covers, she made plans.

Sally went up to the corner and bought some hamburger and some d-CON, and mixed the two together, then made little balls, which she put into the freezer until they were firm enough to throw into the yard next door. And when they were just right, she stood on the back porch, just a concrete stoop with a wrought iron railing, and threw one into the yard where Blackie spent his days. She started with just one.

In the morning, though, Blackie was still there, looking a little less than chipper, but still growling at the mailman who came by the cracked sidewalk and reached over the farthest radius of Blackie's operation and stuck into Citron's mailbox the bills for water and electricity and the catalogues for plastic surgery, mousse, and conditioner, the promotional cans of spray and advertisements for scissors that came "direct from Paris, France."

When she came home from work, stiff and sweaty, she didn't take a shower. She removed three balls of half-frozen hamburger from the refrigerator and tossed them into the yard, and then she took a shower with the water as hot as she could stand it, angry, at the end, when it ran out.

The next night she added another ball of hamburger and then another, all of them gone in the morning, and so she guessed that she could try five at one time and that Blackie would eat them all before the effect of the d-CON made him uneasy enough to stop. She changed the dressing on her dog's wound as she looked out the window. She didn't care what happened, according to her diary, and that all she wanted was justice, a fair percentage for the take at Citron's salon (although Citron, obviously trying to cut a deal, asked for a smaller bite of her tips), just as she hoped that truth would find a way to adjust the outrages it revealed.

She mixed the d-CON and the hamburger like a poor woman trying to make a meatloaf out of ground round and oatmeal. She went outside, stood on her small back stoop with the black metal rail, and threw them, one after another, into the yard next door.

In the morning, a cool fall day with a gray sky and with the trees dark and scratchy against it, Blackie lay on his back, legs stiff, not moving at all. Sally stood at the window and drank her coffee, holding the cup with both hands and put the hot, black liquid to her lips with a delicious tentativeness, almost burning her lips but not quite.

Citron came out the door and walked across that urine- scented earth. "Hey," said Citron. "What's wrong, darling? Did you have a heart attack or something? Did that woman do something to you?" He pushed Blackie with his toe. Then he got down on his hands and knees and put his head to Blackie's chest, but he didn't stay long. He went into the house and came out again with a black plastic garbage bag. Citron unfastened Blackie from the chain, put the dog in the bag, pulled the drawstring tight, and dropped it into the trash can with the tight-fitting lid. This, at least, showed what Citron thought about death. It was like hair swept up on the floor.

Citron's hair was brushed back and moussed. He wore a gray silk shirt that was open to his stomach where his gold chain hung. He nodded to himself. He hitched up his pants, and yet he still waited, and when he was sure that Sally stood there by the kitchen sink, he made a gesture, a quick flip of his fingers under his chin in her direction. He had seen this in the movies. The women in black nodded: yes. They knew what that meant.

Sally's friends at the beauty salons and nail shops were the first to file a missing person's report, and after a while the police went into her apartment but found nothing, that is, aside from her diary, the tape, her clothes, some old magazines, a couple of books that were overdue at the library, and a couple of letters from the library about these books (and "the potential loss of library privileges"). They got a search warrant and went into Citron's house, and in the backyard, right at the property line, they turned up a pair of underwear with Sally's blood on them.

Another woman, a friend of Sally's from a high-end wax shop in Boston, said that Citron had said that Sally wasn't going to be working at the Citron Modèle Beauty and Nail Salon anymore. When this friend had asked where she was, Citron had smiled and said, "I think you better look in L.A. She wanted to be in the movies, you know? Yeah, she wanted her name on the Boulevard, her hand in the cement at Grauman's. What have you got if you haven't got dreams?"

[CHAPTER NINE]

WHEN YOU COME unglued, you are the last person to know it. But emotional explosions have their own revelations, which aren't so obvious when you are flying through the air in the power of the first blast, but the implications are more obvious on the way down, when those details of your life have gone just as far as gravity will allow and now, in the moment of exquisite weightlessness, as in a dream, they turn and fall. In this concussive moment, at the top of the arc, all the tricks I had used, all the devious methods of hiding what I really thought, revealed themselves as the innocent frauds they were.

Of course, as a prosecutor I resisted blowing my top. I had tried to contain what I felt when I held the bloody rags (so conveniently stored in a clear plastic sack) that were brought in from a woman found in an empty lot, or after I had handled, in that same plastic, pieces of bone picked up in the ashes of a wood furnace, or after confronting a man killed over a boom box, a woman stabbed in a drunken argument over what kind of pizza to order, a child dropped out of a window because a boyfriend was angry with a teenaged mother who had bought the wrong kind of microwave enchilada.

I tried to feel nothing. And saved it, just as my grandfather had done, for the late nights when I read Herodotus, Tacitus, Marcus Aurelius, and Thucydides's *The History of the Peloponnesian War.* Those old outrages and vicious events, which were so distant, made it safe to have my feelings about them. I could be appalled by Roman soldiers who had their way with a town that had betrayed them by going over to Carthage. The town thought that when Carthage was winning the war, it was a good idea to make an alliance, but then Carthage lost the war and the Romans appeared. At the sight of the Roman army, the women in the town stood on the walls and watched a battle in front of it, and when it was clear that their men had lost, they threw their children over and then jumped themselves. This reading was an antidote to my remoteness.

Also, in Thucydides I read this:

> The Thracians, bursting into Mycalessus, sacked the houses and temples, and butchered the inhabitants, sparing neither youth nor age, but killing all they fell in with, one after the other, children and women, and even beasts of burden . . . and in particular they attacked a boys' school, the largest that there was in the place, into which the children had just gone, and massacred them all. In short, the disaster falling on the whole town was unsurpassed in magnitude, and unapproached by any in suddenness and in horror.
>
> . . . Mycalessus thus experienced a calamity, for its extent, as lamentable as any that happened in the war.

After thousands of years, Thucydides's grief and horror was still palpable: he was simply appalled, so much so that he was left only with a sadness and fury that descended like a fog.

When I read this, after Sally Sunshine, my own resistance to the horror of the banal, the idiotic smallness for which people died (a TV dinner, a boom box, a slight insult, or hardly an insult at all) simply vanished, and for an instant I was compelled to feel it, as though the ancient historian and I were in perfect communication. And while I had thought that was it, a moment at three in the morning when I was having a slug of single malt scotch before going to bed, I was wrong.

The next day the hand-shaking fury still existed when I played the tape made by the cab driver. I sat at Sally's table with a view of the urine-scented yard. My trick had blown up. I had persisted by reading those old books, but now the feelings I had gotten this way were perfectly combined with a case I couldn't resist.

Something else reverberated back through those thousands of years: she had just wanted what was fair and what was right. The most basic of all desires. Her insistence, with such bravery, left me trembling with self-loathing. I had been cutting deals with people over deaths so tawdry as to seem impossible, and in doing so I had pushed aside Sally's desire: what was right rather than what was expedient, and in this constant bargaining, I had become numb to the possibility of fairness that a woman from Lodi, New Jersey, had insisted on as a basic fact of life.

Where did that leave me? A cynic? A cog in a machine I disliked? Screw it, I thought. That's it.

I sat in my office at home. In the street a garbage truck made a sound like a machine from the underworld that was grinding bones. I should have remembered a line that has come down through the ages, garbled, repeated, attributed wrongly to

Euripides, but certainly could have been from him: "The gods first make mad those whom they are about to destroy." But even if I had remembered, I would have thought that the gods had got themselves in for more than they had bargained for.

We gave the grand jury the testimony of Sally's friends, the fact that Citron had trouble explaining where he had been the night when, as nearly as we could tell, Sally had disappeared. We had testimony from Sally's friends at the Braintree Beauty College, and we had her diary, in which her fury was obvious. We had the tape recording. We had witnesses from the beauty salon who had heard, on a Saturday night, a fight over the split of the take and Sally's threat to open a place of her own.

We didn't have a body and we had no physical evidence, aside from the pair of underwear, which were found on the property line between Citron's house and hers.

All of this, the beginning of my trouble, took place about eighteen months before my father died. So he knew about this part, the trial with such a shaky case, the kind of thing that only an innocent or a man flirting with his own demons would consider. In fact, in the morning before the first day of the trial, I got up and shaved as carefully as on the day of my wedding to Alexandra, who was already dressed and waiting for me in the kitchen, where she had fluffed up some milk for our coffee and where she sat with a posture of understanding, her eyes never meeting mine, since it was unnecessary, although she had said, when I had not only decided that we were going to go ahead with this case but that I was going to try it myself, "You know, Frank, you wouldn't have done this even a couple of years ago. What's eating at you anyway?"

Before I left the house the phone rang.

"I'll get it," I said to Alexandra. "It'll be my father."

"Hey, Frank, how's the hangover?"

"You think I have one?" I said.

"By god, I would," he said. "You'd be amazed how a good, hard-hitting hangover lets you see what your circumstances really are. When you are on your hands and knees and your voice echoes in the toilet bowl as it begs for mercy."

"Not this morning," I said.

"It's not too late," he said.

"To start drinking?" I said.

"No," he said. "To cut a deal. Do it right out in the hall. None of that in camera bullshit."

"I'm going to try the case," I said.

He breathed into the phone. Sucked a tooth. Thought it over. "You know, Frank," he said. "When I got shot down I was coming in low. They can't hear you coming when you come in low. But before I could do anything, I was hit by ground fire. Oil burning in the engine. Smelled like a cheap cremation. Control surfaces hard to move, but I got the plane going straight up, you know, trading speed for altitude so I could jump. You'd be amazed how clear things are when you're up there and when you get out on the wing and jump and you're still going up, boots first, when the parachute opens. It's all clear then, Frank, with the parachute between you and the ground. And down below you see a mess of Italians kneeling and then you realize they're trying to shoot your ass off. See? That's when it's clear what your position is. Blown up, at the top of arc, and these guys want to kill you. See what I'm saying? You need to be smart and you need luck. And the messed-up thing, Frank, is that you are shooting at yourself."

"This isn't the desert," I said.

"That's where you're wrong, Frank. It uses different landscapes, different people, but it's always there. Always."

"I'm not going to stop now," I said.

"Well, that's too bad. A crying shame. Well, come on over when you're done. I'll give you a Negroni."

I wore a gray suit and a blue tie. Shined my shoes.

The cheapness of the business of the Citron Modèle Beauty and Nail Salon, the proxy fight with the dog (and of course I should have seen the danger of this), ran back to those old outrages from thousands of years ago, which, for me, was a perfect reservoir of every bit of suppressed fury I had ever felt about stupidity and cruelty.

I had picked as an assistant a young attorney, Carol Perkins, a smart lawyer if there ever was one, editor of the law review at school, and who could have had her pick of law firms that paid what can only be called real money. But for all her intelligence, she was nevertheless interested in justice. I loved her for it. She was in her late twenties, had red hair, freckles, and green eyes, and everything about her, the way she walked and held her head, the gray suits she liked and wore with such subdued effect, her scent (like baby powder), but most of all her expression of barely contained fury, made her an ideal lawyer to have with me. She was tough with details and contradictions and knew the law.

Citron sat in court with his hair in a ponytail, drawn back and held with a rubber band. He wore a black suit with a tee shirt, although his attorney, Martin Pullagia, had talked him out of the gold chain, but it was obvious that Citron missed it and from time to time reached up to his neck but found only his cold skin. Pullagia had gone to the Sussex Law School at night, represented gangsters, and was involved in things that would get him in the end. Later, he was charged and convicted in a money-laundering scheme. Before he was sentenced, he testified against the men he so frequently defended and finally ended up in the trunk of a car at Logan Airport.

Citron should never have said a word, but Pullagia let him testify. He told a story of such vagueness, of such lack of detail compounded by an inability to remember as to be a gold standard of slippery obscurity.

Citron's voice seemed to have the pitch of a hair dryer. Then I leaned close to Carol, into that scent of innocent outrage, and said, in a voice that was louder than I had intended and which could have been heard by the jury, "That asshole is a lying son of a bitch. And we both know it."

Carol flinched. Pullagia objected, demanded a mistrial. The judge looked at me for a long time. Then he considered the jury, who sat there as though watching an infomercial about something they had absolutely no interest in. He let the trial continue.

"For Christ's sake," Carol whispered in my ear, the heat of her breath showing that she knew I was right. "Will you be careful? Talk to me afterward about stuff like that. You want this to be reversed on appeal?"

The women in black testified, too. They knew what was going on in the neighborhood, and they sat in the witness chair, right on the edge, all of them, one after another, only taking up about as much room as the width of a two-by-four. They had all made their peace with the fact that they no longer were opposed to Sally and to anything that she had done, no matter what her shaving had been, and were now infuriated. They wore their black skirts and blouses, their wrinkled faces and black eyes furious as they pointed at Citron and said, "Him, him!" and with their clawed hands and arthritic fingers they mourned all outrages of history, starting in ancient Greece, where their antecedents had worn black and had intrigued and mourned and disapproved from the Peloponnesian War onward. They hissed. They glared. They accused.

The only physical evidence we had was the underwear, and Pullagia argued that it had been in Sally's trash, that the blood on it came from her period, and that it was outside, on the hard earth, because after Blackie had been killed other neighborhood dogs had come into the yard and had gotten into the garbage cans. It was obvious, or so I said, that this blood came from the night that Citron had killed her. He stared straight ahead, although once he looked at me and made a gesture, slow and languid and with every conceivable aspect of malice, his fingers flicked from under his chin in my direction.

He was convicted.

"Well, that's great, Frank," said my father. "But do you think that's going to hold up?"

And, for a while, everything calmed down.

I went back to my usual work. Pride surely does go before a fall, as everyone with an ounce of sense knows. Pullagia was better than I thought, or at least a lot faster than I had anticipated. In the fall after the trial, Carol Perkins handed me a copy of the *Boston Herald* which said "Citron Modèle appeal wins, prosecutor's prejudicial remarks sets beauty operator free." Citron was released, and when I talked about retrying the case, Carol rolled her eyes and other members of the staff and even the mayor called to tell me to realize I had made a mistake.

Sally's house had a new tenant, a man who drove a dump truck for the city. The place appeared the same, though, the cheap shingles on the roof glittering in the fall sunlight, a blush of green in the hard-packed yard, the old women revolving around the street as though looking for the next error that would cause trouble if you just waited long enough.

I sat in my car, a pint of scotch in my hand, which shook a little as I had one drink and then another, and finally, when the bottle was half-empty, I pushed the button of the tape recorder and the cab driver cleared his throat.

[CHAPTER TEN]

PIA, MY DAUGHTER, was in her last year at Yale, but she didn't have much course work and was doing a thesis titled "Law and the Protection of the Mentally Disadvantaged." She came home for weekends in her yellow VW, music loud, probably smoking a joint. She had gotten the highest score possible on the law boards, had perfect grades, and had applied to law school in Cambridge. We were waiting to hear about her acceptance.

Pia's hair is dark, almost black, which sets off her skin, a pale white that is so luminescent as to suggest the moon, or talc powder. Her eyes are blue, although one has a small section of brown, a quarter of one iris. An example, she said, of heterochromia.

Everything about her was large, not in the sense of size but something else, as though every conceivable gift had come down through the ages to her. She was an athlete, and when she was home from school, we went out on the Charles River, each of us in a single. She rowed beautifully, as though it wasn't a boat but a violin. I had taught her, and she had taken to it in the same way she had to everything else, with a variety of soothing exuberance as though her excitement was something that she passed over to me: it was a thrill to be there, in that water like something out of a painting by Monet, all little chips of light, tinted with green from the grass along the bank. She had perfect catches, the blades cutting into the water like it was a solid, like butter. When she was fourteen and fifteen, we rowed together, but by the time she was seventeen I had trouble keeping up and soon she blew right by me, her hair bright in the sun, her breathing hardly noticeable, her long legs pushing against the stretchers.

She resisted the overly civilizing effect of the boarding school we sent her to, and it left her with a variety of grace. Her vitality had its own imperative, its own dignity, which no amount of crypto snobbery could injure. She enjoyed, for instance, the summer she worked at a drive-in restaurant outside of Cambridge, next to a low-income project. The men who lived in the project worked in the last factories around Boston, on the waterfront and as plumbers. Her frankness with them when they came to the drive-in, her smile, her genuine interest, beguiled them, and soon they were on her side, wishing her the best. In those days before she went away to college we'd argue or discuss those things she was curious about and which she understood better than I did.

Fermat's theorem, for instance. She said, "Because there are an infinite number of equations, and an infinite number of possible values for x, y, and z, the proof has to prove that no solutions exist within this infinity of infinities." She said this and smiled at me. It was her smile that really made her deadly: a full, large mouth that turned up at the corners when she smiled. It was like turning up the thermostat on a cold morning. "Don't you see, Dad? It's pretty obvious why German mathematical academics spent so much time on this when you get down to cases . . . "

We had gone every now and then, on a weekend when she was in school, to that piece of land my father owned on the Delaware River, or the five hundred acres that were left after he had sold the thousand acres to the Girls Club.

On a trip there a year or so ago, ten months before my father died (the clock was already ticking), Pia and I had our one really bitter argument. As bitter as the taste of ashes in the spring after they had been left in a fireplace all winter. We did our best to pretend that it had never taken place, but it fits here, too, and I guess was part of her license to behave the way she did.

This fight had been coming for a long time, and, in fact, it had been building with the same, perfect cadence that drove her from being a girl to a young woman. This, of course, meant that she slowly stopped considering the prospect of having children as an abstract and distant if not impossible circumstance to one that was as real as a stone. We argued about what she called the Mackinnon stain. Mixed in with this bitter fight was the fact that she was the end of the line. I would die. That left just her. If she didn't have children, that was the end of all of us, the living and the dead. No future. Nothing but entropy. And she wondered at my fury.

We went the usual way, out through Hartford and then on 84 to the Delaware Valley, which you could see from above Port Jervis and which had, on this trip, a blue mist that hung in the ridges. We were going to stay in that stone house that my father still owned and hated, and which I liked to go to, if only to have a little time alone with Pia so we could talk and hike, and go down into the stream on the land, Trout Cabin, where we used to see the copperheads coiling on the rocks.

On the place where Trout Cabin ran into the Delaware, it flowed through a piece of flat land, a couple of acres that my grandfather and grandmother had, as nearly as I could tell, given to my cousin. Or someone my grandmother and father had told me was a cousin, a poor one, I guess, whom they had taken in and raised. About fifteen years younger than my father. This, I guess, is one of those places where secrets live. Or where I should have been aware enough to know that a secret was here, but why should I have doubted my grandparents?

Here, on that flat land, my cousin had built a place from hoods of cars that he got from a junkyard, pieces of plywood he had picked up after dark at construction sites along the river, and some corrugated roofing material you see in Mexican border towns. He had a Coleman stove he cooked on, although he had power, too, and a laptop computer that he used to watch the Nature Channel and clips of alligators and snakes, zebras and sharks. One time, he made me watch a lion eat a zebra in large, shredded chunks.

On the afternoon of that bitter fight, we stopped at my cousin's house. The place was empty, although the door was unlocked. At one side he had a pile of sardine cans, which he was saving, I guess, to make a new roof. He existed mostly on sardines. The pile of them looked like an enormous mound of fish scales.

"Guess he's not here," said Pia.

"Wait," I said.

Upstream, in the Delaware, something came through the water that went around the rocks where big fish waited. Still, that creature emerged from the glare, which finally lifted like the sides of a circus tent. That is if the tent was made of foil. Jerry emerged from it, and we came down to the river to meet him. He stood in about a foot of water, in a patched pair of waders, but he wasn't fishing. Just looking around. Maybe he had set an eel trap.

Jerry's shirt was sun-bleached, a blue that was the color of a piece of glass from a milk of magnesium bottle that has washed up on the beach, and it perfectly matched his eyes. His hair was straight, and even though he was balding, he left it long. Still, he smiled with a sincerity that was as intense as the stars.

Now, he said, his lips moist, his hair slick with sweat and his own personal oil, "Well, hell, hell, hell, hell . . . "

"Hello," I said.

"No. No. Don't say that. I can say it. Don't do that. Don't. I hate it."

I swallowed.

"I'm sorry," I said.

"Just let me be . . . ," said Jerry. He swallowed. "Cousin Frank. How are you?"

"Hi, Jerry, how are you?" I said.

"Well, you know me. I'll fight till the last dog dies," he said. "And look who you've got with you. Why it's Pia. My favorite cousin. How the hell are you, Pia?"

"I'm fine," she said.

"Well, you know what, that's fucking-A great."

"You better fucking believe it," said Pia.

"Come on," said Jerry. "Let's do our drill."

"Some other time," said Pia.

"No, no, no," said Jerry. "It's how we say hello. Like some handshake at Yale. Look into my eye."

Pia stood opposite him, nose to nose.

"You see it?" he said. "You see the brown part in my eye? Like a quarter of a pie? Just like yours."

"Yes," said Pia.

"We're like two peas in a pod," said Jerry.

Cars went by on the highway with that ripping sound, like something that arrived not by speed but violence.

"I see you're still driving that Audi," said Jerry to me. "Der Grauer Geist, your dad calls it."

"Yes," I said.

"You want to hear the other German I know?" he said. "*Schießen Sie sie in der Rückseite des Ansatzes*. Your dad taught it to me when we used to drink together."

"Yeah," I said.

"It means 'Shoot them in the back of the neck,'" said Jerry.

Jerry's skin was red from the suntan dope that he cooked in the back of the shack made from those hoods of cars and with that solar panel to watch the nature movies on his computer, which, I think, he bought from a man in Matamoras, just across the river, who had passed through here a couple of years ago, one jump ahead of the police.

"Yeah. That's one thing your father told me . . . He had some other things to say about Russians. You want to hear them?"

"I think I've heard his war stories," I said.

It was a misty afternoon, but not the kind that leads to a thunderstorm. Just that silver water in the river because of the mist.

"Looks like we're going to get a storm," said Jerry. "See?"

"See what?" I said.

"Sort of purple over there," he said. "Like we're going to get lightning."

Pia stood there, light in light.

"What's the storm look like?" she said.

"Can't you see it?" said Jerry. "Getting darker, like smoke, like some chemical is burning . . . the color of an iris. Or something that grows at night."

He bit his lip and looked around as though he was in the midst of vertigo, or that the entire landscape had begun to swirl around like water going down the drain.

"Everything is turning purple. Blue . . . ," he said.

Jerry blinked at the distance: the sky was clear, blue, as clean as a baby from the bath.

"Building a little," he said. "Funny. Can't you see it?"

"Yes," said Pia.

"Frank," said Jerry. "You remember what you read to me?"

"I remember," I said.

"God's grandeur flashes out, like a dapp-dapp-dappled dawn dawn—drawn . . . "

"Falcon," said Pia. "Falcon."

She stepped forward and behind him.

Jerry's eyes rolled back in his head and he went stiff. He seemed to resist it, like a deer just hit by a car, but it was just too big. The tremors already swept his arms and legs. He fell backwards, an ironing board slapping the water. His head went under and his feet kicked, but even so, in bubbles and in sheer volume, he clearly said, "ah, ah, ah, ah." Dawn drawn, I thought, dawn drawn . . . The bubbles of his voice rose and burst, the surface of them smeared with a rainbow. It appeared that we had an enormous fish and that it thrashed as it tried to get away. I reached down and Pia did, too, our fingers touching under Jerry's back, and as we pulled him up, Jerry's convulsions quickened. Like an increasing earthquake: if we had been in a house all the dishes and glasses would be rattling. Although in the rattling, I felt the ebb and flow, the waves of them, each one becoming stronger than the next, as though that half-hidden malice in the landscape had rolled down to the river and into this man.

Silvery moisture, part drool, part river water, came out of Jerry's mouth.

His legs kicked into the dry weeds on the shore, and he jerked harder, as though he knew he was on hard ground, and made that sound, which was the worst part, that "ah, ah, ah." Jerry banged his head on the stones in the weeds, and I took off my jacket and put that under his head, but his blood was already seeping into the cloth and on the ground, surprisingly red on the dry grass of summer. It made a sleek line through weeds until it mixed with the water of the Delaware.

His bridgework came out when I put my handkerchief into his mouth, and so I pried open his mouth to get the teeth before he choked on them. Pia picked up the imitation teeth and put them into her shirt pocket with an infinite, considerate gentleness. I put my hand into the pinkish foam of Jerry's mouth and the teeth he had left cut me.

The "ah, ah, ah" came out as an infantile burbling, a choking and perfect cry of surprise and horror.

Pia used her phone to call the local rescue, and as she said "Just down river from where Trout Cabin comes into the Delaware," Jerry stopped breathing.

With my ear on his chest I could hear nothing but the river, the cars on the road, Pia's clear, calm voice as she explained exactly where we were. The artery in Jerry's neck made a faint and irregular pulse, but then my fingers, where he had bitten me, were bleeding, and maybe it was just the throb of my own heart. I put my head on his chest again. The river seemed blue beyond the grass. Even the current seemed slow and sluggish, but obviously wearing down those stones in the middle, which had been there for thousands of years but which the river would reduce to dust.

"Dad? Dad?" said Pia.

Jerry's nose had a bulb, and I squeezed it with one hand and held his mouth open with the other.

"Clear the vomit," she said. "Turn him to the side to make sure it isn't blocking the airway."

We turned his head into the light and his mouth was a conglomeration of slime, of red flesh, of his tongue that was a color I had never seen before. It was warm and wet, and yet I didn't want to press too hard, to do anything that was going to make it worse. Then I turned his head back, relieved to see that he was still bleeding from his scalp. But maybe less than before. Did that mean he had bled out from an interior wound? Was his blood pressure falling? I held his nose and put my lips against his, into the sheen from his drooling, as bright as the river. Then I blew into him, still holding the nose, once, then waiting, and then again, the chest rising and falling. The blood from my fingers ran down his cheeks and into his mouth. I used my handkerchief to wipe it off his mouth, but the cloth was filled with grit, and then Pia pushed my hand out of the way and said, "I'll do it."

She brushed away the slime and the blood from my hand and took Jerry's nose the way that one touches a newborn. She squeezed Jerry's nose, not quite so hard as I had done, more as though she knew precisely what she was doing. She took a deep breath, put her lips against Jerry's, held the odd-looking nose with her thumb and first finger, and breathed into Jerry's lungs. The chest rose. The breath came out with a gurgling wet sound, a sort of bubbling that made me think Jerry had swallowed some of the Delaware, but then it seemed possible this was a death rattle, river-like but still having that same, wet horrifying quality, all the worse for being in the sun and that silver glare.

Pia's lips were covered with blood and slime and she shook her head, as though she knew what I was thinking after all. No, she seemed to say, No. I don't think he's dead. Then with that same, infinitely gentle movement she put her lips against Jerry's again, squeezed that nose that looked like an old rubber bulb, and breathed in, not too hard, not too soft. The chest rose and fell with a quality that was at once regular and yet frightening.

We sat face to face, covered with the slime and blood. An occasional gurgle came from Jerry's throat. Up the river from the next town, Pond Eddy, came the siren with its ululating whine.

I managed to get the handkerchief around my fingers enough to keep them from bleeding, and as Pia sat up, I reached down and took the nose, Pia letting it go not because she was reluctant to go ahead, but because of something else: a gentle suggestion that said, All right, all right. It's going to be all right. Or, at least, if he is going to die, it is going to be in the ambulance, not on our hands, not with us demonstrating our incompetence.

The siren came along the river, but the ambulance passed us, went a quarter of a mile down river, stopped, turned around and came back. It was an old Ford van that had been outfitted with a used siren and a cheap light.

Jerry's eyes opened. He breathed on his own.

I let go of his nose and rocked back on my heels, and as Pia and I faced each other the second wave of the seizure hit with a power that made us both flinch: Jerry stiffened again, like some new, previously unknown material. He touched ground in just two places, like a yogi, just the back of his head and his heels, his back and legs completely free of the ground. You could have run your fist under there without touching his back. The seizure came in earnest, trembling, shaking, and the odd voice of it was like a prayer, or an expression of fear.

One man and one woman in uniforms that must have been at one time jumpsuits for a gas station, the kind that had Bob or Sam stitched on the front, now came through the dry grass, which in the sun appeared with filaments of red, like a toaster. Jerry's cry was constant, so articulate and yet so meaningless.

The woman was Mary Drucker.

"I'll bet he stopped taking his pills," said Mary. Then she opened his shirt pocket and took out a pharmacy bottle, an iodine-colored one, and held it up. Then she read the number of the pills, the date, shook it again. "Look. Look. You see that?"

The man opened his bag and removed a syringe, took off

the top that protected the needle, and put it into Jerry's arm, the plunger coming down with a slow, soothing movement, the silver liquid, as bright as the glare, disappearing into Jerry's arm.

The seizure stopped.

Then they checked to see if he was able to breathe, if the airway was clear, and when they were satisfied that Jerry was breathing, they went up to the ambulance and brought down the stretcher on wheels. Pia and I sat back, our faces bloody and covered with slime.

The stretcher bounced through the dry grass and rock, looking for all the world like a small boat afloat on a dry sea. Mary Drucker and the man loaded Jerry onto it, tied him down, covered him, and took him up to the road, where they slipped the gurney into the back of the cheap ambulance and slammed the door.

Mary turned to me and said, "Nice to see you Frank. Where you been keeping yourself?"

"Boston," I said.

She shrugged. As though that was all there was to say about anyone who abandoned a small town along the Delaware for a place like that. Then she shrugged and said over her shoulder, "I told Jerry if he doesn't take the phenobarbital, this is going to happen. I told him."

"I mentioned it to him," I said.

"Mentioned?" she said. "Well, the only way he is going to listen is if you mention it with a two-by-four." She turned to the man who had given Jerry the shot. "Mentioned? Did you hear that?"

"I called the hospital in Port Jervis," said the man. "They're waiting. He doesn't like the way the pills make him feel."

"What the hell does that have to do with the price of bread?" said Mary. "What does feeling have to do with things like that? You do it or you don't. Don't talk to me about feelings." She turned to me. "Isn't that right, Frank?"

"Yes, yes," I said. "Sometimes."

She turned to Pia.

"You know what I mean, don't you?"

"Yes," said Pia. "I do."

"The only one with any sense in this group," said Mary. "You do your job. Let other people do theirs."

They got into the van and slammed the door, and then it took off, that wailing louder than ever, at least when it turned around, but then it receded, the sound having an odd throb.

"What do they call that?" I asked Pia.

"The sound?" she said. "The Doppler effect."

"Yes," I said. "That's what it is."

She nodded. Sure. She remembered. It was like those moments when she explained Fermat's theorem: it happened as fast as a memory triggered by the scent of honeysuckle or an orchid, but then the sound and scent of the river came back.

Jerry said the seizures came first as a blue light, as though it was the exhaust of a flying saucer. Or sometimes he said it was like a storm, one of those cells out of which the tendrils of a tornado come, rich with the shape and color of the tentacle of an octopus. It came down and touched the earth, at once black and contradictory, like smoke and the ink of a squid. Sometimes it was like an eclipse, when the moon covers the sun, but the shadow was as violet as a gentian.

He didn't really stutter, although some words gave him trouble, and while he had a disability check and while my grandfather had left him a little money, I still sent him a check every two months. Well, not a check. A stack of twenties held together with a rubber band. When we were together, we played a game, and he said "One," and I said "Two," and then he said "Three," and we went on that way until we got to nineteen, since he couldn't quite understand how it went from the teens to the twenties, then thirties, then hundreds. Still, he liked geometry, and he glowed when I showed him a proof.

Pia and I washed our faces in the river.

"Dad," she said. "You understand, don't you?"

"What?"

"I will never, ever have children. Period," she said.

"Wait," I said. "They've got all kinds of genetic tests . . . "

"Don't," said Pia. "Don't give me any lawyer bullshit. Or any bullshit. For once, I want you to listen to me. Can you do that for once?"

"What is that supposed to mean?" I said.

"Just listen. Don't ask questions. You heard me," she said.

"But . . . "

She was standing on the bank, a little above me, and so we stood nose to nose. Her eyes were the same gray color as mine, maybe a little bluer, although that could have just been anger.

We turned away from each other and got into the car, and drove to the hospital in Port Jervis. Jerry was fine. Then we drove home, back to Cambridge, and we didn't say a word until we pulled into the driveway.

"Have you heard what I said?" she said.

"Yes," I said. "The end of the line."

"Good." She swallowed and closed her eyes. "Is there any other way? Is that what you want? Seizures? Incapacity? Madness?"

[CHAPTER ELEVEN]

IT WASN'T THE best of times or the worst of times, but some other combination altogether. Or maybe it is better to say that it was the best of times, but fate, or darkness, or that substance Thucydides tried to define, if only by events, was waiting to do its worst. The first detail of it had to do with a dinner Alexandra made five months before my father died.

Alexandra put pasta on the table, linguine with a white puttanesca sauce, some tomatoes with fresh mozzarella and basil, a white wine, Orvieto Classico Superiore. Then she sat down and smiled. Well, I thought, at least she is making an effort. She put the pasta onto a plate and handed it to me, and in that moment we both held that white plate, when we both tugged it at the same time, I felt some firm, definite pull. I have lived with my wife for twenty-five years, and I know that pull, that insistence, which is so perfectly mixed with hesitation.

Alexandra taught film production at Boston University, and for a long time she had wanted to make a documentary film about Marinetti, an Italian Futurist who, to my mind anyway, was simply bonkers: he and his followers, at the early part of the last century, embraced the worst aspect of the modern age with a sort delusional pleasure. For instance, they thought that the sound of a machine gun as it mowed down soldiers was a kind of music, or the music of the age. The new symphony. My wife was as amazed by this as I was, and for a long time she had tried to interest people, like WGBH, in funding the project. I had even written proposals with her.

"This is good," I said, with the pasta on a fork.

"Yes," she said. "Isn't it?"

"I wonder if you have heard anything about the funding for the Marinetti?"

"I can't fool you," she said. "How do you do that? How do you know I've heard something?"

"The way you cook," I said. "So?"

"Well," she said. "It's not the funding. But close. I've been invited to teach a course at the University of Rome. American film of the twentieth century. Frankly, I'll have to go quickly, since someone else backed out on them for the spring. I'll have to be there next week."

"Oh," I said.

"It won't be that long," she said. "I'll be back before summer. By late spring. I know it might be tough for you, after losing the Citron case. Pia will be at school. I skedaddle to Rome . . . "

I went on eating, and as I rolled the shiny linguine on my fork, I thought of Via del Corso, the monument to Marcus Aurelius where I always went to eat a gelato. Well, I thought, well. Maybe she will have a good time.

"OK," I said. "That's great. Have you told Pia?"

"Yes," she said. "Pia's all for it. And you're really glad, aren't you?"

"Sure, you'll be able to look into Marinetti. There must be an archive or something at the University of Rome."

"Yes," she said. She rolled some pasta on her fork and put it in her mouth. "That's right. There is an archive."

"And Pia comes home for weekends," I said. "How bad can it be?"

The wine tasted of those Italian hillsides and that constantly changing light.

"Do you think a time comes when your kids decide to finish you off?" I said.

"We're not Eskimos," said Alexandra.

"Don't be too sure," I said.

"It's possible," she said.

"Maybe it's like Newton's laws of motion. Big objects attract small ones. Here, if I'm a little shaky, it attracts events that have just been waiting for it. Like if I'm vulnerable, then the natural thing is for Pia to push back. Maybe she's not even aware of it. Maybe it's easier to face up to a father's death if you diminish him first. Or just defeat him in some way. You don't even know you're doing it. That's how natural it is."

"Frank," she said. "I'd relax if I were you. Stop thinking for a while."

"Yeah," I said. "That's got to be right. Too much thinking around here."

A week later I stood in our bedroom, where she packed her new Tumi bag with sheer underwear, dark and red, with small ribbons, matching brassieres, and other items, clinging black dresses, which she folded neatly, as though these things were part of a promise. She was in her forties, but more attractive than she had ever been. I helped her close the bag. And in the morning, she said, "I know you have to be at work. I'll take a cab."

In the kitchen the coffee in my cup got cold as silence flowed into the house like fog. If I had been more alert, the silence should have tipped me off, but I saw it as just the lack of sound, not the announcement of the beginning of trouble, which for me always has an almost ceremonial peacefulness, that is, it seems like peacefulness but is something else altogether.

I went to work and tried to use those old tricks, desperately employed to be indifferent or at least numb to the lingering effects of the Citron case, those bodies found in trunks, in the cold and dusty parking lots at Logan, in Dumpsters, trash cans, storm drains, storage rentals, old refrigerators in junkyards, or just left out there on the sidewalk for people to step over. My hands started shaking. That should have been a sign, but, of course, I believed that everything was going to be fine. So, you're a little shaky. So what? You've made your mistakes, paid for them, with interest, hard interest at that. You are growing wise before you grow old. The rest is pure gravy, right? Why be worried about Mackinnon's First Law of Emotional Gravity? That wounds attract trouble?

Aurlon Miller, a.k.a. the Wizard, and Pia came for a visit in the middle of January. A winter so odd and warm they hardly had to wear coats. I sat in my office with its view of the drive. A gun case stood at the end of the bookshelves with my editions of Marcus Aurelius (and a bust, too), Livy (*The War with Hannibal*), Xenophon (the *Anabasis*), Herodotus, the complete works of Tacitus, and the rest. The guns that had come down to me from my grandfather and the ones given to me by my father were stored there, an L.C. Smith field-grade twenty gauge, a Holland and Holland twelve gauge (which had turned from a field piece to a collector's item), and that Mannlicher, 6.5 mm with open sights. In the kitchen, I dug around in the refrigerator. Would the Wizard like Roquefort cheese? A pear tart? Salmon on cream cheese with capers? I pushed the bags of plastic one way and then another, like a miser uncertain about the count of his gold.

Of course, Pia and I had an unspoken language, and the item we never mentioned was that nothing is more dangerous than the wrong man. Nothing. I wasn't uninformed about this, either, since I saw the police logs, and the investigation reports (the 34-1-A forms) that were filled out for rape, assault, robbery, murder, murder with mayhem, with mutilation, and for various scams that were still being used, such as the Murphy.

The odd, lint-colored light of a New England winter flowed in from the window. I had pushed the plastic bags around in the icebox, my head stuck in there like a bear in a trash can. So, Aurlon and Pia came in, with a whiff of smoke and cold air, while I discarded the salmon, the cheese, the capers, and the rest. Booze, I thought. That's best.

Pia sat on the leather sofa and Aurlon stood at my desk, where he looked down at a manila file that I had left closed, but which was now open. With the tip of one finger and his thumb, as though he didn't want to leave any fingerprints, he turned the pages of a case I was trying to make a decision about. I had left *The Pearl Fishers* playing on the gray, matte-colored electronic equipment I had installed, and Aurlon sang along, not missing a word as he turned a page in the file. This was a summary of a murder indictment: a woman had killed her child and tried to put it, one piece at a time, down the garbage disposal. Her attorney, a public defender, wanted to cop a plea.

I stood in the doorway.

Aurlon was almost six feet tall, slender, as though he had been built to wiggle into small spaces, and his gray eyes and dirty blond hair were oddly familiar. Kurt Cobain? Was that who he looked like? His face was oddly handsome, his acne scars making his complexion rough, his entire aspect at once vulnerable and yet tough. He looked as if he had been in jail, not a penitentiary, just a jail. His hair smelled of Pia's shampoo, and he looked as though he had taken a shower and then put on his dirty clothes. Gray shirt with a sort of cape over it.

"What are you doing?" I said.

With one long finger he flicked the file shut.

"Hi, Dad, this is Aurlon Miller."

"Just Miller is OK," he said. "Some people call me the Wizard. You know, just for fun."

"Don't look at my papers again," I said. "Is that clear?"

"Oh," he said. "I didn't understand all that legal stuff anyway."

"Miller knows a lot of opera," said Pia. She had that look, too. *Don't,* she seemed to say. *Just be nice, OK?*

"You got a lot of nice things," Miller said. "Very cool sound."

"I'm glad you like it," I said.

He turned an ear to a speaker. "Great sound. Really great sound."

The second act, the most beautiful duet, came on. We listened, although Miller kept his eyes on me to see just what effect beauty had. Was that a weapon?

"I see you've got a chess set. You want to play?"

He spoke like a three-card monte man who stood behind a card table at Harvard Square and fleeced the suckers who came in from the suburbs. And, of course, a three-card monte man is what he was. He had a tensile, cobra-like intensity, a toughness that while seeming to be a stance, might have been more than that.

He took two pawns, one black, one white, and put them in his hands behind his back.

"Pick," he said.

I got the white. He smiled.

"Good," he said. "I guess we'll see what you know. I guess it's possible to make a living playing chess, but most chess players are so broke it's hardly worth it."

What would we play for, he seemed to be thinking, after he had let me win a couple of games and then suggested that we make it a little more interesting. How about twenty bucks? How about what was in the gun case? That twenty gauge? The computer? Is that the way it would work? He considered each object in the room, his eyes sweeping along the books (already thinking, or so it seemed, how much he could get for the books at the used bookstore up the block), the desk, the pen there, the paintings on the walls, and then, with a barely perceptible but still acidic smile, he glanced at Pia.

Did I understand? We were going to play for her. This was his horror and his charm: he could take any small action, any small gesture, and fill it with the ominous.

I opened with a king's pawn. He answered. Basic setup, move for move. He made a clumsy attempt at a fool's mate, the moves made with the expression of a douser who is looking for water. What was down there, under the surface?

I had played a lot of chess when I was an undergraduate. At school a Russian grandmaster put on an exhibition, one of those occasions where the grandmaster (in his French suit and with his Russian girlfriend who looked as though she would turn heads in Moscow) played twenty people at one time: it came down to him and me. Of course I made a mistake, but it was close to the end and the grandmaster had had a good scare, but he was still a gentleman, in the old style, and so he wiped his brow, looked me in the eyes, and said, "You play well."

Aurlon and I went at it, and while I tried to avoid trading pieces, just to see how dexterous he was with a lot of possibilities, he traded as often as he could, doing it by the book, taking each small advantage as though it was money in the bank. After all, I thought, why not make a couple of mistakes, just to see if he is up to it? He was. It was five moves to mate, then four, then three, then two.

"I guess that's it," he said.

"You play very well," I said in a voice that I tried to make sound precisely like the grandmaster. "Why don't we try it again?"

"Sure," he said. He looked at Pia. "I've got a little time."

"Let's make it a little more interesting," I said.

"Oh," he said. "I never play for money. It's just the beauty of the game."

"Why not keep it friendly?" said Pia. "It's just a game."

"Yeah," he said. "But I'm being nice to your dad."

"How much do you have on you?" I said.

"Fifty bucks," he said.

"And how much in your shoe?" I said.

"How did you know about that?" he said.

"Lucky guess," I said.

So, we sat there for a moment. He looked across the table with those non-colored eyes, his bad skin, his breathing slow and regular. He nodded to himself, and in that moment, like a sudden breeze on water, he had a little doubt. Was he the mark, or was I? He took off his shoe and took out fifty dollars and put it on the side of the table along with the fifty he took out of his pocket. I moved them to the desk. The money from his shoe smelled like a gym.

"Pia's a nice girl," said Aurlon. He pushed the hair out of his eyes. Then he looked at me so there would be no misunderstanding. "You know what I mean?"

"I can take care of myself," said Pia. "People make that mistake all the time."

"Sure," he said. "I'm sure you can. Let's play."

The house made a slight ticking that you could only hear when the silence was absolute. A dripping in the downstairs bathroom, which I was going to have to get fixed. Every now and then a car went by on Brattle Street with a tearing, ripping sound. Aurlon drew white. King's pawn opening. If he was any good, I could play for a draw, but then he glanced at Pia, at her legs. She looked away, out the window. Then back at me. Was that where it began, in that little defiance, in that moment when she wanted to show me that she could deal with this and any other trouble that might come her way? Or were we still bitter about the end of the line, and did that contribute to her anger?

I pinned a bishop, gained a move, set up according to Aron Nimzowitsch, all slashing angles, from each side, still keeping the pin.

"I've never seen that before," said Aurlon.

He began to sweat. He bit his nails. He put his nose down to the point where he almost touched a rook. His fingers touched a bishop, tilted it on the base. Then he left it alone. He looked at me and then at the money and then at the things in the room.

"Well, well," he said.

He made his move. Five to mate, then four, then three. He knocked his king over.

"Maybe we should play for real money. Or something else," he said. That glance at Pia.

"Sure," I said. "Sure. If you want. I'll give you a chance."

We sat in the silence of the house. The dripping faucet. The creak of the old timber. The ripping of tires on the sidewalk. The sound from the house next door, where my neighbor and his mistress met every Saturday afternoon and got into bed.

"Naw," said the Wizard. "I got to get going."

"Here," I said. I held out the money. "I don't want it."

"You won it," he said. "I should have seen you coming. Serves me right."

"Take the money," I said.

He put out his long, slender, even beautiful fingers and took the bills, and he divided them up as before, half in his pocket, half in his shoe. "You wouldn't believe the people who are crawling around in the square." Then he glanced at Pia and back at me, but this time he dropped that blank, three-card monte glance that was almost cheerful. No, he seemed to say, I'll have to find another way to settle this. He looked at Pia again.

"I'll think of something to do," he said to her. "I'll call you."

He stood, stretched, looked at the chessboard, nodded to himself, and said, "You going to let that woman cop a plea?" He gestured to my desk.

"I'm thinking about it," I said. "Come back to play some other time."

"I plan to," he said. "See you, Pia."

He closed the door.

"You didn't have to do that," said Pia.

"No?" I said. "Why not? You want to bring a hustler in here and let him take me for a mark?"

"You could have been more graceful," she said.

"Is that right?"

"Yes," she said. "I can take care of myself. Don't you think I know what he is? Don't you know me at all?"

"Yes," I said. "I know you. Who would know you better?"

"I've done everything ever asked of me. You wanted a good student. You got it. You wanted someone to row with. You have it. You wanted someone to do well at school. To get the highest score possible on the law boards. You've got it. And you know what?"

"What?"

"I'm tired of being a good girl. How about that? I'm fucking tired of it."

"That doesn't mean you have to be stupid."

"What are you calling me?"

"I didn't mean it like that," I said.

"You know, I can feel confined by you all the way down to the genes. I can feel them, from you, twisted on each other like chains."

"All the better to end-the-line of us then," I said.

The silence seeped into the room like a gas.

"I'm sorry," I said.

"You know I'm never going to have kids. So maybe I can have some fun. Have you ever stood at the edge of a cliff? Wasn't it thrilling?"

"Look," I said.

"Do you know what an ion channel is?" she said.

I closed my eyes.

"An ion channel is a part of a neuron that allows sodium, calcium, potassium, and chloride to move in and out of the cell. An imbalance here is what causes a seizure, but hundreds of people are walking around with the genetic mutation that is known to cause seizures, and nothing happens . . . no one knows. Some do, some don't. So, that's a pretty thin reed, wouldn't you say? And this condition is associated with a lot of other things, too, but the associations are unclear. You want me to go through the list and the biology, the electron flow? Let's start with the specifics of how a brain cell metabolizes sodium, calcium, potassium, and chloride. Get out a piece of paper. I'll show you the formulas. And the irregularities that we know about so far . . . Well?"

"Look . . . ," I said.

"I warned you. Don't underestimate me. And you think you know who I am?"

So, we stood there, almost nose to nose.

"Can I ask you a question?" I said.

"Sure," she said. "Go ahead."

Still on her way up, getting angrier.

"Why are you interested in a guy like this?" I said.

She tossed her hair over her shoulder, then seemed to listen to the silence of the house.

"You want to hear?" she said.

"Yes," I said.

"I like the way he smells. I like the way he is in bed . . . "

"Wait, wait . . . "

"I thought you wanted to hear," she said. "He does something to me. It's hard to describe. Like something that runs right into me, and then I wonder if everything I've done is a mistake. How can anyone, who is so obviously wrong for me, make me feel this way?"

She stood in the doorway, her expression the same as when we had had minor disagreements, or so I thought: a little insistent, piercing, one eyebrow raised. The kind of look she would have given me if I had started to resist her explanation of Fermat's theorem. Or if I had said she was rushing the slide in her boat. Of course, that's the way it began.

She raised a brow, and I knew that if I did what I could to get rid of the Wizard, if I went to friends on the Boston police force and had this jackass arrested, and without any trouble at all, since he was obviously selling drugs or fencing stolen computers or working some silly game, this would be nothing.

So, the rules were clear: she'd see how far she could go, and I'd keep my mouth shut.

So there it was: not the thing I was always afraid of, but a new aspect I had never dreamed of. And it's at moments like this, when you stand at the abyss, where all the potential is right there, that you realize what it means to love someone. The shock, of course, is that you think you understand this, but you don't really until that dark tentacle, that change in light, that possibility of a horror that is at once so ordinary and so appalling has made itself apparent. It walks in the door and tries to look like Kurt Cobain.

Even then I still had hope. Or at least I hoped she knew the Wizard was some kind of cheap thrill. But, of course, something else had stirred in the depths: it was as though when she was young and we went rowing together, or when we talked things over, that we had been too close, too sympathetic, too much like each other. We had been pals, and that was coming back to haunt us: she had wanted a violent, intense rebellion, and both of us had avoided this, if only because we had both hoped, in some grown-up way, from an attitude that was too smart for the way things really happened, that we could get around the rebellion part. We had liked each other. Now, though, we were up against what we hadn't done. And this mixed perfectly with the pure, sweet animal attraction she felt for him.

I swallowed. When you get to be all grown-up you learn how not to cry: you bite down. You swallow. You look into the distance.

She got up and gave me that daughterly peck on the cheek and then turned and left the room, her hips swaying in that spandex, her ponytail bouncing. Now just what the hell was I supposed to do? She was twenty-one.

So, that's how we started: the delayed rebellion would be played out through what she would tell me, and I would take it, stand up to it. If the rebellion was late, we were going to make up for lost time. The trouble was, of course, we had the weapons of an adult. Or she did. She had the future of the Mackinnon family in her crosshairs.

[CHAPTER TWELVE]

"WELL," ALEXANDRA SAID in an email from Rome. "Let me tell you about the apartment they found for me. Two stories, that is a main floor with a living room and a bedroom and upstairs I have a small office from which I can walk out to a roof garden and where I can sit at night: earlier, I had a glass of wine and a pigeon flew from the street below, from the gray shadows to the air above the building, which was filled with light, and the bird suddenly seemed to be covered with gold. Of course, when I saw it, I wanted to turn to you to say, Frank, look. But you weren't there."

Yes, I thought. But even as I missed her and wondered about how she spent her nights, I considered something else. For the first time in my life, I had a chance to be with my daughter, to make decisions on my own, to be closer to her than I ever had been before. Somehow, with everything else that had gone wrong, such as the Citron conviction being overturned on appeal, I wanted to take some action, to be clear-minded, to show my daughter how much I cared.

Pia and I understood the risk, and yet, in the warmth and the intensity and wallop of her smile, in that intelligent expression in her eyes, which suggested that this would be all right (as though intelligence was a way out, when, in fact, as I know, it is often behind the worst things that happen), this understanding of danger only made this all the more attractive. But the risk was real, too: fury and the loss of love could make a dark place where almost anything could happen. We weren't there yet, but we waited at the abyss. Because both of us knew, within an hour of the talk we had had, that if she told me the wrong thing, if Miller was up to something that I couldn't take (and this, I guess, was the boundary, the limit of what we were doing with one another), I'd snap again.

And what would that be? I'd load that L.C. Smith shotgun or that Mannlicher and walk out to the front room when Miller was here and put a 6.5 mm through his head and then reach down to touch those places where the bone had turned to a kind of granulated sugar from the impact. That was my risk, or the risk of having woken up and having allowed myself the reactions to those things I had seen rather than approaching them secondhand, through Thucydides, Xenophon, Tacitus. And, I suppose, this was part of the trap, since if I tried to tell her that I had changed, that I wasn't the reasonable man she had always believed me to be, I would be reduced in her eyes, and if there was anything I craved, that was keeping me in one piece, it was my daughter's approval.

So, we were playing with the scale of the darkness that would allow this to take place, and I thought of the despair, the depths of fury that would take what I had with my daughter, those chips of light on the Charles, the smile, the delight in being perfectly understood and to turn it into that black, appalling place in which everything we don't want is lurking and ready. So, yes, we were getting the contest we never had, although we had learned that truth does hate delay, and that by putting this off, we had made it worse. And maybe my original notions were right: a child has that mystical instinct for that psychic bruise, as though the mind was a pear with a soft spot.

Miller came back to our house the next weekend and Pia made him some pasta puttanesca, which he ate with good appetite. When I came into the kitchen he had a glass of wine that I had been saving for Alexandra's return, and he toasted me. And he had that look as before: he was going to work now, and we were going to settle things that needed to be settled. He wasn't a young man who liked to be defeated, not if cunning and deviousness could be brought to bear. In my office they listened to *Madame Butterfly* and then the Ramones.

"You like this oldy stuff?" he said.

"It gets better as the time goes by," I said.

"Yeah," he said. "I guess."

Then Pia went upstairs to change before they went to a movie, and as she ran up the stairs, I wondered what it was: her diaphragm? Is that what she needed? Miller raised an eyebrow: yeah, he seemed to guess that was it.

"All right," I said. "You want a drink?"

"Sure," he said. "Let's be gentlemen."

He stood in my study and put his hands in his pockets. The books, on three walls, appeared orderly, brown, with titles in gold and red. I poured him a drink and he took it while he went along the shelves and said, "Lot of books."

"Yeah," I said.

"Is that what you read when you are getting ready for a case, huh?" he said. "By the way, what did you do with the woman? You know, the one who wanted to cop a plea."

"I haven't decided," I said.

"Must be tough to lose a case," he said. "I read about one in the paper. What was the guy's name? And that woman. Sally Sunshine? Is that what they called her?"

"What's it to you?" I said.

"Nothing," he said. "Just making polite conversation."

He finished his drink as Pia came down the stairs, jumping two or three at a time, even though she was in good shoes with a heel. That innocence, if that's what it is, was still there, no matter what she did. She came into the room with a faint whiff of perfume—gardenias? Some other flower? She smiled at me as though to say, Well, all right. This is the first test. You seem to be standing up to it all right.

"I might be late," she said.

"We're going out dancing," said Miller.

"Be careful," I said.

"Sure," she said. "See you later."

They went outside, where they laughed ("Careful?" he said. "Why, where is the fun in that?") and got into her Volkswagen. The sad whack of the doors of the car as they slammed came into the room and then the puttering of the engine left me with the tick of the house as the silence settled in, the residue of her perfume. The gun case opened quickly and I took out the Mannlicher and threw back the action, which was so perfectly machined, so goddamned German, that it moved with a kind of fluid grace, a perfection of engineering. A rifle Hegel could have loved. A box of ammunition sat on the top shelf and I picked it up, feeling the sudden heaviness, the weight, as though death was congealed here, made into an intense sense of gravity.

Alexandra and Pia had given me a piece of stone with a fish, a fossil, about nine inches long, itched into it with all the perfect weight of time. I used to look at it when I was working on a case, or when I needed reassurance, but now, when I reached up to touch it, the thing was gone.

Just like that: two hundred million years. Just vanished. Had Aurlon put it in the pocket of his down coat that leaked feathers from time to time?

• • •

In the first week of February, I stopped at the card table in Harvard Square where the Raver sold handprinted epigrams that he had picked up in a flying saucer. ("Look to the beauty in yourself and look to the beauty in universe. They are related.") The fossil of the fish sat next to some secondhand books, *Dr. Spock's Baby Care*, *Goodnight Moon*, *Physics for the Practical Man*. The stand was missing, but it sat on the table with all the power of time made real. I got it for a tenth of what it was worth and then bought a new stand at an art supply shop and put it back on the mantle. When Miller came to visit his eyes stopped on it, then on me, and then he smiled.

"That's a nice fish," he said. Then he looked around the room and came back to it. "Yeah, that's nice. Can I pick it up?"

The shape of the ancient fish, so perfectly etched on that stone, sat in his long fingers, and he moved it up and down, as though its value could be determined by weight, or that movement was a kind of assay. Then he said, "It's probably not worth that much, I guess. In terms of money. Maybe it's just more sentimental value."

"You could say that," I said.

"It's funny about that," he said. "How people get hurt. Why sometimes things get going wrong and you don't know where they're going to end up."

That smile again. And yet, he carried himself with an air of the tragic, or the romantically doomed, his hair long, his skin pale as moonlight, his entire aspect one of intensity in the face of long odds. Yes, it was Kurt Cobain. That was the look.

"Your daughter really thinks the world of you," he said. "Do you know that?"

"Are you threatening me?" I said.

"Oh, Frank," he said. "What do you take me for?" He brushed his hair out of his eyes.

[CHAPTER THIRTEEN]

NOW, AFTER MY father has died, and I think of him in those months before that piñata party, I realize he was dying right before my eyes. It was as though he was facing an enormous, black accordion and it was closing up, getting closer, until it would be flat against him.

So, in those months when my difficulties began to build, he came to see me, but I missed the details that should have told me the time was getting closer. Fourteen months. Twelve months. Getting closer. He seemed gray, although I thought this was just a hangover, and sometimes he stared at nothing, or through the world around us. He could hear the clock. I could not. Sometimes, though, he seemed to carry an odd whiff, as though he wasn't all here, or he was part of some experiment that left him marked in a way that only those about to die were marked. More a mood than a fact.

So, the winter when Aurlon showed up, when he began his work, we had no snow and unseasonably high temperatures, and we didn't even have snow on the land my father owned. It was so warm the bears were out, too.

We knew this because the Girls Club was taking advantage of the open winter. They sat around the fireplace in what had been my grandfather's house, sang songs, toasted marshmallows, and took walks in the woods that were gray, but at least not snowy. The springs were already running and the stream, Trout Cabin, wasn't frozen. But a particular bear was out, one my father and I had known about and seen for years, and he was hanging around the Girls Club, digging through their trash, scaring the ones from Scranton and such places to death. Then the bear, old, enormous, waddling, but seeming malevolent to the Girls Club, walked across the property line of my father's land and disappeared into the swamp there.

The Girls Club's camp director called twice a day. "We just can't have this," she said to my father. "What would happen if the bear mauled a girl? What then?"

So, in the midst of this dogfight with my daughter, when my father was getting closer to that explosion in his head, his pink Cadillac, the one he would later run into the Charles and which would end up in a junkyard, pulled into my drive, the car leaking hydraulic fluid as always. The car came to the end of the drive, the tires locking when my father pulled on the brakes. Then he kicked open the door and stepped out in his retro preppy pants and a hunting jacket, a khaki coat with a Pendleton blanket lining, which he always said would have been handy in Poland. Now, he came up to the door, opened it without knocking, came into the study, where I sat at my desk with a file (bones found in a furnace, but the DNA showed they were not related to anyone in the house where they were found). He opened the gun cabinet, took out the Mannlicher and the ammunition, and said, "You know, Frank, I let you keep this. And it's sort of yours. But I need it. And you, too. Come on. I've got a problem. You know, there are times when I've had it up to here with problems."

He put a hand under his chin and drew it across the skin as though he was cutting his throat. I should have known what this meant: what is life but a series of problems with moments of unbelievable happiness? The happiness was gone. That black accordion was made up of problems. He was gray. His eyes were bloodshot.

"You know how much one of these 6.5 mm cartridges cost?" he said. "Four dollars and fifty cents. So we better make sure we don't use too many. Get some jeans on. And old shirt. Boots. A red jacket. Come on. It's Saturday, so I know you don't have to work."

"What's going on?" I said.

"Just get your stuff. I'll have a drink while you get dressed. How's Pia?"

"Fine, fine," I said.

"Glad to hear it," he said. "I think we'll drive your German piece of junk. Der Grauer Geist."

"Where are we going?"

"To the farm. Those Girls Scouts, or their leader, the one with the butch haircut and those glasses with black frames . . . "

"Buddy Hollyette?" I said.

"Is that what you call her?" he said. "She's complaining about a bear—it eats their garbage, and she says it was following a girl who had her period. Do you think that's true?"

"Could be," I said.

"Well, she says the bear comes from our land and that we've got to get rid of it. It's a nuisance, she says. And since I have the hunting rights, she wants me to do it."

"It's out of season," I said.

"You know, for a lawyer, you don't see things very clearly. The law is made to be bent, to get what you want. I'll show you. Come on."

So we drove the Audi to the farm, out 84, to the ridge of mountains along the Delaware Valley, and because the weather was so warm the mist hung there, over the river, like some ominous smoke.

The Delaware was as constant and indifferent as any river on earth. We went up the dirt road that leads to the farm from the river and I drove through the woods, white oaks mostly, where a deer ran over the gray leaves left from the fall. We stopped in front of the stone house, the one built for my father's dead brother.

The main room was musty and a snakeskin hung over the mantle. The wood stove stood in the corner. One bedroom, where my father would sleep, was under the loft, and in the main room sat the dusty sofa. This is where the snake was supposed to live in the furniture's wooden frame, where I was supposed to sleep.

"You don't mind a little snake, do you?" said my father.

It was just dusk and that blue was about to absorb everything. We went outside and my father said, "That goddamned Girls Club. What do they think bears are? Stuffed, in the museum of natural history."

"If they're eating garbage, they aren't afraid of people," I said.

"Just whose side are you on?" said my father. "You'd think that bear would have enough sense to stay away from them. But I guess they are picky eaters and throw away a lot of good stuff. Bacon. You know a bear loves bacon. So, the two of us, you and me, we're going to settle the bear's hash. Screw it. I'm ready to make problems go away. Bang. I've got other things to worry about."

"Me, too," I said.

"No kidding, Frank?" he said. "Well, when the problems get bad enough, come to see me. I'll set you straight."

That blue light darkened a shade: you never saw it change, but there it was, slightly more opaque.

"By the way," said my father. "Has Pia got a boyfriend?"

"Some jackass from Harvard Square," I said. "Thief, three-card monte stiff, small-time dope dealer, I guess, maybe a pimp for runaways . . . "

"Why don't you call Tim Marshall. I'll bet he's got some bad medicine for this twit."

"She's already warned me about that," I said. "Have you ever played chess with her?"

"Boy, was that a mistake," said my father. He swallowed. "Does she worry about Jerry? Does she think she is stained?"

"Let's stick with the bear," I said.

The bear had a lineage, since it must have been the son or daughter of the bears that used to run around on this land when it was owned by my grandfather, large black bears that left scratches on the trees as they marked their usual paths, which they followed each day with astonishing regularity.

So, as we started our walk in the evening, we didn't need to say anything. My father was trying to decide whether or not to kill the bear, at least this one that had survived in spite of the houses that were springing up along the northern boundary of the land that my father still had left. More people came to poach deer on this land than even a few years before, but I didn't mind that so much since in the closest town, where the railroad had failed, a lot of people were hungry. What got to my father about the poaching was the fact that the people who killed these deer ground them up and mixed them with hamburger helper.

We walked in that smoking gloom of dusk, and as we went,

he didn't speak, although I now know he wanted to talk to me. He didn't have enough money, and time was collapsing in front of him. Maybe he had done some funny stuff with the money that had been left to me. Was it time to talk about that? No. That wasn't his style at all. Deny it to the end, which he knew was coming.

So, we went looking for that bear, which was a stand-in, I guess, for a lot of problems like the money. My father's attitude, his movement, the color of his eyes still linger (his eyes were blue, but pale, as though they were part of a man who is only partially here, who is so clearly only passing by this way, who has only the most tenuous grip on life).

I thought I should just be quiet. And now, when I think back, it haunts me. Could I have comforted him? Well, probably not, given that the first part of comfort is admission of wrongdoing, and that would never happen. So, maybe that added to the bear's chances: that my father was trapped by his own way of doing things. Me? he'd say. You're barking up the wrong tree. I began to think that bear was in more trouble than previously. Here, my father could say to the director of the Girls Club. Here's the dead body. It's all yours.

The wood road we took had been built two generations ago to drag logs to a sawmill that was long gone (nothing left but a saw blade rusted to the color of a scab), and now it was only a trail, but like a formal garden, since the trees made a bower over it. At the bottom a spring ran in this warm winter, and the air was filled with the scent of the early watercress. My father stopped in that ammonia scent.

Above the spring an abandoned apple orchard had been overtopped by pines, and the apple trees looked like skeletons, the wood without bark, ghostly and white there in the increasing blue light of the evening.

"See," said my father. "Without a place like this, what have you got? But the taxes are killing me."

"I'm sorry," I said.

"Don't you dare be sorry for me," he said. "I'm hanging on to this place so you can have a little of it. Don't you see? I'm trying to give you something."

"I didn't mean it like that."

He stopped in the blue light, under the bower of trees, where the scent of watercress was so strong.

"You know, Frank, I'd like to talk to you about something . . ."

"Sure," I said.

"Well, a little money was left . . . ," he said.

"I know," I said. "Three hundred a month."

"Yeah, yeah," he said. "Well, that's right. Technically . . . "

"So?"

He brushed the leaves with his boot one way and then another, and he made an open space on the ground just like a buck rub.

"You wanted to say something?" I said.

"No, no," he said. He shook his head. "I'm keeping records. It's all there. I'll store them carefully."

"Where?" I said.

"Down in the cellar. I'm getting it waterproofed . . . "

Then we walked through the orchard and into the woods where the ash and oak were so big you couldn't get your arms around them, and where, at this time of the year, the trees stood up from a layer of gray leaves. The entire landscape was gray, the bark of the tree, the leaves, the stone that stuck up: the only color was greenish lichen which, on the rocks, was the color of oxidized copper. A wild turkey pawed at the ground for an acorn. My father kept right on walking until he came to a spot that he liked.

"Might as well cut down some of these trees. Have some logger in here," said my father. "Get some money out of them.

Why should we leave these trees here for the next guy to sell? That is, when you get rid of the place."

"I didn't say I was going to do that," I said.

"I didn't tell my father I was going to sell a thousand acres to the Girls Club." He shrugged, as though seeing a dead friend on a road in Poland. It was a gesture far beyond despair. "You may think money isn't important, but let me tell you. It comes back to bite you."

On the way back to the stone house, the bear came out of the shadows. We were at the spring where the watercress grew, and the bear was a blur on gray black, and its fur was the color of a can of black shoe polish, with that muted sheen. It came out of the abandoned orchard where the trees looked like what had been left over after a forest fire: trees without bark, just that hard white wood. The bear moved with a steady, sloppy gait. It was fat from grubs and, I guess, the garbage. Usually, at this time of the year, late winter, bears have just woken up and are skinny. But this one wasn't skinny. Maybe the Girls Club threw away donuts and cheesecake, bacon fat and pancakes. Its belly swung from side to side and it moved its head one way and then another, its path going downhill, toward the stream. It stopped at a deadwood, a tree that had died a long time ago, and the bear tore at the trunk, its claws as white as the dead apple trees in the orchard, and as the punky bits came out, you could see the chips, the shreds, the black debris of half-rotted wood. Like something exploding. The bear found a grub here and there, ate it like a man consuming peanuts, and then continued downhill.

It stopped. It was as though the bear was tasting the grubs, or what it had found in the deadwood, or maybe it was thinking about going all the way down to the bottom of the gorge, where it would just have to climb up again on the other side of the stream. Maybe it was getting tired of the routine, of that struggle to get to the top of the other side of the gorge. Then the bear turned its head with a muted and yet piercing fatality, his eyes going over the landscape with the most profound sense of farewell, of letting go of the place where it lived, although when he came to us, it stopped. The bear's eyes appeared, with the white snout but black fur above it, like an entrance to a world we could never understand. The eyes had a sheen to them, like black marbles. Then the animal stepped toward us, its fat sides swaying just a little in that measured gait, which so clearly showed a sort of rumination, a thinking that was done not in the mind but in the body, in the way the claws touched those cinnamon-colored ferns, the way his old and probably arthritic joints squeaked, in the lingering taste of the grubs.

"Stay still," said my father.

The thing kept on walking, coming back up to the watercress, where it stopped to have a drink in the spring and then went back to staring at us. My father stood without moving at all, not a quiver, not a breath, his pale eyes showing some deep consideration, some memory that he was still trying to make sense of: the flak that rose around him, his time in the air, swinging in his parachute like a target in a shooting gallery. I was just beginning to learn something about regret, just the first hint that there are things hidden away in the future and that we are trained not to think about them. For my father, the future had arrived.

But there it was: he got through things by keeping his mouth shut or telling lies. And, of course, what did I know about that ticking clock, how the hand was moving, getting ready to point him out?

The only movement was a few strands of hair on the side of his head that lifted and settled, feathers falling from a shot bird. The bear was close enough for its smell to come downwind: the entrails of a deer, the clean, silver scent of the stream, like dirty socks and the bitter sweet stink in the bottom of a garbage can, and something else, too, a wild, arctic perfume, not smelled but felt as when you can feel that snow is on the way.

That odor became stronger, and for a moment it reminded me of a fish market, of the ocean. The bear breathed with a slow, laboring effort, all the more alarming because it seemed to be unexcited. It kept its eyes on my father, as though it knew (by scent, by my father's gray hair, by his old clothes) that this was between the two of them. The bear stepped closer, not so much that we could touch it, but enough so that the nose was dark as a piece of coal.

"The color of flak," said my father. "Right after the red part, after the explosion."

The bear made that slow, steady *huff*, *huff*, and it was cold enough for the breath to show. Its head dropped, as though something important was on the ground, and when it looked up, its eyes settled on mine. The eyes fixed me, like the lens of a camera. I stared back, even though a bear takes this as a sign of hostility, of evidence that a fight was coming.

In the woods, in front of the bear, my father turned his pale eyes on me, their expression one of mystification, not so much as in what he understood, but in his inability ever to sum it up. I guess all he really wanted to give me was the refusal to panic. He hadn't panicked ever, not even in Poland. In fact, just the opposite was true: at the absolute worst, he panicked the least.

"All right," he said. "Let's take care of this fucking thing."

The bear turned away, its fat belly swaying, its claws clicking when they touched the field stone that stood up between the trees, and as it walked downhill, a black snake flowed downhill, too, its skin like patent leather, its eyes like beads made of coal. It flowed around the stones, water going downhill.

"Timber rattler. Just out of a den," said my father. "Aren't many left."

The bear looked over his shoulder at us, taking inventory. Yes, it seemed to say, we'll meet again.

And so my father and I walked up to the stone house, where we got the stove going, and with the damper open it made a *huff, huff, huff*, just like the bear. The stove had been made in Sweden, and it had three compartments to hold the smoke, one on top of another to get all the heat.

"So," said my father. "We've made the hard decision."

He sipped his drink. The stones of the house began to warm up and he sat there, looking out the window where he expected to see that bear.

He gestured toward me, one hand out, fingers open, as though offering something and asking for something in the same moment: the sound of the stove, that *huff, huff*, so much like the bear now that it seemed like a hint of mortality. Did that make the coming moment, which could take almost any form (an exploding piñata, for instance) all the more real? Was he trying to tell me it was coming? Was that it? If I wanted to speak, I better do it then? So, I was left with the bear, my father, the unspoken thing, whatever it was, all in that sound, so asthmatic, so desperate for air.

He sloshed more bourbon into my glass, although, at least, he didn't add sweet vermouth. The stove made that *huff, huff, huff*. The clinking of ice in his glass matched that huffing, mean-spirited, ominous sound. He seemed to be back in Poland, because he said out of the blue, "Blood sausage." The snow in Poland, the camps, the barbed wire, that violent, ghastly world that everyone seemed to think was disappearing but that was really just reconfiguring itself, finding new places to emerge again, to do its worst. I thought about that young man who had found a way to get between my daughter and me.

"Tomorrow we'll deal with that bear," said my father.

We knew what the bear's run was. We even knew what its mother's run or its father's run had been, since we had been here for generations. We had bacon and eggs and toast, the eggs cooked in the grease in the pan while the stove made that sound. That *huff, huff, huff*. My father looked at me across the table when we ate those basted eggs, clouded over from the hot grease he had used to cook them. We sat there, as though we had nothing to say, which is how people appear when they have everything to say. Then we went out the door in our coats, our blue jeans, our boots, my father with that Mannlicher. We closed the wooden door and it made a sucking hush in the frame.

We went downhill in that light just before dawn, which is not the darkest but the most blue, with the trees emerging like imploring shapes, the limbs black on blue as though that world where all the phantoms exist gives up its hold on the earth grudgingly, and no more grudgingly than when a man and his son go out into the blue light to look for a bear. We went down the path, going almost by smell, since the watercress was strong after the cool night. The woods were silent, although as the black became dark blue, the first of the birds made a noise, but it wasn't cheerful, wasn't anything but a sound that pierced me, since here we were, in that dusk, in that chaos before the light.

We went along that formal path, and then we turned uphill, into the woods that were a combination of red oak and white oak, bark as gray as an elephant. Spruce grew here, too, the needles as green as money. We kept to the high ground, up there where the rocks stuck out and where the lichen showed on them in gray-green blotches. And all along my father went ahead, bent over a little, going slow, carrying that Mannlicher (round chambered, safety on) in his right hand. Then he turned to me. His eyes were filled with tears.

"What is it?" I said.

"Oh, you'll see," he said. "Give it some time."

He bit his lip and then we started along that ridge that went above the stream.

We were halfway up the slope, surrounded by that timber he thought we should sell some day, the trunks tall and cathedral-like. Down below, at the bottom of the gorge, the stream, Trout Cabin, flowed along, not frozen either in this odd, warm winter, from one pool to another, one silver spout above another. Then the sun began to rise and long slanting rays cut through the haze. We sat there, breathing, the mist from our breath rising.

The bear came out of the haze with that gait, its fur looking as though it had been tinted silver by those spots of water that slipped from one pool in the stream to another: the silver of silvers, the shine of shines, that existed here only for the moment when you are up against something that cries out to be said but can't be heard. Mortality, love, the power of one generation being passed to another: all these things were in that silver glint, which seemed to flow back and forth with the bear's lumbering gait. I could smell it, since we were downwind: a sort of damp, moldering odor, like the stink of a deer that emerges from the snow in the springtime, a sort of vague rotting, dog-like scent that has something else underneath it, the reek of vitality, of attraction, of resistance. Its breath seemed to carry along, too, and it had been eating some garbage or carrion, or maybe more grubs found in the logs.

The bear went right along beneath us, its head swinging a little from side to side, its claws flinging out and flopping down in a way that was almost funny, but maybe that was just the work of perception of all those movies that tried to make bears cute. This was not cute. My father slipped off the safety of his rifle.

"Head or heart?" he said.

The bear stopped next to one of those pieces of stone that

rose out of the ground like the prow of a sinking boat. It looked one way and then another, and with the sun rising behind us, we must have been hard to see, but nevertheless, in spite of the wind, in spite of the difficulty of the light, it stopped and faced us. Its eyes were filled with the double suns, one in each eye. It raked one claw over the ground, as though a grub could be found there. Behind us, from a roost, the wild turkeys descended, and the flap of wings, like some unknown presence, shuddered down to the ground. The bear glanced from the birds to us. It waited.

"Head is faster," I said. "No blood trail to track."

"Yeah," said my father. "It's a harder shot, though."

"It's not much range," I said.

"No," said my father. "Not much." He swallowed. Then he shrugged. The sky above the trees was precisely the color of his eyes, and a black cross appeared here and there: a hawk looking for something to eat.

He put the safety on.

"I'll tell you what," he said.

The bear moved its head from side to side.

"I'll leave this bear for you to kill one day. You may have to. Even though you don't want to. You'll be alone. You'll have done your best. It might not be good enough. That's what haunts."

The bear turned to the side: it was as though he was offering the perfect shot, just behind the foreleg, right where the heart was. He waited, his head turned toward us. He was doing his part, and what about us? Then he looked uphill where more wild turkeys fluttered off the roost with a rush of wings, and then the bear went into the mist and turned downhill, toward those silver spouts in the stream.

My father unloaded the Mannlicher, the bright hulls wheeling like gold coins in a pirate's hand. Then he gave it to me.

"It's yours now," he said. "Not just to keep in your study. But yours for good. You're going to need it."

The open woods appeared like gray fur, although here and there the ferns had yet to grow and were a rusty color. The turkeys moved.

"Strange weather," said my father.

[CHAPTER FOURTEEN]

THE NEXT WEEKEND, early February, a greenish puddle of hydraulic fluid formed on the apron beneath the Audi in front of my house, as though to make me feel that as much as I had tried to escape being my father's son, this liquid, so slimy and yet critical to the way things worked, was there to remind me that I had been kidding myself. His character was sneaking up on me not only in my impulses but through my cars, too. Well, I wasn't going to take it the way he did. That is, I wasn't going to drive around with the emergency break and, as he would have put it, "a wing and a prayer." Or in his case, maybe just a prayer.

I got down on my hands and knees, in my blue jeans and a sweatshirt that Pia had given me ("It all depends on conditions," it said), and then flipped over on my back and pushed under the car to avoid that green lagoon, that pool of fate, and put my fingers here and there, into the tubing and lines, the cast aluminum, the wires and bolts to see where this stuff, as slippery as the side of a trout, was coming from. Of course, the engineers had fixed things so nothing fell in a straight line, but, instead, ran across some pump, or crossbeam, or clutch housing, and then dripped to the black apron in front of the house. Nothing clear. Nothing definite.

The shoes that moved along the side of the Audi belonged to Aurlon Miller. Brand-new Nikes, white, clean, somehow cool in the way they laced. They walked to the front of the car, then back to where I was stretched out, flat on my back, the odor of that fluid strong under the car, like the scent of the mechanical age. His head slowly appeared next to the ground.

"These Audis," he said. "The maintenance will make you crazy. It's like having a kid, right?"

"It's leaking hydraulic fluid," I said.

"Sure it is," said Aurlon. "I noticed it the other day when I was here. Even looked under the hood. And you know what? You're going to have to replace the power steering pump. Take it from me. It's curtains for that papasan. What do you think it's going to cost?"

"I don't know," I said.

"A shitload," he said. "Going to be three grand. I'm telling you, Frank, it's not going to be a dime less."

"Maybe not," I said.

His face disappeared and the Audi creaked as he leaned on the roof. Writing something down, I guessed. His shoes were pointing directly at me, as though he was getting ready to give me a kick. If I slid out, on my back, it would be less than ideal: that's the last way I wanted to appear, knocked out and trying to get up before the count.

"Here," said Aurlon. He pushed a piece of paper, torn from

the *Daily Racing Form*, under the car. In block letters he had written, "Bargain Auto Parts, Stanislav Ivakina, Prop."

"That's where to go if you don't want to get beaten on the price for a pump. That's the place. Believe me."

He held out the scrap of newsprint. I wanted to tell him the precise spot of his anatomy where he could roll this up and shove it, but then, with a sort of genetic resignation, since my father loved nothing more than a bargain, I took the thing and put it in my pocket.

• • •

"You know," said Aurlon on the other side of the chessboard, a black pawn in one hand, the white in the other, both held behind his back. "That attack you used when we played before? That was from Aron Nimzowitsch. It took me a while at the library. Why, you have to push those geeks away from the computers, but I looked at a couple of his games. What a devious guy. Why, you could never tell what he was up to. Is that why you like him? The countermoves were B to K3, R to Q1, then you castle, and KN to R4. Pick."

Pia read a book on the sofa. Miller and I sat opposite each other, his eyes on Pia from time to time, the fullness of her hair, the way she tucked her legs under herself as she read, the way she tucked her hair behind ear, all of it done with a grace that charged the room.

"Pia and I were thinking about her taking some time off before law school," Miller said. "Go out to Montana, Utah, Wyoming. See a little of the country." He held out the pieces.

"Is that right?" I said to Pia. "Have you heard anything from the school?"

"Yes," she said. She kept her eyes down.

"Well, what did they say?"

"I got in," she said. "Nice fat envelope."

My calendar showed it was February 12th. She must have known for a while, a week anyway.

"Why didn't you tell me?" I said.

"I don't know," said Pia. "Harvard Schmarvard."

"Harvard Schmarvard?" I said.

"Pick," said Aurlon. "Aron Nimzowitsch. You won't catch me again with that, papasan."

"Did you tell them you had accepted?" I said to Pia.

"Yeah," she said. "But . . . I've never been out West."

Is that what we were playing for? That Pia would forget law school? Or was Aurlon looking for a psychological advantage, and when he had it, we'd play for five hundred dollars? Of course, I underestimated him, but if you don't know all of the vipers on earth, how can you recognize each one? After all, an Australian brown snake, the most poisonous on earth, looks pretty bland.

"We could go on the road, Pia and me, make some pottery," said Miller to me. "Macramé. Tie-dye. You know? Hit the crafts circuit. Sell some other stuff."

"So, it's money you want?"

"You've got to have money, Frank," said Miller.

"Sure," I said.

We set up the pieces.

"Maybe we should make it more interesting," I said. "Maybe you don't have to worry about making pottery."

"You're nothing but a hustler," said Miller. "Jesus, I've got to watch myself around you." He looked over his shoulder. "Hey, Pia, you were right. He wants to play for money."

She shrugged and looked down at her book.

"Sure," he said. "A hundred." He put five twenties on the table. "Pick."

I drew white. Fast opening. Then we started in earnest. He had gotten better, and he played with a sureness that had been lacking before. He didn't touch the pieces anymore while he thought about a move. He rocked back and forth a little, nodding to himself, then moved the piece with a gesture so final it was as though he was stamping a form at the post office. Maybe I could let him win five hundred, a thousand, would that do the trick? Or maybe I could take him aside and just write him a check. No, cash held together with a rubber band. But he would use it two ways: against me while taking advantage of it. Here, he'd say to Pia, your old man is trying to buy me off. What do you think of that? Come on, let's buy a VW bus, you know, see the country. You ever been to Ennis, Montana? Nice town.

He traded pieces whenever he could to get to the endgame. The sounds disappeared: no cars on the street, no ticking of the old house, no dripping faucets, just that silence filled with possibilities.

He knocked his king over.

"Well, well," he said. "I thought you were just a one-trick pony."

I took the money that was on my desk.

"Oh," he said. "Taking the money, too. Frank, you must be getting more serious. A lot more serious."

"It's just a game," I said.

Pia glanced up.

"Maybe," said Miller. "Come on, Pia. Let's take a drive."

"I've got work to do," said Pia.

"You can do it later," said Miller. "Give yourself a break."

Pia closed her books.

"Maybe you're right," she said.

Her car made that slow, sad puttering out to Brattle Street, and the brake lights glowed as she waited to make the turn, and then disappeared into the stream of traffic. At least, on Sunday, she'd go back to school, since she hadn't graduated yet, although I wondered if he was going back to New Haven with her.

• • •

Usually I went to the Audi dealership, and sometimes my father came along to use his prison camp German with the mechanic, who had been born and trained in Stuttgart. The mechanic enjoyed my father, as most people did, although like everyone else the mechanic misunderstood him and didn't have a clue that when my father spoke to him about the Audi, my father was thinking of those lines of barbed wire, like lines of music, like notes against that yellowish air beyond the prison camp fence. Now, though, I drove to the Audi place on Mass Avenue alone. They wanted $2,891.89 for a hydraulic pump. Not labor. Just the pump. Miller's handwriting had swirls for the cross stroke of a *T*, and loops for the tail of a g, but the address was still legible. I was a sitting duck: tired of getting screwed for $2,891.89. As though nothing else was involved.

Braintree is pure strip, miles of muffler shops and donut houses, but not new, not promising cheap convenience, but rundown paltriness. Here and there an abandoned car sat in front of a house with a collapsed porch, missing asphalt shingles, and a dented trash can, without the lid, sideways in the gutter. Men stood in front of a donut shop, each with an extralarge Styrofoam cup, which they drank from as the cars, with doors obviously locked, went by a little above the speed limit.

The sign out front said Bargain Auto Parts, STANISLAV IVAKINA, PROP. A fence, not wood but fiberboard covered with plastic, went around about an acre, although cars showed here and there, fifteen feet in the air, windshields with the mark of the modern age: that spider web of cracks that had been made by someone's head. The gate in the fence was open, but topped with razor wire like the rest of the fence. It looked like an outpost in Afghanistan.

Stanislav Ivakina's office wasn't too much bigger than a booth for a parking lot. He had a crew cut that had grown out, acne scars that he tried to cover up with makeup, was heavy in the arms and chest, and he wore a black sweater under a black leather coat. It wasn't that cold, but he had a space heater in the corner, the filament as bright as the hot wire of a toaster. And in the corner, on a piece of fiberboard held up on sawhorses, sat a samovar. Or what I thought was a samovar: it was like an urn to keep the ashes of an ancestor, a brass thing with handles, but it had a little spigot. Next to it sat a cheap stainless steel microwave with a digital clock and some hieroglyphics, little stars, and clocks, and something that looked like an exclamation mark.

"Come in, come in," he said.

It was hot inside, and as I took off my coat, a woman pushed in, too, and sat down in front of a Mac that was next to the samovar. She was tall with pale skin, made all the more obvious because of the black hair and blue eyes. She spoke Russian to Stanislav Ivakina, but he just shrugged and made a gesture of dismissal with his left hand, the one that didn't hold a cup.

"Give my guest a cup of tea," he said to her.

"Aurlon Miller sent me," I said. "He said you might be able to help with a part."

"Aurlon, Aurlon . . . ?" said Stanislav to the woman with pale skin, black hair, and eyes the color of a purple iris.

"The guy in Cambridge," she said. "You know, the one who brings in an air . . . "

"Oh, him," said Stanislav. "Yeah. Yeah. I know the guy."

The woman took my coat, glanced at the label, and put it

over the back of a chair. Her fingers were cool when she handed me a cup of tea.

"My friends have tea when we do business," said Stanislav Ivakina.

I took the cup. The woman turned her back and sat down at the computer and began scrolling through pages of auto parts, although she left a scent, a musky perfume that suggested the steppes, or maybe just Russia, those churches where incense has been burned for years and which makes the atmosphere seem different than just air. Death and beauty.

"You must be Stanislav," I said.

"Stas," he said. "No one around here can say Stanislav. When I go to the dentist I know it's my turn because the nurse starts mumbling. Sit down."

The woman said something in Russian. Or was it German?

"She says you have a nice coat. So what's a guy with an Armani coat doing in Braintree?"

"I need a pump," I said.

"For an Audi, right?" he said. "I see that's what you're driving. Took a dump on you, I bet. Goddamned things. And you want to talk about expensive? I bet they wanted three grand for it."

"That's right," I said.

"I can do something for you. Aurlon was right to send you," said Stas. "Don't you like your tea?"

It was pungent, and it had that same musky scent and hint of the exotic that came from the hair or skin of the woman who typed at the Mac. She spoke again, but Stas shook his head.

"Looks like a new one," he said. "Your Audi. Isn't it covered under warranty?"

"It's just expired," I said.

"That's the way of the world these days," said Stas. "They've got it down to a science. Am I right?" he said to the woman.

"You're right," she said.

"That's Yana," said Stas.

She just touched the palm of my hand with her fingers. Then she went back to typing, the keys clicking with a languid pace.

"I'll see what I can do about the pump," he said. "It will take a day. Where can I reach you?"

I held out one of my cards. He took it between the tip of his thumb and forefinger, read it, and then said something in German to the woman at the computer. She turned around and looked at me, from my hair to my shoes. Then she looked at the Audi, then smiled at me, and said something in Russian.

"So," said Stas. "A district attorney."

He stood up and for a moment I thought he was going to kiss me on each cheek. But he shook my hand, bowed a little, then sat down.

"I know a joke about a lawyer," he said. He gestured toward the junked cars outside, as though that's where the joke was. He had a ring, too, a gaudy diamond in a lump of gold.

"I do, too," I said.

"We'll tell them some other time," he said. "When we need a laugh."

The woman went on typing.

So, we sat in that overheated room, drinking tea from the samovar as that woman typed, as she used the mouse to scroll through parts, and from time to time she made a phone call, either in Russian or German, although before she began she turned to Stas and said something in Russian, and he answered and said to me, "You don't speak Russian or German do you?"

"No," I said. "My father speaks German."

"Where did he learn it?" said Stas.

"Prison camp," I said.

"We know about them," said Stas to Yana.

"You could say that," said Yana.

She knocked on the plywood. *Bang. Bang. Bang.*

"Three AM express," she said. "Siberia next stop."

She went back to the phone.

"She's talking about some private stuff," said Stas. "Women's stuff."

Some leaves were left in the bottom of the cup, and when I put it on the counter, Yana leaned over me so her hair brushed my cheek. That scent of the steppes. The fragments of tea were green and black, like metal flecks from a machine that was coming apart.

"What do you see in them?" I said.

She rolled a shoulder, pushed her hair out of her face, pursed her lips. Outside the cars were piled up like statues on Easter Island.

"You've got to recognize a chance when you see it," she said. One of her fingers touched mine. "Don't hesitate."

"I'll call you when I have the part," said Stas. "We'll fix the krauts. Better yet. Just come back tomorrow."

Yana offered her cool hand.

"Nice to meet you," she said.

"Come back tomorrow," he said. "I'll have what you need. About this time." A calendar with Russian script hung on the wall. "Yeah. February 14th. I'll have it then."

"Good-bye," said Yana.

Stas spoke Russian to her and she sat down at the Mac and started typing again, her hands long and the fingers pale, too.

The next day he had the part, and he had a mechanic, too, who was ready to put it in, and so we sat there, in that small office, the woman typing as before, although she turned to listen to what I said. The mechanic hammered and worked with his power tools, which were hooked up to an air compressor that made a repeated effort, like someone straining. Stas told me about Moscow, in the Soviet era, when no one could buy a dog, since that was too bourgeois, but after the regime came unglued you could buy a dog on the Arbat, where people sold them out of baskets. Did I like dogs? He was thinking of getting one for the junkyard to keep "the creeps out." He spoke to the woman and she said, over her shoulder, "A German shepherd."

"That's an East German for you," said Stas. "You ask about dogs and she wants a German shepherd. What about a pit bull, for Christ sake? Don't you think one of them would do the job?"

"Only half German," she said. "My mother was Ukrainian. Ukrainians know about fate. They know about hunger."

The mechanic came in and said the car was done. It wasn't too expensive, but it wasn't too cheap. Just the right amount. I'd saved about a thousand dollars, and somehow, saving that money, when everything else seemed difficult, felt much better than it should have. I wrote the check.

"So," he said. "Come around sometime. We'll have tea. Maybe a pastry. Don't be a stranger."

So, that's the way it began. In the last two weeks in February, as Alexandra studied in Italy, as my father was away (as the spy he was demanded), Pia went out with Miller, as she missed some classes and stayed in Cambridge and came home at midnight and then one and then two and then three in the morning, wobbling up to the front door, still only drunk, but giving me worries about what was coming next, I went, when I could, in the evening or on a weekend, to that place in Braintree with the razor wire, the warm office, the samovar, and the stainless steel microwave. Sometimes the woman, Yana, was there, and sometimes it was just Stas and me, each having a cup of tea, although sometimes Stas had a bottle of vodka, and he took off the top and threw it away, and we drank, like Russians he said, having a shot.

"A genie gives three wishes to a Russian. So the Russian wishes for a new pair of shoes, a new roof, and then the genie says, 'Well, you only have one last wish left.' And the Russian says, 'Can you make my neighbor's cow die?'"

He had a drink. Poured one for me, too. Sometimes we just sat there in front of the space heater, the vodka in small glasses. He didn't say anything then, as though just being together was enough. With me he was able to have the feeling that he was in touch with other things aside from the problems he never mentioned, not really, aside from some angry talk in Russian to Yana, and when he spoke to some men, in dark clothes and long coats, who came to the junkyard and said a few words in Russian and then they got into a new Mercedes and drove away. He asked if I knew that there was a problem with women from Eastern Europe being smuggled into the U.S. Had I heard anything about that?

He told me too that the stolen-car-parts business was expanding. That's where there was growth, real potential. They were a sort of unofficial consortium for distribution, headquartered in Miami and Atlanta. Of course, he never said he had anything to do with these things directly, and when we discussed them it was as an abstraction, the way an investment banker might talk about a factory in India or a textile factory in Pakistan. Still, the office with the tea and Yana was a place to go, to get away, that was so far from the details of my ordinary life as to seem like a trip to Kurdistan.

From time to time, Yana put her hand on my shoulder, leaned over so that her hair brushed my face, and said, "It's always nice to see you."

One evening, during those two weeks in February, Pia waited for me in my study. She sat in the chair on the other side of the desk. Her cheeks were a little red from the touch of a heavy beard.

She looked up, her eyes a little red.

"Dad," she said.

"What?" I said.

"I don't know how we got started on this," she said.

"Oh, I do," I said. "There's something that goes on between fathers and daughters. Each is fighting for a little respect. That's all. Pretty simple when you get down to it."

"I've got something to tell you."

"What's that?"

"You know, I was just thinking . . . "

"About what?" I said.

She shrugged. She got a drink from the little tray in the corner and gave me one, too. She watched me drink it.

"I don't know," she said, "about this lawyer business . . . "

"What lawyer business?" I said.

"The going-to-law-school business," she said. "I thought I'd take a little time off. Like Miller says. See the country. You know, all I've ever done is study and do the right thing. Get a job as a waitress or something. Take it easy. Get a van. Drive around."

"You mean like Miller's parents?" I said.

She shook her head.

"I'm trying to talk to you," she said.

She put her head into her hands and started to cry, and when I came around she let me touch her but she didn't lean into me the way she used to.

"I just don't know," she said. "Maybe I want to take a chance."

In the morning, the Volkswagen made that ominous puttering as she drove back to school.

"How is Pia these days?" wrote Alexandra.

"All right, I guess," I wrote back. "Don't you see, I am showing her I love her, that I am there for her, that I have dropped any semblance of restraint, that I will do anything for her . . . Don't you see?"

"And what's happening?" Alexandra wrote.

"I think things are getting worse. How can you win?" I wrote.

"Maybe you can't," wrote Alexandra.

So, the next day, late in February, I went to Braintree. There, at least, out the window of the auto parts place was the evidence of a thousand people who had made mistakes so large and so long-lasting as to make a sort of pyramid of disaster, those piles of smashed cars and cracked windshields and those air bags that had deployed and then faded like a used condom. Somehow, being in the presence of a disaster that wasn't mine made me feel less alone. But how can you get control of things at this moment, how can you go on when everything you try to do, either carefully thought about or spontaneously, still leads to that same downward swirl, which feels like being on that silvery water that goes around the drain in the sink?

Stas came in and sat down, his acne scars prominent in the light that came from the window.

"Everything is fucked up," he said. "You can't trust anyone to do a fucking thing. People owe you money, and what do you have to do? You have to go and knock on the fucking door and scare some dumb shit in front of his wife and kids. You know, the kids start crying. See?"

Then he swallowed and looked down.

"Sorry," he said. "I didn't mean anything. I got screwed on a load of transmissions. It was easier when I was shipping this stuff to Afghanistan. We used to get a big truck, fill it up with junk in Holland, and drive straight through . . . "

He said this while he looked out the window.

"Tell me," he said. "What's with you?"

"That Miller," I said. "You remember? The guy who sent me out here?"

"Yeah," he said. "I remember." He let me see his eyes again, which were the color of mold.

"I wish he'd go away," I said.

"Would that make you happier?" he said.

"Yeah," I said. "If he was just gone."

Stas looked across the table, opened a bottle of vodka, threw away the top, poured me one, then one for himself. He drank it in that one quick gulp, like a snake swallowing a small rat. My hands were shaking as I picked up the drink on the table.

"My daughter's not going on to law school because of that asshole," I said. "And it's not that. My daughter and I were close. Not anymore."

Stas stared out the window.

"You know the best thing about being born in Russia, in the time of the Soviets? You understand small gestures, like the look in your neighbor's eyes when he's just made up some lies about you to tell to the KGB to get a better spot on a waiting list for an apartment. You understand the hidden, unseen connections."

"I guess that's right," I said.

"There's no guessing," said Stas. "I understand you, Frank. Like no one else. Who understands outraged innocence the way a Russian does? Look. You lost a case. It meant something to you, didn't it? An innocent woman, who just wanted the right thing, and look what happened to her. Some thugs got away with it. And I know you feel that as a sort of darkness that's behind things, like a gas, that taints everything."

"Maybe," I said.

"Sure. Maybe. And now that same darkness, the same toxic, hidden thing, like a ghost, but a dark one, like all those things you've been trying to pretend didn't bother you, is now coming right into your house and not only that, it's coming right between you and your daughter. And you're telling me I don't understand."

He poured me a drink. I didn't even feel the warmth as it went down.

"So, am I right?"

"The kid is dangerous," I said.

"Sure he is," said Stas. "I understand. I'm sorry you're having trouble."

Outside, in purple lights on the yard, the wrecked cars with their cracked windshields had an icy sheen. Torn metal, a black stain here and there, like a bottle of ink had been broken. The wind made a whistling moan as it blew between the piles.

That was it. We finished our drinks and we sat there for a while. Stas put a microwave burrito into that stainless steel machine and when it was hot he put it on a paper plate and pushed it over to me.

I ate the thing with some hot sauce he had on the fiberboard desk next to the Mac. Not bad, when you get down to cases. It was hot and the inside of my mouth was blistered, which seemed worse as I drove along the Charles River, by the Cambridge Rowing Club, where Pia and I had gone in the mornings in June, just nine months earlier, when the water was so perfectly scalloped by the light breeze, when the birds, the gulls, wheeled overhead and the runners jogged on the path that went along the grass. What could possibly have gone wrong? Weren't we everything that was right, the father in a racing single, staying in shape, performing some service for the community, a daughter who was possibility itself, both of us moving along and leaving a thin, silver wake in those scallops of light?

So, Pia came home the next weekend, just like always, and

waited for Miller. Why didn't he call? He usually called every day when she was in New Haven, but she hadn't heard from him. Pia stayed in her room, stretched out on her bed, and on the computer she had some old rock and roll, which was like the music that she must have heard at some retro club she and Miller went to. She had her cell phone on the nightstand, and as she waited in her room, her ear turned toward the distant sound of traffic on Brattle Street, she seemed to be somehow shrinking, getting more pale, more withdrawn. I asked her if she wanted to row, since it was so warm for early March, but she just looked at me and shook her head. The only thing we could do was cook, and I looked up new recipes. In the kitchen we made shrimp with fresh ginger, red snapper with brown butter and capers, with a dry white wine. She looked, for a moment, like herself as she peered over a small skillet, watching the lemon pulp dissolve, but when her phone rang, she took it out and flipped it open, like someone with switchblade. Then she closed it again, disappointed, and turned back, with a sort of resignation, to the pan where the butter had almost burned.

Pia and I went to the movies and sat in the dark. There, at a silly romantic comedy, the tears made shiny rills on her cheeks, the silver quality of them all the more obvious because of the light that came from the screen. Then she pulled herself together, blew her nose, and bucked up. We drove home and then sat in my study, where she had a drink and said, "How could anyone do that? You know, just disappear? Not even a good-bye."

"I don't know," I said. "Is that what Miller did?"

She looked at me. Then she took down a copy of Thucydides and flipped through it, going from one year of the war to the next, and sometimes she stopped and read a little something out loud, dwelling on those occasions when someone on the Peloponnese or someone in Athens had someone assassinated, as though this was an indictment of some kind. One of these men, who had been killed, stabbed outside a temple, was described as "pestilent." Then she closed the book and went upstairs, where at night she got up and walked the halls, making the old boards creak. It was like a sound of regret, one perfectly modulated by time.

The next weekend, Pia went to the house where Miller had a room but his things had been moved out. The landlady had been threatening him with eviction for a month, and when he stopped coming around, she moved his clothes, old sweaters, and blue jeans with holes in them, a couple of Bose radios that didn't work, a TV with no knobs on the front into the cellar with the dust and rats. The landlady said she'd keep them until Miller paid what he owed. She was even going to paint the room, she said, and get a nice young woman to move in. In the evening, Pia ate the food I made her, and then she went upstairs to listen to her music and sit with her cell phone.

In Braintree, Stas wore a new black shirt with his black jacket, and his skin condition had improved.

Yana typed at the Mac. The lists of car parts scrolled by on the screen, and next to them there were pictures of brake shoes, carburetors, fuel pumps, hydraulic pumps, air bags. The air was heavy with that scent she wore, which seemed so much like the steppes.

Yana scrolled down the lists of auto parts.

"So," said Stas to me. "How are things?"

"All right," I said.

"How's your daughter?" he said.

"Better in some ways. Worse in others," I said.

"That's always the way. You just can't win. But," he said, "what about that guy she was hanging around, that lowlife from Harvard Square? Is he still in the picture?"

"No," I said.

"See," he said, "everything comes to the patient guy. It all works out. You want a burrito?"

The driveway of my house was quiet. A light was on downstairs in my study and one was on upstairs, too, in Pia's room. Otherwise the place was dark. It had always seemed, when Pia was growing up, that the place was warm, that even in the dark it still glowed with domestic certainty, like a rock that had been in the sun all day and was still hot hours after twilight. It didn't look that way: just dark and a little cold. Now, in March, the fog came in some nights and the house seemed to be suspended in shreds of mist.

Pia came downstairs when I was in my study. She wore an old bathrobe of mine, and she had her hair in a ponytail. No slippers, and she tucked her long feet under herself as she sat in a leather chair on the other side of the desk.

"I want to ask you something," she said.

"What's that?" I said.

I looked away, though. She went right on staring.

"I want the truth," she said.

"From me?" I said. "When have you ever gotten anything but the truth?"

"I'm not sure," she said. "Not anymore."

The poison, like the presence of dry ice, was working through the house: doubt and suspicion. I bit my lip, if only because while the poison was spreading, I still had plenty to resist it. After all, if I looked into my heart there was plenty there: goodwill, love, the desire to be honest, and yet it all seemed to be wrapped up in that cold fog, that stinky mist from the river. How to get clear of it, to get back to what we had had before?

"You want something to eat?" I said.

"No," she said.

"How about some shrimp and garlic, sautéed in butter with a little french bread to dip in it? Some sliced tomatoes. Maybe a little lemon sorbet for dessert?"

"No," she said.

We sat there. The house ticked. Outside, in the distance, a car went by on Brattle Street with a long, shrill honking; I guess a drunk had been in the street or an old man or old woman, lost in the fog.

"I've been thinking," she said.

"About what?"

"You," she said.

"What about me?"

She shrugged.

"I want the truth," she said.

"Sure," I said. "If I can give it."

"Did you have anything to do with Aurlon?" she said.

"Like what?"

"With his disappearing?" she said.

"Me?"

"Did you have one of your cop friends scare him?"

"No," I said.

"No?" she said. "They didn't take him downstairs someplace and let him have it with a phone book? Isn't that the usual thing? Wouldn't that get him on the first bus out of town? Or do you have something more high-tech than phone books?"

"No," I said. "I don't do that. No one I know did that."

Her eyes were so piercing I felt the touch of them, like the point of a pin on my face.

"If I ever find out that you did," she said, "or if you had anything to do with making him disappear, I promise you'll regret it."

I swallowed. The house ticked.

"I won't take betrayal," she said. "Not from my father. You understand?"

"Yes," I said.

She started crying, and when I went around the desk she pushed me away.

[CHAPTER FIFTEEN]

THE TISSUE ON the physician's examination table was like the paper of toilet seat covers found in airport bathrooms. Stiff, crinkling, and obviously sterile, as though the germs were just waiting to take a whack at you. I always had this physical in the middle of March to see what the winter had done to me.

The diplomas on the wall were from Berkeley and the University of California Medical School, and so I was able to take a little comfort that where education was concerned, I didn't go to the medical version of a junkyard, surrounded by barbed wire in Braintree, as though in Uzbekistan, but to the medical ghetto in Boston, out by Brigham and Women's Hospital. My doctor, Michael Stevenson, came in, the tape of the electrocardiogram in his hand: a starched lab coat, cheeks recently shaved, hair precisely trimmed, skin at dermatological perfection. He glowed.

Now, though, with that strip of the electrocardiogram in his hand, he looked into the distance.

"How did your father die?" he said.

"Stroke."

"That makes you the last of the line," he said.

"I have a daughter," I said.

"Is she going to have kids?" he asked.

I shrugged.

"So?" I said. "What's the verdict?"

"We've been friends for a long time, Frank," he said.

"That doesn't sound too good," I said.

"Some irregular heartbeats," Dr. Stevenson said, "according to a study in *The New England Journal of Medicine*, are related to specific emotional states. For instance, when a man or a woman has had an unfortunate affair, a particular irregularity may show up in the heart. Or if you're concerned about someone you love, the rhythm may show up, too."

"That's what I've got?" I said.

"To fix it, we do what's called an ablation," he said.

"What's that?" I said.

"We burn the part of the heart that's causing the problem," he said. "We do it by going in through the artery in the groin."

"You mean you're going to stick a toaster filament in my leg and push it into my heart and then fry it?"

"If the arrhythmia doesn't go away. Who are you worried about, Frank?"

The paper wrinkled when I moved a little, just to have something to do.

"We don't want to wait too long," said Dr. Stevenson. "The heart has a memory. It starts doing something and it doesn't forget it."

I put on my clothes.

"Otherwise, you're fine," said Dr. Stevenson. "Make a follow-up appointment on your way out. We'll keep an eye on this . . . "

"Maybe my heart will forget . . . ," I said.

"Maybe," he said. "Maybe not. I guess you're still upset about that case. The one that was overturned on appeal."

"I think about it," I said.

"Maybe you should take up a hobby," said Dr. Stevenson.

"Yeah," I said. "Sounds good." I buttoned my shirt. "Have you ever read Thucydides?"

In my study, at home, I poured myself a drink and pushed the play button on the answering machine, and Stas said, with the keys of Yana's computer clicking in the background, "Hey, Frank, come on out to see me. I want to talk something over."

The barbed wire at the top of the fence was spun in perfect spirals, like DNA. That's how Stanislav must have seen this place, like a camp on the taiga.

The samovar was hot and the office, with its wooden walls and the odd blue light from that carport roofing, had the bitter scent of tea. Yana was paler than before, and her skin was almost transparent in its delicacy. She pushed her heavy hair to one side as she looked over her shoulder at me and smiled. Then she went back to typing and scrolling through the images of auto parts on the computer: transmissions, clutch housings, air bags. She spent a lot of time looking at air bags.

The tap on the samovar made a little trickling sound, like a leaking boat, as Stas filled a cup and passed it over.

"Frank," he said. "Well, I was wondering when you were going to come see your friends."

"Uh-huh," I said.

He knocked a pile of repair manuals for Audis and BMWs off a chair and shoved it in my direction.

"You know, Frank, you should learn to put a sugar cube

between your teeth when you drink. It makes it sweeter. Doesn't it?" he said to Yana. An air bag was on the monitor, but she said, "Yes. Sweet is nice. If you can get it."

"Yeah, getting sweet is always hard," said Stanislav.

"What do you want?" I said.

"You're not sitting down," said Stanislav.

I sat down. The tea was hot and bitter.

Stanislav spoke to Yana, who shrugged, picked up her jacket, and said to me, "I've got an errand." Then she glared at Stas.

She put on her jacket and went out the door, into the muddy earth, and up to the gate and by the rolls of barbed wire at the top of the fence.

"Let's talk things over. Like friends, so no one gets hurt."

"Who's going to get hurt?" I said.

"You," said Stas.

He said this as though it was a fact of life. There are birds and bees and ants and when they get together, the boy and the girl ants . . . The irregularity in my chest was a small tick, or so it seemed, although it was hard to be certain if it was there or not. Maybe the ghost of a click.

"You know the heart has a memory?" I said.

"Yeah," said Stas. "Pushkin says something about that . . . It's a Russian thing."

The tick came and went. Or was it just irregular?

"I never asked you for anything," said Stas.

"What would you ask?" I said.

He pursed his lips as though trying to figure the price on a hot air bag. We drank our bitter tea.

"Let's start with the basics. You haven't got any more trouble with that guy who was bothering your daughter. See? You don't have a problem. I thought you wanted it to go away."

Outside the cars went by on the highway with that tearing sound of rubber on asphalt, and it seemed that the wind, in the piles of wrecks, made a long, barely audible whine, as though something lingered from those hours when people waited, after an accident, for the arrival of an ambulance.

"You were in a tough spot, Frank," said Stanislav. "So you ask me this favor, a pretty big one. And that guy, Aurlon? He's gone."

He stood up, went over to the Mac, typed, hit enter, and then scrolled through the video that played until he came to a section where I sat and talked about Miller and what he was doing to my daughter.

"Maybe I'll send a copy to *The Boston Globe*. Or the *Boston Herald*. And if anyone finds out I sent it, I'll just say I let a lot of people see it . . . Who knows if anyone took you up on it?"

"And?"

"Well, maybe they might ask a favor, too. After all, that guy Aurlon is just not around anymore. Where do you think he is?"

"I hadn't given it much thought," I said.

"Maybe you better," he said. "Maybe it's really worth thinking about. Maybe some reporters, that is, if they saw this, might try to find out where he is."

My heart made a small tick, like a chick's wing against the side of the nest. The tea was bitter, cooling off, but still exotic, still hinting at the steppes.

"And you want something?" I said.

"Who doesn't want something?"

The beating in my chest had that same *thump, thump-thump, thump, thump-thump*. The lightness of it, the betrayal of it, spread as a variety of trembling. Like when you have almost been in an accident.

He shrugged, made an expression with a pitted chin.

Yana walked back and forth in the cold beyond the window, her breath trailing her, her skin pale, her eyes so blue, even at this distance. She looked in the window. In her hand she had a plastic bag from Walgreens.

"If you don't play your cards right, Frank, you could end up on a bridge someplace, you know, like you see on the news. Some guy getting ready to jump . . . everything gets to be too much . . . the scandal will hurt someone's family, wife, child . . . why, a clean jump makes all that go away, doesn't it?"

He shrugged.

Yana came in the door and brought with her the cool air, the scent of her hair, and the fragrance of those smashed cars, which was a combination of oil, rotting leather, and something else, too, which was the stink that is left after someone has been killed: not a physical thing, but something else, like the darkest gloom that comes when the lights are turned out. Yana sat down at the computer and went back to scrolling through the varieties of air bags.

Then the samovar hissed. Stanislav didn't bother to get up or open the door or do anything but sit there thinking things over.

"Take care," he said.

"You, too," I said.

"Frank," he said. "I can start over anywhere. Florida. Arizona. Illinois. But you, you're trapped by being somebody. That's the difference." He looked out the window at the rolls of barbed wire. "When I ask for a favor, you better listen. That's the message. Now get out of here."

Outside the cool breeze blew through those piles, which reminded me of statues on Easter Island, or just large figures that suggested meaning that was hard to understand. The seats of the Audi squeaked in that leathery way, and then I drove over the dried mud outside, through the doors, and underneath those rolls of barbed wire. Yes, I thought in that breeze around those piles of cars, What penance had Henry II done after his exasperation with Thomas Becket and his rhetorical question, "Who will rid me of this priest?"

[CHAPTER SIXTEEN]

EVEN IN LATE March, Pia was still waiting. Maybe Aurlon would show up? On the weekends, she slept until noon, her figure under the blue duvet like some enormous chrysalis. When she woke up, she loaded an iPod and went into my study, her eyes on the driveway as though Aurlon might walk up to the house with his lupine gait, his ponytail bouncing, his smile as beguiling as ever. Chocolate, or so I had heard, had a beneficial effect on a woman who had experienced an unfortunate affair, and so Pia came into the kitchen and picked at her schoolbooks while I separated eggs, mixed the yolks with sugar and melted chocolate, and then folded them into whipped egg whites, the peaks like the tip of a Diary Queen cone. The scent of the chocolate soufflé filled the kitchen, and as Pia tried to look away, as she went out with a huff and even slammed her door upstairs, she still came back when it came out of the oven, and I served her a section with whipped cream, which she ate, unable, in the moment, to keep a smile, a small one to be sure, but a smile nevertheless, off her face. Then I moved on to other things, a crown roast of venison with a broccoli soufflé, roast potatoes, and a wine I had been saving for years. She picked at it in the beginning, but then had a taste. The small, begrudging smile appeared again.

"What's with all this cooking?" wrote Alexandra from Rome. "You used to cook that way for me when we were first going out. What gives? Are you trying to talk Pia into something? I know your tricks. So, what is it?"

"A little fun," I said. "What is the purpose of life anyway?"

"It won't wash, Jack," Alexandra wrote. "You can't pull the wool over my eyes. You're up to something."

From the *Larousse*, I cooked duck and pâté, and then I went through an Italian cookbook I had bought in Rome: lobster and potatoes, or black pasta with garlic oil and sprinkled with parsley. Pia now sat at the table, not quite holding a fork in one fist and a knife in the other, but obviously wanting to.

"I'm gaining weight," she said.

"So, let's go for a row," I said.

We went down to the boathouse and got out the racing singles, long, narrow boats, with a sheen of light on them. Soon we were going neck and neck until she blew by me. The light shone in those bits like an impressionist painting. I was making an argument that she understood. Life was meant, in many ways, to be enjoyed. Food to eat. And slowly, with a sort of begrudging admission that maybe there were other things than a thug from Harvard Square, she went about her business.

But not completely, and so I decided it was time to go nuclear.

One afternoon, I said, "You know, I'd like to tell you something. It might be helpful."

"There's something funny in your tone, Dad," she said. "I don't know if I like that."

"Maybe not," I said.

The phone rang, and when the beep was done, Stas's voice said, "Say, Frank. Have you been thinking about things? Why don't you come out to see me? Let's get this settled, right?"

"Business," I said. "Nothing."

"No kidding," she said. "Sounded Russian or something . . . "

"Look," I said. "I think you're old enough to know something. All right?"

"There's that tone," she said. "Are you sick? Have you got cancer or something?"

"I wanted to say that when I was young, before I met your mother, I thought I was in love," I said.

Pia looked down at her shoes.

"I'm not sure I want to know this," she said.

"I don't want to say my heart was broken, not exactly," I said.

"What was her name?" said Pia.

"Pauline," I said. "You know she went around in sort of goth clothes before it was goth and liked to flirt with trouble. She knew right what to do to me."

"You're not going to tell me, are you?" she said.

"No," I said. "Not that. I wanted you to know that I understand. That is, I was sick for a while. That's all."

She stared at her shoes.

"And that's it?"

"Well, no," I said. "I had a friend who was a shrink. And when I couldn't forget about her . . . "

"Pauline?" she said.

"Yes, Pauline," I said. "I asked him if there was a trick. Something I could do to make it go away."

"And?" she said.

"You sure you want to hear this?" I said. "It's pretty strange."

Outside, the clouds dragged with those ragged puffs of late winter.

"I don't know, Dad," she said.

"Well, he said that what I should do is get a picture of her, put it in the toilet, and take a leak on it."

"What?" said Pia.

"What can I say?" I said. "The guy was a shrink."

"Did it work?" she said.

"I never tried it," I said. "But he said it was the last resort. A sort of romantic fail-safe."

We sat in my study. The garbage trucks worked. The bicyclist went by in streaks of color like a fireman's jacket. Then Pia went upstairs and made some noise in her bedroom, a sort of shuffling, searching sound, a flipping of papers. The bathroom door opened. I went up stairs and waited in the hall. The house creaked. The small graveyard in the backyard was visible from the upstairs window, the stones as gray as a rain cloud. The toilet flushed and Pia came out, and no matter how hard she tried, no matter that she trembled with the effort to keep a straight face, she put her fingers to her lips and giggled.

"Well?" I said.

"It's hard to say," she said. "But I can tell you this. I don't think I would have tried unless I was so angry I had already started not caring . . . "

"So, how about a chocolate soufflé?"

"You know, Dad," she said. "I don't think that's going to be necessary. I think, after all, that I'm going to go to law school just like I had planned."

I swallowed, looked at my shoes. Nodded.

"And I got an email from some guy in my law school class. Robert something. He wants to have a drink."

"Why don't you do that?" I said.

"Maybe," she said. She shrugged.

Downstairs, when I touched the button, Stas's voice came into the room. Not threatening. Just a sort of faux friendliness.

Of course, the clock was running down. My father was closer to that piñata party. Somehow, you think people are like furniture, that they aren't going to disappear, but they do.

In May, even closer to that piñata party, on a day that was warm and filled with that endless promise of spring, as though every bloom was concealed in that first warm breeze, a taxi pulled up in front of the house and Alexandra got out, her hair golden in the afternoon sunlight, her smile somehow satisfied and soothing. She walked with the most lovely womanly swagger, hips swinging, her hair tossed over her shoulder like those women on Via del Corso or in the Borghese gardens or as they go into the gallery where they stand in front of *The Rape of Proserpina*. She rolled her suitcase up to the door, and in one hand she held a plastic bag from an *alimentari*—a Roman delicatessen—the plastic stretched out as though a five-pound stone was in the bottom. She came through the door, all perfume and energy, her smile infectious, her vitality unstoppable. She carried with her, by her attitude, by just being alive, an essence that would vanquish all the worries that had piled up since she had left.

The bag held a five-pound piece of Reggiano, and I made linguine alla vongole, just like they do in Rome: poaching the clams in wine, letting them open, cooking the pasta molto al dente, and finishing it in the pan where the clams had cooked. And as I cooked, as I checked to see that the clams were open and as she sat at the table, she looked around the kitchen and then at me as though taking stock, summing up. She was hungry, and we ate the pasta with some freshly ground cheese, and as she rolled it on a fork and put it into her mouth, as she closed her eyes with the taste of it, she nodded to herself, as though agreeing with her initial assessment, and as she ate, in the taste of the food and wine, I was reminded of that first golden light when I had seen her years ago, and which I saw again in the golden atmosphere around the birth of our daughter, in buying a house and making it a place to live, in the gardens we had planted, in the odd, private languages we spoke (a teacher at Pia's school, whom we referred to as the Vampire, or the parents of Pia's friends, whom we referred to as the Ghouls), all of it coming down to that kitchen where we ate.

"How was Rome?" I said.

She swung her hair and took a sip of wine.

"All I can say," she said, "is that it's wonderful to be home."

"Yes," I said.

"And you had some time with Pia, too," she said. "How are things?"

"Fine," I said.

"Good," she said. "Let's make all this last. Let's not have anything go wrong."

"I've got something to talk to you about," I said.

"Can it wait a little?" she said. "This is so nice."

The domestic has such a tug, such a gravity of the ordinary and warm. After dinner, Alexandra came into my study and curled up on the sofa, her legs under a fleece blanket she got from a sporting goods store, and I sat at my desk, reading through the paperwork for an indictment: it's all in the details, in precision, in not making a mistake, although as I sat there, in the midst of what seemed to be just that, I tried to let the warmth of the room, the gentle shifting of Alexandra under her blanket, the tick of the book she was reading as she turned from one page to the next reassure me, and for a moment it did. I could almost convince myself that it was all right.

Then I told her everything.

She looked down.

"I'm not a lawyer," she said. "Why don't you call your father? God knows he's been in enough trouble."

I dialed my father's number and told him that Alexandra was home, that everything seemed fine, but there was a legal matter, nothing important, or at least I didn't think it was, but maybe I could come by the next day, in the afternoon, and we could talk it over. I didn't think I was in trouble, but maybe we could talk things over.

"Well, sure, Frank," said my father. "My Latin American students are going to be here for a piñata party. We're going to have some fun. They don't think I can hit that thing, but you know what, Frank, here's the trick: you listen for the wheels of the pulley that control the piñata. Wait for it to come down. Then, wham! It rains candy. So, yeah, come by tomorrow."

[CHAPTER SEVENTEEN]

ON THE DAY before my father's funeral, which we were going to have at the farm, I drove the ashes from Concord in that red gift bag. Of course, because I didn't get to ask for my father's help didn't mean I had stopped wanting it. If he had been able to handle Poland and the Germans in the snow, he'd have been able to help. And so I was left with that constant desire to reach across the gulf between the living and the dead, that invisible wall that keeps getting closer.

The ashes gave off that stink of a half-smoked cigar, and the box vibrated from the engine. The light came in the window and made the slick paper of the bag glow, as though it was water with the sun on it. The ashes sat on the seat, in that bright party bag, and I had the sensation of my father straining, as though he was just on the other side of that darkness that confronts us all. And that goddamn bag: it made me think of the store where these things were for sale, as though these cheerful, foil receptacles were there for an endless number of boxes of ashes. The bags lined up, an almost infinite number, like a vision of children in the dark before life, that is, in the gloom of time before they are born.

In the car, I reached over and touched the box, which was a kind of primitive moment all by itself, that is, the son reaching out for the spirit of the father. I touched the box and asked for forgiveness. What, after all, can a father give to a son more than that?

The bag had the aspect of a Buddha, an object that suggests knowledge if you are just smart enough, just keen enough to understand, and so I kept looking for the right question, the right method of asking, of imploring, from one generation to another.

At least we'd bury my father, or what was left of him, near that piece of land along the Delaware.

The director of the Girls Club still wasn't as cordial as she could be, not after we didn't kill that bear that was getting into the garbage. But that's a fact of death. Yeah, she could be pissed about the bear still running around, and yeah, she could be pissed at my father (and me, although I don't know if she knew I had been along), and yeah, she could wish she had never agreed to any entanglements, like letting us store things in the farmhouse with the white siding, black shutters, and with the trout ponds in front, but when a son asks if he can use the house where his father grew up for a few hours before they bury the father, she couldn't say anything. And, I guess, in the background this was part of the negotiation for me killing the bear.

That wild green and shiny foliage lined the road I took up from the Delaware with the box on the seat next to me. Then the car ticked as it sat in front of the porch. The new hydraulic pump worked just fine. The lawn chairs that my grandmother and grandfather had used were still on the porch, although peeling now, a little rundown, but my grandfather had sat there with his mint juleps, his mind filled with schemes of one kind or another, and which I listened to when I was eight and nine and ten years old. He never mentioned any problems he may have had when he was young, or younger, and away in South America while his wife was alone.

Charlotte was a woman in her eighties now, so heavy she had to throw her weight from side to side when she walked, but she had worked for my grandfather and my father, too, her age showing when she came out to the front porch in her green cardigan sweater, her hair in a white bun, her skin like a shrunken mushroom. Her husband was dead and gone, and yet Charlotte still seemed to carry his presence with her, as though he had been reduced to a scent. I had the feeling that if she had to, she could open a beer bottle with her teeth.

She came out of the house and took my hand.

"I'm sorry for crying like this, Frank," she said. "It's just for everything. That goddamned Girls Club. Your grandfather and mother, your father. That bastard time."

She took a damp handkerchief out of her pocket and blew her nose.

"It's a hard job, Frank, to bury a father. It's the last thing they ask you to do. There aren't any harder. Have you cried yet, Frank?"

"Not yet," I said.

She stood next to me and put her head against me, just the slight pressure making me feel a little better, as though this touch was something I could depend on. "Don't you see, Frank, why you have to be so considerate and loving with your kids? You're going to ask them to bury you. That's a hard job for them and so you've got to show them how much you love them, or anyone who would do that for you."

She took her handkerchief from her pocket and twisted it, as though she could force some final element, like saying good-bye, into a more comforting shape, but it only made her seem useless, and so she put it back her in her pocket and said, "Well, come in."

The living room was clean, and yet it still had the air of a camp, and maybe this was because the furniture was mismatched, worn out by years of squirming Girls Club members who were so excited to be away from the cities of New Jersey that they couldn't sit still. Charlotte went over the small loaves of bread, the chicken salad she had made, the smoked sausage she had gotten in Port Jervis. She said she was going to roast a turkey and a ham, and that she'd have a tub of potato salad with parsley. White wine and beer. A few bottles of liquor.

"It's a mixture of the comfortable and the cheap. But I got one really good bottle of scotch, just to keep them guessing. Just the way you, father would have liked it. He loved to keep them guessing. Was he the sharpest man we have ever met?"

"Yeah," I said.

"I've got brand name Kleenex here and there," said Charlotte. "Extra wastebaskets. Here's the bill for what I spent," she said.

The twenties and fifties in my wallet were wrinkled and old, and I counted them out, giving her two hundred dollars, which she tucked into the pocket of her dress.

"Well, god bless your father," she said. Then she shrugged. "We'll be ready for the people after the church. I'll clean up after. God bless his miserable heart."

The party bag, with its red sheen, made a little rustle as I went through the woods and around the swamp that was between here and the stone house where my father had held his hunts and which had been built for his dead brother. Somehow I didn't think I could leave it in the car, and yet bringing the box out here seemed to be the height of folly, of sentiment, and yet I went through the mountain laurel, the low brush, and came out on the stone house road.

I sat in front of the stone house and some turkeys made their way through the field above it, their burnished feathers in the mist of the late afternoon. The stone house had walls of cobbles up to shoulder height and then the roof went up from them. I sat on a stump in front of it, the bag on the ground at my feet, both of us alone.

• • •

Alexandra already had a room in the motel in Sparrow Bush, a town about ten miles away. And when she traveled to places like this, she brought snacks: good blue cheese, sardines and crackers, olives, cold chicken in a hamper, a bottle of white wine, napkins, all of which she had in the room. It was the culinary version of the difference between us, a way of being devoted to details that showed how much she loved me or how much she loved our daughter. The details that made for comfort.

"Is Charlotte going to help?" she said.

"Yes," I said. "All set."

She got into bed with her book, just like home.

I brought the bag with the ashes in it and put it on the cheap dresser and then got up and put it in the closet, but as I sat there, Alexandra got up, took them out of the closet, and put them on the dresser. She glanced over at me and I glanced back, and that was another of those moments that held us together.

"Here," said Alexandra.

She passed a bottle of single malt scotch from her bag over

to me, and then she put down, next to the box, two small glasses from the motel bathroom.

"I only need one," I said.

"Pour one for him," she said and got back into bed with her book.

I poured scotch into the other glass and shoved it at the box. The odd thing is, he seemed to appreciate it.

On that early June morning, one my father would have loved, the trees so green as to tint the air, I left the bag in the car when I got to the chapel with the white siding, the green shutters, the brass fixtures on the door, the pitched roof covered with slate tiles, and, of course, the building sat in the middle of a churchyard where the stones stood up like a model of a town. The river, with its rills and bone-white boulders, deep pools and long rifles, was a hundred yards away. The chapel had pews on three sides, small ones with a little door in the rail that went in front of them, and then in the middle ten rows of benches were arranged in front of the altar. I had had help with this, in that Charlotte had hired a friend to order the flowers here, and they were on the altar and here and there in front of the pews, nice white ones, carnations with ferns, and some lilies, too, although my father had always hated lilies.

I stood by the front door to greet the mourners. Alexandra did too, her expression one of gratitude for people attending mixed with her natural dignity, her dress a dark blue, her blond hair showing like some vision from the painting of a chapel in Italy where the angels hover overhead. She even handled Ginny for me, Cal's wife, who came in with an air of sexual uneasiness, as though she was reminded by funerals of why her husband jumped off the bridge.

Billy Meerschaum, the Cambridge cop, came in, dressed in a suit that he wore for weddings and funerals, the thing smelling a little of the mothballs that he packed it in between these events. He took my hand and gave it a squeeze, and then looked around the chapel, giving it the once-over to see where drugs might be hidden. Then he waddled up the aisle and sat in the front, his eyes on the altar, straight up, dignified and alert.

Tim Marshall, the inspector with the Boston Police Department who had been on the bridge when Cal did a Dutch job, was there too, a little drunk in the morning, which he allowed himself as a good Irishman on his way to a funeral.

Marshall said, "I'm sorry, Mackinnon, for your troubles," and then he sat down, right next to Meerschaum, the two cops finding each other in the crowd like two members of an Eastern European tribe, Croats or Serbs, who send out a kind of radio signal that can be picked up only by other members of the group.

Jerry came in a blue fishing shirt and his hair slicked down with what looked like a bottle of Stay Comb that must have belonged to my grandfather. He took my hand, let me smell the scent of his hair, blinked, then let the tears run down his face and said, "*Schießen Sie sie in der Rückseite des Ansatzes.*" No stutter. And, for a moment, I wondered if I taught him German if he could speak that without any trouble. But he sat down, too, his Stay Comb bright as the sheen of a bowling ball.

Pia came in, her eyes set on mine as she said, "Oh, Dad, you know I'm sorry. Please. Let's spend a little more time together. OK?"

I nodded, not trusting my voice.

"I'd like you to meet Robert McQuire," she said.

McQuire was tall, with perfect posture, and a nose that was so beaked as to make him look like a bird of prey, a peregrine, I guess, and he had a look in his eyes that suggested a variety of smoldering anger, as though, in advance, you were warned that you better not give him the least cause for trouble. He took my hand.

"I'm sorry," he said.

"Robert's a rower," said Pia. "A classmate, too."

"We'll row together sometime," I said.

"Anytime," said Robert.

"You better get ready," said Pia. "His splits are under 2:00."

She cried, too, and they went in and sat down, Robert's tall, blondish head above the others.

So I sat in the cool air of the chapel, scented with flowers and the newly dry-cleaned clothes and perfume worn by some of the women. Out the window, the churchyard had gray stones sticking up like boulders cracked by frost, covered with lichen, and beyond the black metal fence of the churchyard the current in the Delaware showed as a slight braid in the otherwise green and dark water, and above it all the sky was smoky, as it always is at this time in the spring. Bare trees, the sudden frost.

About a hundred people showed up, mostly older than me, men and women of my father's generation who came to funerals as a sort of endless dress rehearsal for the one they weren't going to be able to attend, at least not on two feet, and who looked around with a sort of sad accounting to see who, among their friends, had fallen aside. The minister was the chaplain at Yale and he spoke of my father's service in North Africa, his skill as a hockey player at Yale, his instinct for "fun," which we all knew was a way of admitting that the man we were saying good-bye to had been a drunk. The minister seemed to be keeping his eyes on the otherworld, as though by doing so, he could avoid having to address the pitfalls of this one.

Men in dark tweeds and women in gray and black dresses sat here and there, the men from the school where my father had taught law and diplomacy, although everyone knew this was a front for his CIA stunts, and the friends and associates from that aspect of my father's work stood around at the sides of the chapel, not wanting to sit down, I guess, because they had been trained not to get comfortable in any place where there was only one exit. They looked a lot like the professors and academic administrators who had shown up, although the CIA ones appeared more like an academic who had just published a book that had gotten a bad review in a journal that was important for scholarly success. Or maybe it was more intense than that: the men looked like they had been sleeping with a graduate student who was about to spill the beans. A constant worry and a sort of dread.

At the back stood two men whom I thought might have been the next generation of spooks, or maybe the CIA had gone democratic, since these men had obviously not gone to Groton or Saint Paul's and Yale, but came from somewhere a long ways down the academic and social river. They wore black suits and one of them had a gold earring about the size of a golf ball. They both had bad skin and wore their hair slicked back, and from time to time they turned to stare out the door or out the window at that array of headstones that seemed to be dying, too, absorbed into the earth, eaten by lichen.

Fifty or so people who cry at the same time is not a comforting sound, but perhaps a necessary one. Pia cried harder than all the rest, so much that I thought she would dissolve, that she would just disappear in the silver streaks that came from her eyes, and when she wiped them away, it seemed that she cried for my father, whom she had liked, for me, and for everything else, too, having been seduced by a punk, having made a fool of herself, and out of relief, I guess, that even here she had a chance to start again. Robert looked straight ahead, although when he touched her hand, she seemed to take comfort and to lean against him.

The men with the slicked hair and the bad skin stood at the back, more like morticians than mourners. One reached for a cigarette and the other gave him an elbow in the ribs.

We filed out. The ashes were in the back of the car, and when I picked them up, I was oddly reassured by the weight of the box, as though that, at least, gave me some momentary connection to my father.

The two men in dark suits with the lousy skin stood right behind me, their backs against the black fence with the small points, like spearheads that went around the churchyard. In the distance, around a hole near the back of the place, the mourners gathered in a sort of disorder.

"Hey, Frank," said the man with the earring.

"Sorry about your trouble," said the other one.

"Thank you," I said.

I held the box in both hands, my eyes set on the churchyard, the gray stone and that ragged circle of people. My feet moved a little in that dusty, brown soil, and as I held the box, felt its weight, smelled the cheap cologne these two were wearing, I said, "You're from Stas, aren't you?"

The air seemed a little heavier, a little more ominous, and the sun, for a moment, seemed filled with ill will, as though while it gave life, it had occasions, too, when it was ready to do its worst.

"Can we talk for a minute, Frank?" said the first one.

"I asked you something," I said.

"Listen," said one. "You can call me Semyon. This is Timofei."

"Sorry for your trouble," said Timofei.

"Thanks," I said.

Semyon, his skin rough in that gray light, put his hand on my arm, although he didn't touch the box. At least he had enough sense not to do that.

"Get out of my way," I said. "I'm busy."

"We know that, Frank," said Semyon.

"We understand," said Timofei. "But you can imagine how important this is if we'd talk to you now."

"About what?" I said.

"Well, that's complicated," said Timofei. He put his hand across his chin. The people in the churchyard glanced at us, not impatient, not anything, really, aside from the fact that they seemed to look like people just before a bomb goes off, or before someone yells fire. The men from the CIA glanced at the sky, the river, the hole in the ground.

"We want to remind you of that favor," said Semyon.

"It was an important one," said Timofei.

"Aurlon Miller? Remember?" said Semyon. "And so we may ask you for help. That's all. One hand washes the other."

"That's what we have to say," said Timofei.

He stood back.

"We'll be in touch," said Semyon.

"You know, maybe some friends of ours who are having legal trouble in Boston might need some help."

"Listen to us," said Timofei. He put his hand on the box, as though he was going to take it from me. I looked at him, in the eyes. He stared back.

"Don't," I said. "Don't you dare . . . Let go."

Semyon smiled.

"Go on about your business," said Timofei. "Pay your respects to the dead. They need it. We'll talk to you some other time."

"Let go," I said.

I put the box on the ground and stepped toward Semyon, but he opened his hands, as though blessing me, and then stepped back. Timofei did, too.

"These guys causing trouble?" said Tim Marshall.

"No," I said.

I made my way through those stones, the box in my hands, in that smoky air with the sun hanging there like a lemon on a gray sheet, the haze so thick it felt we were already in the underworld, where the mists of the dead hung with such infuriating vagueness: here was the atmosphere of eternity, but it wasn't definite enough to get your hooks into. The path between the stones was covered with a little sandy gravel, and my shadow moved along it, a shade over the film of light that came through the gray mist.

The crowd turned toward me. Alexandra stood by the small hole in the ground and stared at me: I felt the caress of her glance, her steadfastness. I came through the gate. It was about thirty yards from the entrance to the churchyard to the hole in the ground, and as I approached it, a car door slammed behind me and then an engine started. The crowd seemed to open up, to pull back, and I carried the box in two hands, and as I went, I wanted to put it down and open it up to look in at the dust and the chips of bone to ask my father just what the hell I should do now.

I stood next to the hole. The box fit in perfectly. The grain of the box looked like the current in the surface of the river, and then I stood up, missing my father more than ever, although I'm sure if he had been here he would have only insisted on more delusion, on denial, on the notion that if we all just had another drink everything would be fine.

We all picked up a handful of dirt, my father's old CIA pals sad and somehow exhausted, as though burying each other had come to the point of being as much part of the job as the work they had done fucking up governments in South America. They came up to the small hole and reached down, their hands shaking, as they picked up the dry dirt and dropped it in, letting it fall through their fingers like the flow of regret itself.

On the other side of the fence the car had been pulled into gear, and the engine faded away as the two men, one with an earring, drove along the river, the sound getting fainter and fainter, like a memory that one wanted to hang on to but that was nevertheless disappearing no matter how hard you tried. The car had burned a little oil and the mist of it, like a black cloud, hung in the air.

Finally, with that dirt on my hands, I went to the back of the crowd and waited for the rest of my father's friends to be done, to stand there with a handful of dirt so as to say good-bye as it slipped through their fingers and onto that sad, lonely box.

Alexandra took my hand with a squeeze and said, "Well, that's the worst of it." Then she glanced at the car that had driven away. "Is that the trouble?"

The air was smoky blue, that odd fate-tinted color that you usually see in the fall, but which was nevertheless here in the spring. Not like fog, but more like a cataract in a blue eye, at once ominous and blind, and all the more ominous for being that way, as though fate didn't care what it was going to do so long as the bang was loud enough. I often felt this when we hunted deer, or when I had hunted deer with my father, and in that Oo-Bang of a center-fire rifle, and when a deer had been shot through the chest and ran into the woods, it was more keen than I could say, but still there for all that. Once, at that moment, an old friend of my father's had said, looking at the deer like this, *Why, he's heartshot. Dead and still running. Well, he'll find out soon the way things are.*

"Yeah," I said. "Part of it."

• • •

In Cambridge, the next day, the usual assortment was out, street musicians in tie-dye shirts and torn blue jeans, the three-card monte boys, the guys with card tables covered with used paperbacks and fold-up umbrellas made in China, a guy with a portable amplifier plugged into an outlet of a head shop. The coffee I held in a paper cup was so hot I had to move it from one hand to the other. The Raver came through the clutter, his gray cape flowing behind him, somehow regal in its sway and flap, his eyes gray, too, his hair thinning a little, but it was obvious he accepted this as part of things. He nodded to the men with card tables, the musicians, stopped in front of the Burger King and knocked on the window, to say hello. The women, in the uniforms, looked a little sour. Then he turned to me.

He handed over a scrap of paper, a little dirty, as though he had used it to clean a windshield, which he did now and then and if the driver didn't give him some money, he had another sponge filled with oil that he would swipe across. "Ying and Yang," he called it. The Raver stood next to me and then he said, as he looked at a woman through the window of the Au Bon Pain, "Do not act as if thou wert going to live ten thousand years. Death hangs over thee. While thou livest, while it is in thy power, be good. How's the heart?"

[CHAPTER EIGHTEEN]

SO, A WEEK after the funeral, the dust, like a gray boa, trailed from Tim Marshall's new Subaru on the dirt road to the gun club. The gun club is where Marshall liked to talk: no one around, the scent of gunpowder, which to him was like the aroma of fertilizer to a farmer. But even with the windows rolled up in the Audi, the grit still got in, and it made a little crunch between my teeth, and it probably got into the gun case, too, where I kept my grandfather's L.C. Smith field-grade shotgun. Marshall had a custom-made trap gun, a pump that had started out as a Remington, but he had the trigger fixed so he could, as he said, just think about it going off, and bam! That's the secret, he said: you think more than shoot.

I stayed in that dust, and we pulled up to the gun club, which was nothing more than a wooden shed on one side, a cement house that held the machine to launch birds, and a dusty parking lot. Beyond the blockhouse, the landscape sparkled with broken birds and scrub that seemed as though it should grow in the Mojave or the Kalahari, on the edge of death but knowing that patience was its only hope. The Bulgarian who ran the club launched the birds. He usually wore a wife beater and said the blockhouse where the birds were launched reminded him of the apartments he had rented in Bulgaria. "Same smell," he said. "Wet concrete."

Marshall wore a pair of khaki pants, a blue work shirt, some boots with steel toes that a longshoreman would wear, as though to show that this was all unofficial. He had on his day-glo vest, with a pocket for shotgun shells, which hung with the weight of them. Just us here today. He took his shotgun out of the car, the port already open, so you could see no round was chambered, and then said, "Frank, we've got some trouble.'"

The Bulgarian said, with an accent that seemed sort of generic European spy, "You ready?"

"You ready?" Tim repeated to me.

I held my grandfather's field-grade L.C. Smith shotgun.

"I mean for the birds. You aren't going to be ready for this other thing."

The Bulgarian went into the blockhouse.

"Pull," said Tim.

A hard shot right away, a passing one to the right so you have to swing away or against the right hand. The clay pigeon flew in that line like a line drawing. The bird disappeared in a puff of smoke, like the flak my father had described to me. Tim pushed another green hull into the port.

"So, why are you curious about this guy out there in Braintree. Stanislav Ivakina, right?"

Of course he knew the name.

"Yeah," I said.

"So," said Tim. "What are we looking at here?"

"Domestic violence," I said.

"Pull," said Tim. Another bird, a hard shot, straight to the right, vanished in the flak-like smoke. He took another green shell and tossed it up and down, up and down. Then he put it back in the pouch and turned those blue eyes toward me. They were at once oddly fatigued and utterly blank.

"Frank," he said. "I've been a cop for thirty years. And I've been lied to by guys who beat their wives to death with an iron, by wives who put d-CON in their husbands' hamburgers, by kids who raped a ten-year-old girl, by men who put bodies into furnaces, by mobsters who dropped bodies out there in the Atlantic. And you know what, Frank? After all those years, you learn something."

"Yes," I said.

"So what do you learn?"

"If someone is lying to you," I said.

He put the green hull into the shotgun and said, "Pull." The bird disappeared in that pigeon-colored smoke.

"Now, you can tell me all kinds of things, Frank," he said. "But if you think you can say you're interested in this guy in Braintree because he's pushed his girlfriend around and have me believe it, then you better remember who you're talking to. So, let's cut the bullshit, Frank. You know what I'm like? A sex therapist. I've seen it all. Every fucking thing you can imagine. So, don't tell me any lies, Frank. It just pisses me off."

The Bulgarian sat in the blockhouse, just glad to be under cover.

"Pull," said Marshall.

Dead center: like magic, just a little smoke, which drifted away. The field looked like the back of a failed pottery factory in Rumania.

"It's personal," I said.

"Hmpf," said Marshall. "That's the first honest thing you've said."

My ears rang with the shot. The puffs drifted away and I thought of my father as he came in low, so they couldn't hear him, those men around a general's headquarters in the desert.

"I'm close to retirement, Frank. I've got a nice little place in New Hampshire where my wife likes to grow flowers. Snapdragons, delphinium, astilbe, hollyhocks. It's nice to sit out there when the fireflies are in the flowers."

"I'll remember that," I said.

"So, here's your friend Stanislav. Guys like him don't start out at the end of the spectrum. Chopping guys up and putting them in Glad bags to put out in the landfill. They sort of work up to it. But it happens fast. We haven't got enough to indict this guy, but he's on the move. Won't be long. And, of course, we're always a little behind. That's the hard part. Keeping up to date."

The Bulgarian said from the blockhouse, "Are you done?"

"Pull," said Tim.

The bird disappeared in that puff of black smoke.

"You want me to pick this guy up and take him someplace and have a talk, you know? We can go up against him hard. Maybe in some room downstairs in a suburban precinct. I'm not saying like the bad old days with a phone book, but let me tell you, that was a piece of work. Around the kidneys. When they start pissing blood, why you'd be surprised how they want to talk. It's not the blood. It's the fear. So, even though I'm looking forward to those fireflies in the snapdragons, I'll talk to this guy. You want me to do that?"

"No," I said.

"What's he got on you, Frank?"

"I don't know," I said.

"There you go again," said Marshall.

"Yeah," I said. "I guess I'm on my own."

"That's right. You're on your own, then," said Marshall. "You poor son of a bitch."

"Do you have a daughter?" I said.

"Sure, I do, Frank. My little patty-cake," he said.

"What would happen if she suddenly thought less of you? A lot less. Like some kind of scum?"

He put a green hull into the port, closed the action, and just stood there, the barrel over that gritty landscape, which was a perfect combination of dump and cheap graveyard.

"I'd do a kervork," he said. "A first-class Dutch job. But I'd do it so my wife got the insurance. You want help with that?" He touched the barrel of his shotgun. It wasn't too hot. "So it looks like an accident? So your wife gets the money?"

"We'll see," I said.

"Pull," said Marshall.

That flak- and pigeon-colored smoke appeared.

"After thirty years on the job, Frank, you realize what your job really is. It's to see how things are connected, underneath, not where you can see it. Like poetry, see? Do you read Yeats?"

"Yes," I said. "I read Euripides, too."

"What does he have to say for himself?" said Marshall.

"Cleverness is not wisdom," I said.

"Hmpf," said Marshall. "Maybe."

Another explosion like flack.

"So, we got something else. What do you make of this?" Marshall said. "A lot of people from out of town are ending up dead. Why would someone bring someone to Boston to get rid of them? Why not do it in Florida or Arizona or wherever these people came from? Just think of the money that's being wasted on airfare and car rentals. It doesn't add up."

"No," I said. "I guess not."

"Pull," he said. We stood in the aroma of burned gunpowder and that black flak.

This man, said Tim, sold stolen car parts in the South that he got from the Northeast, from Boston and Hartford, New York and Passaic, and he had come north for what was supposed to be a vacation and to do a little business. Firm up connections. Maybe he brought to Boston a list of what he needed: air bags, fuel injection, DVD players, parts for Audis and German cars and Volvos, which parts cost a fortune if you import them. The usual stuff, said Tim.

"You drive an Audi," he said. "Don't you?"

"Yes," I said.

"Parts expensive?"

"Yes," I said.

"Like how much does a power steering pump cost?"

"$2,891.89," I said.

"$2,891.89?" he said. "Hmpf. Handy the way you have that number."

Tim looked over at me: not suspicious, not curious, just that lingering glance from a man who had been a cop for thirty years.

So this guy from Miami, said Tim, brought his wife along with him, a heavyset woman with bleached hair and a tan that looked more like a leather coat that had been left out in the sun too long, and his kids, too. They all wanted to go to the amusement parks in New England. They called it the Six Flags tour. They rented a car and went from one amusement park to the other. The guy from Miami sat in the parking lot and read the *Daily Racing Form* with a pint of scotch and a hot dog he got from the concession stand while the wife, even though she weighed two hundred and fifty pounds, went with the two teenage boys on the roller coaster and the Gravity Defier. He waited in the parking lot of the aquarium in Boston, his *Daily Racing Form* spread out over the steering wheel, and someone came to the window and shot him. Didn't open the door. Didn't go over the body. Didn't do anything like that at all. It took a while, but the police were able to arrest two men, each of whom had bad skin and who had a long list of minor and not-so-minor violations. Eastern Europeans. It was pretty obvious that they had done it, especially since one of them had been stupid enough to keep the gun that had been used.

"I've never seen anything like these guys," said Tim. "Smug, you know, like they've got nothing to worry about. They said they had friends. What do you think?"

That same look: he had seen everything there was to see, and so it wasn't curiosity, just a sort of running through the catalogue of possibilities. Sort of like dreaming with his eyes open.

Tim faced the rubble of that field.

The Bulgarian brought us two bottles of beer and one for himself and then sat on the overturned bucket and faced that landscape.

The Bulgarian picked up a handful of the dirt next to the bucket and let it sift through his fingers, just like the yellow loam of the graveyard where my father's ashes were buried. I was left with the memory of those bloody feet in Poland, wrapped in rags, the blackness of the bore of the pistol that a German guard in a coat had put against my father's cold head, those moldy papers that my father had left to disguise the fraud he had pulled off and for which he obviously wanted my forgiveness, and the memory of that funeral dirt as it slipped between my fingers. Now, when I needed to reach across that gulf between us, I was faced with silence. I picked up some dirt, too, and let it sift away. I was left with the smell of gunpowder, so much like flak, and the litter on the ground was like the cigarette wrappers and condoms in the pigeon shit that was the last thing Cal had touched before falling away, a skydiver in a business suit.

When you drive to think things over, just to be behind the wheel of a car, as though having your hands on a machine gives you a grip on some difficulty, you don't really think of a place you want to go. You just drive. And so I found that the Tobin Bridge was green as it ever had been, sort of pale, like insect killer in a glass jar. The cars went by when I pulled over, next to the spot where Cal had waited in that scum of guano and fast food wrappers, bits of Styrofoam and sticks from ice cream bars, and other items people threw from cars, parking tickets, bills, advertisements. The wind blew, but even so the river still had that stink of diesel and salt air, chemicals and garbage. The two hollows in the guano where we had sat were still there, not yet completely filled in with bird shit and junk. The gulls hung in the air. I got out of the car and stepped closer. The wind carried that harbor aroma and I came closer yet. Down below, where the bridge went above some houses before it crossed the water, the streets were cluttered with debris. Further out the haze seemed to be waiting. The metal of the bridge was cold.

A cop turned on his red and blue lights and stopped behind my car.

"What are you doing out here?" he said.

"Just thinking," I said.

"No kidding," said the cop. "This isn't the place for thinking. Let's see some ID."

I took out my wallet.

"Well, Mr. Mackinnon, if I were you, I'd go home. Am I making myself clear?"

"Yeah," I said. "I'm going to be late."

• • •

In the evening, with the Audi in front of the house (with its new hydraulic pump no longer leaking like my father's cars), I sat in the golden light of my study. I ran my fingers across the spines of the books. Thucydides, Livy, Xenophon, Herodotus, all said the same thing: nothing, once started, just disappears. Be careful what you start, these books seemed to say, as a chorus, since you never know how it is going to end, and when it does, it's usually not what you wanted. Xenophon, Thucydides, and the rest liked to show how the machine of history grinds, not only fine, but with perfection, as though some beautiful and frightening thing decides to show itself in the details of malice. And then, if you are alert, one day you find the machine has turned your way.

[CHAPTER NINETEEN]

FLOWERS ARRIVED ONE afternoon in June at our house in Cambridge, sent to Pia from an address near the law school. Card included.

"Who's this Robert person?" said Alexandra.

She gave me the card. I thumbed the edge and put it back in its green plastic holder.

"He was with her at the funeral."

"Oh," said Alexandra. "Him."

She said this as though it explained everything.

Pia had rented an apartment in Cambridge, not far from the law school, but she took her time in furnishing it, and sometimes she came home to our house from IKEA or Target, the plastic bags like a hump an ant carries after finding a sugar bowl. Then she'd ask if she could have some towels, some sheets for a double bed she had bought. Sometimes she didn't come home at all, and Alexandra and I were left with the modern lifeline: her cell phone. I learned to text. So, I sent a note to Pia, my big thumbs hitting the wrong letters on my Droid X. "Flowers for U here. Can U pick up?"

"Did you ever send me flowers?" Alexandra said.

"Of course I did," I said. "Roses, orchids. You don't remember the orchids? They had the scent of paradise."

She took my arm. "Of course I remember. You've got to recognize a joke. See, someone says something and you see it isn't what it really means, but something else. Like a guy walks into a bar . . . "

"I get it," I said.

"That's my boy," said Alexandra.

The flowers were an array of delphiniums, spiked, blue, haunting, the petals like an illustration of some genetic fact, some structure associated with DNA.

"So, every day I find a message from that guy in Braintree. Stas?" Alexandra said. "What are you going to do?"

"I don't know," I said.

"Well, I'll stick with you. Thick and thin. Remember? I'm not some frail reed like Ginny."

The flowers stopped coming, but this just meant that Robert was sending them to her apartment, which is where she stayed now. Then the call came.

"Mr. Mackinnon," said a voice when I answered the phone in my study. "You may not remember me, but we met at your father's funeral."

"Sure," I said. "Robert. You're a classmate of Pia's."

"I wanted to say how sorry I am about your father," said Robert. "I didn't really get a chance to say that at the time."

"Well, I appreciate that," I said. The rows of books, Herodotus and the rest, seemed like a chorus now: a polite young man, they seemed to say. What the hell does he want?

"Can I take you out to lunch?" said Robert. "I want to discuss something."

So, a couple days later, the oak chair squeaked in front of the rolltop desk with the green blotter that still had inky hieroglyphics from signatures and notes my grandfather had blotted there. An atmosphere flowed from the old joints and polished wood of the desk, part of it the stink of the ashes of cigars that had been rubbed into the wood, although nevertheless perfectly mixed with furniture polish: the scent of genteel mischief. But it had a lower depth, a monstrous substance like a demon that wants to escape that dark, stinky, bone-filled lair, where all the death and disaster are hidden. I faced this presence when I had to see things as they really were. Or when my solitude was complete. What were the details of the deal I was going to work out with this Robert? Just what did he want? Had Stas gotten to him? The books on the shelf looked down on me with a certain harsh reminder of just how wrong things could go.

Locke-Ober is at once oddly European and keenly Bostonian, all white linen and silver utensils for serving, large egg-shaped covers the size of an ostrich's body, all reflecting the light in the place and the painting on the wall, nude, antiquated, and oddly sultry as though there are some constants in the universe. Surely, sultriness is one of them. But even so, as I went along that hard sidewalk in front of the place (concrete always seems hard at the moment of decision or action) I was alert to mischief. Or, at least, uncertainty, which in many ways is the same thing.

Maybe my hands were shaking a little, between my own worries and the possibilities, made up from nothing, of what I would say to Robert, that is, if he knew anything he shouldn't.

I came up the street to the glass doors, the polished brass, the reflection in the windows that revealed me in that moment I usually avoided: my hair was turning gray, and some new lines showed in my forehead and around my nose. My expression was troubled. I looked ripe to be sold a graveyard plot. Nothing fancy. Just the basics. And at the door, in the reflection of the glass, Cal's figure showed, arms out, tie fluttering over his shoulders, legs bent back, the ground approaching, as all good schoolboys knew, at thirty-two feet per second per second: the last, critical fact. Schoolboy knowledge that comes back to haunt.

I had reserved a table in the café downstairs, and I sat with my face to the door, the bar on my right, the silver trays and covers looking almost medical in their sheen. I sat there in my suit made in New York, in my best shirts from Fifth Avenue (four-hundred-thread-per-inch cotton), in my most soothing silk blue tie, and to kill time (an ominous way to put to it) I added up my life, one side and then the other, pro and con, and as I did this, never coming up with the same answer, I brooded more about Stanislav with each run through the past. At least I came to this: I didn't think my grandfather or father (putting aside the war and just considering his fuck-ups here) had been in quite the same deep shit as I was.

Robert wore the same suit as mine, same tie, although his shoes had a better shine. I stood up. We faced each other.

"Well, it's great we could get together," I said.

Robert's shirt was the same as mine, too.

"Yes," he said.

He was already sweating.

Maurice, the waiter in his apron and his white shirt, arrived, his head gleaming in the light, his dentures as white as piano keys, his paunch seeming to advertise the wiener schnitzel, the panfried potatoes. He brought us both a drink, single malt, my favorite, and said, "Well, have you got any money in the market? It's taking a dive today."

"Too bad," I said.

"They're going to be jumping out the windows if this keeps up," said Maurice. "Any place high up. Bridges. You know."

"Thanks," I said.

Maurice had a waddle, and it showed mostly when he walked away.

"Well," I said to Robert. "It's nice to be able to talk."

"Yes, sure," I said.

"Is this really convenient for you?" said Robert.

"Sure," I said.

"You seem a little worried," said Robert.

"Nothing out of the usual. You know."

His expression was so familiar I thought I was having déjà vu until I realized it was the same as Tim Marshall's. Of course, I saw this as a sign that more caution was in order. Robert didn't believe me either.

"Of course," said Robert. "I understand."

"Do you?" I said.

"Yes," he said. "But I don't want to intrude."

"Well, what do you want?" I said.

"I want to talk to you about Pia."

"It's best to do that alone, that is, just the two of us," I said. "You can't really do that with Alexandra and Pia around. You know the joke about the minister in New England who took up the collection and found three pennies in the offering plate? He looked over the congregation and said, 'I see we have a visitor from Scotland with us today.' And a man stood up at the back and with a thick accent from northern Scotland said, 'Yes, there are three of us here.'"

Robert sipped his drink. He looked me in the eyes.

"My family is from Scotland. Campbells," he said.

"Me, too," I said. "Sinclairs."

"Maybe we should have worn kilts," he said.

"Hunting or dress?" I said.

"Hunting," he said. "Do you have a dirk? You know all the clans were horse thieves and murderers, at least in the nineteenth century."

"I'd heard rumors about that," I said.

"Not rumors," he said. "Bloodthirsty thieves. They were as bad as the tribes of Afghanistan."

I wonder if this had occurred to my father when he was a spook who had encouraged the Taliban against the Soviets. Maybe that's why he felt so comfortable with treachery.

"Well, I don't really put much stock in genealogy . . . ," I said.

"Me, neither," said Robert.

Robert sat so still I thought he was posing for one of those Civil War photographs. His eyes were on mine, and as he tried to see beyond them, into me, I realized what was happening. I'll be damned.

"I want to marry Pia," he said.

"I can see why," I said. "But just between the two of us, I think you should talk to her about this."

"I have," said Robert.

"Oh," I said.

"Yes," said Robert. "She says that she doesn't want to get married, ever. It is not me. It is not ambition. It is not any kind of political thing. She just said she can't."

"Oh," I said.

"So, I wonder if you have any influence with her?" said Robert.

"Me?" I said. "Pia and I have just been through the worst fight of our lives. I don't think I'm the one to ask."

The crinkles around his eyes had a slight sense of the tragic.

"I've come to be honest," he said. "To offer what I have."

"I think she's the one to listen to that," I said.

He shrugged.

"I think I need some help," he said.

"We all do," I said, before I could stop.

Maurice appeared in his apron, with that head shiny as a bowling ball, his hands behind his back. He never wrote anything down and just nodded when we asked for the wiener schnitzel, the panfried potatoes, creamed spinach, a salad, and a little apple strudel for dessert.

"Why do you want to marry her?" I said.

"That's pretty obvious," he said.

"How do you know you love her?" I said.

"I feel sick when I leave her. When I'm not with her. Cold and sorry."

We sat in silence, looking into each other's eyes.

"So, what's the difficulty?" he said.

"You'll have to ask her," I said.

"She avoids it," he said.

The shape of his fingers, the texture of his hair, his eyes (and just what intelligence did they suggest?), the way he moved, his posture, all those qualities that, if you are smart enough, showed something critical about a man.

"I think we should talk honestly," he said.

The word "honestly" emerged just at that moment when everyone in the room was quiet, and it hung there like an unexpected expression, not "fuck" or "cunt," but something unusual at Locke Ober's. The other men in the room glanced at Robert with a wary concern. Honesty was not a Bostonian virtue.

"I want to tell you something."

Maurice brought our lunch. A faint sound of the plate hitting that tablecloth. Then, sensing that we were at some critical juncture, Maurice vanished.

"I went to Stanford on a track scholarship," said Robert. "I will probably do well at law school. What I have is prospects, not money. That is what I have."

"Of course," I said, although I wondered, with that sense of turning into my grandfather, what the hell does that mean?

"I understand that you read Tacitus, Xenophon, both the Latin authors and the Greek."

"In translation," I said.

"That's what Pia told me," he said. "Have you read *The Agricola*? It's one of my favorites."

"Tacitus?" I said.

"Yes," Robert. "A panegyric, or maybe a funeral oration for his father-in-law."

"Yes," I said. And, of course, there it was: no one lives forever, and here was a young man who understood that, and who was offering his concern for me, too.

"So, what's wrong? Why won't Pia even talk about it?"

"I think you better ask her," I said.

We ate our lunch in silence, then the apple strudel. I paid the check and we went outside, into the small side street and then up to the commons, where the trees had come into leaf and where the street had a sheen, like a green light on a woman's skin.

"So," said Robert. "You haven't answered me. About Pia. I think you know."

Then we went into the street, where the capitol glowed in the afternoon light like a bauble of gold in *Paradise Lost*, and as we came up to the corner, a garbage truck pulled in front of Robert.

Robert stood straight, in the same way, I imagine, as his ancestors had done when marching with swords and bagpipes in

Scotland. Just a straightening of the shoulders, the eyes a darker blue, like that tint in the sky when something odd is about to happen. And, if the garbage man had had any sense, he would have stopped the truck, gotten out, and apologized. Robert's posture should have shown what the garbage man was facing. Instead, when Robert stood that way in the crosswalk, the garbage man spit into the street.

Robert said, "Watch where you're going."

"What the fuck did you say?"

"Watch your language," said Robert. He stiffened more and squared his shoulders. In the park, on the other side of the street, boys on skateboards went downhill but watched the truck. A mugger who waited on a bench glanced away from a limping old woman and turned toward the man who stood in the street with such square shoulders, right next to the garbage truck.

"My fucking language?" said the garbage man. "Listen here, you dumb shit. Why don't you go fuck yourself?"

He spit into the street again, but this time on Robert's shoe.

"Mr. Mackinnon," said Robert.

"Call me Frank," I said.

"Are you sure you aren't having trouble?"

"No," I said. "Nothing special."

He nodded. And then, as though showing me how things could be handled, he said, "Did we hear this truck driver clearly? Did he say what I think he did?"

"Yes," I said, although my voice had a defiant sadness, which I remembered as being like the one my father had used when we faced that lonely bear and he had passed over that rifle: here, get ready for trouble, it seemed to say.

"Let me show you something," said Robert.

"What the hell are you two jackasses jawing about?" said the garbage man.

"Listen, you asshole . . . ," said Robert.

"What did you say?" said the garbage man.

Robert put his face up to the garbage man's.

"Fuck you," said the garbage man.

Robert turned back to me.

"Listen to the man," said Robert. "Why, it takes your breath away."

Robert opened the door of the garbage truck, and as the man inside lunged out, Robert put his elbow, with a sharp, perfectly practiced movement, into the man's stomach, right there under the rib cage. Even from a distance and over the sound of the traffic, the cabs going by with the drivers leaning on their horns and with the kids in the park on their skateboards, the air came out of the man's body like someone stepping on billows. Robert reached across the seat and the wheel, took the keys from the ignition, then stepped down, still holding them, and in the momentary silence of the stopped engine, he walked about five yards away to a U.S. mailbox.

"Ah," said the garbage man. "Ah."

He put out his fingers, the gesture at once supplicant and desperate.

Robert pulled back the door of the blue box with the little sign on the front that gave times of pickup. The keys swung back and forth over the open maw of the box.

The garbage man struggled out of his seat, and then Robert raised a brow at me and dropped the keys into the box and let the door slam shut. The garbage man struggled for breath and shook his head. "Those were my fucking keys," he said.

"Watch your language," said Robert. "Do you want me to get tough?"

The garbage man gagged.

"What?" said Robert. "I didn't hear you. Speak up, for Christ's sake."

"No," said the garbage man.

"No, what?" said Robert

"No, please," said the garbage man.

"And don't you owe an apology to the man I'm with?"

"That's all right," I said.

"I'm sorry," said the garbage man.

Then Robert and I went through the commons, the horns honking at the garbage truck sideways in the street, the leaves in the park making a slight, almost kissing sound in the light wind, the two of us strolling along as though we had had a satisfying and successful lunch.

The horns around the garbage truck, even at a distance, became more intense: the drivers were all in sync now, *honk, honk, honk.*

"I have a favor to ask," said Robert.

"Sure. I'll talk to her," I said.

"That's all I ask," said Robert. The sky had that misty blue that made the statehouse dome so golden, so elusive as to seem like a dream. Now, dark birds flew around it in a spiral.

"Thanks for lunch," he said.

• • •

In the evening, Pia came over to the house on Brattle Street, her hair bright, her gait showing a bounce, a delight in movement, as though she was on a planet where the gravity was a little less than here. We stood in the hall, next to the table where the mail was piled up.

"Robert said you had lunch," she said.

"He wants to get married," I said.

"I told him about that," she said.

"He wants something more than just a no," I said.

"All right," she said. "Invite him for a weekend. To the farm. Jerry will be there, right?"

I nodded. Fine. All right.

Then she picked up a letter from the pile of mail: it was a generic envelope and addressed in a large, sort of drunken script, with a return address that said Pauline Martin above some numbers on a street in Florida. Pia tapped it against her teeth, then dropped it into my hand.

[CHAPTER TWENTY]

OF COURSE, I should have worried about Mackinnon's First Law, since its truth hid in the shadows, or just behind the surface of things. You see them not by their math, but by their effect. Events don't take place with an even distribution, but just the opposite: each human activity, each moment of difficulty, has its own gravity, and the larger the event, the more it attracts other things. Both large and small, like a star pulling in galactic dust along with an asteroid or a comet. I forgot the essential element, the critical thing, which is the way in which trouble attracts trouble.

I agreed to invite Robert to the farm. Pia went out the door. Then I sat down with the mail in my study at the rolltop. You never forget the handwriting of someone who has said, in a letter or a note, "My darling, I love you. I would die without you. Simply die without your scent, your touch, the way I feel after you have come in me. It is like something that brands me, that leaves me changed forever."

The rolltop had the scent of an old-time lawyer: difficult to describe, but still definite once you have experienced it. Similar to a briefcase that you have found in an attic and inside you find not only some old briefs and onionskin paper and a half-used pink eraser, but the remains, too, of a tuna sandwich that someone took to court on the day he died and which was stored in the attic with that briefcase: fishy, but after all this time, sort of blended into the general atmosphere of old leather and only half-remembered grievances and injustice. Or that's the way it seemed when I sat with that letter on the desk's green blotting paper with its mess of inky hieroglyphics.

Dear Frank:

It's been a long time since we were in touch, but I haven't forgotten about you, not for a moment. I have followed you from a distance, and I always felt something between us, as though what happened some time ago, when we were close, has bound us together. It is a kind of scar, always there. Sometimes, at night, I can feel the itch of it, as though I could run my finger along the pink, slick ridge, and that in the silky caress I can feel the touch of your lips. Your ear. Or something more intimate, which I think about. You never forget those touches. Of course, I have missed you and I have often thought of what my life might have been if you had been able to understand me, but then I didn't love you for understanding. It would have helped, though. Still, the scar torments me and I can't get over it, even now.

I am not sure why I am writing now, but then we all have regrets, which seem to exist as a kind of invisible shroud, not obvious, yet still there for all that. I feel it, too, like a fog you can't see.

Do you ever think of me? Do you remember the scent of my hair or what we smelled like after we had been in bed?

I often think about you and so rather than brooding, as I often do, I thought I would send this to you to see if I get any relief. I think, too, of that time I broke the window to get the diamonds. The glass was in the street, glittering there like a bracelet, and then I held what I wanted for a minute, dangling from my fingers like all the hopes I had that came to nothing. I wanted to say that this is one of my regrets. That you wouldn't get me the diamonds, that you wouldn't give me a sign.

Well, we all grow up, I guess . . .

With my memories of you, sometimes in the most intimate places, Pauline.

Of course, I wondered what the message was here, not so much what she had to say as something else, which was that as an adult you like to think you are somehow immune to those passions and delights that you see in younger people, but this is an illusion, and the letter came to remind me, I supposed, of things hidden so carefully and buried so deeply as to make you think they never happened, that is, until that little tick sounds one day beneath the mail slot.

I put the letter to my nose. Was there some scent of her skin there? Some lingering essence?

When I was an assistant prosecutor, just out of law school, I went to a party in a shotgun apartment on a side street in Cambridge: women in short skirts, legs white as powder, and yet the smell of dope mixed with the cooking of an Italian family that lived in the building, the sautéed garlic, the simmering tomatoes imbuing the aroma of dope. The usual complexity of American life. It was a cool party, and what can't cool get away with?

Pauline's spiked black hair set off her blue eyes, and she wore tight-fitting clothes that showed her small figure, her tight, sinewy stomach, and she carried herself in such a way as to suggest that she judged you by how you overcame your fears. This, she seemed to say, not giving into fear, was the purpose of being alive.

"You want a sip?" she said. She passed her glass over where the ghost of her lips was on the rim. "I haven't got any cooties."

I put my lips on the white ghost of hers.

"So," she said. "A risk taker. You know what? I like risk takers."

"One sip doesn't mean much," I said.

"You'd be surprised," she said. She shrugged. "So, what do you want to talk about? All my best stories are about men," she said. "Does that bother you?"

"No," I said. "Like what?"

"One time I was with a guy and we were trying to break into a pharmacy to get some spermicide for my diaphragm, and we stood out there and threw a rock through the window and then the cops came. I was just trying to be responsible."

At her apartment, she took off her clothes and threw them on the floor, and then she lit a cigarette while she sat on top of me, slipped me into her, took a long drag, and then put her mouth over mine so that she could breath into me. Then she laughed and contracted, squeezed me. "Does that feel good? Well, maybe that's a lesson. We fit."

She tapped her forehead against mine and said, "Where have you been? I've looked so hard for you."

Outside, in my yard in Cambridge, in that small graveyard, I sat on a stone with that cheap paper in my nose. Surely the deaths of these children were one of those moments of incomprehension. And, in the mossy, almost dusty odor of the old stones, in the gray colors, in the midst of that fence, with the bars that were turning to rust, I felt Pauline's laughter, her tight squeeze, the touch of her nipples as she leaned forward to breathe that smoke into me. It was what she did to deny a place like this small cemetery, her actions at once so dangerous as to be almost equal to the dreariness of the stones, as alive as this fenced-in square was dead. And, I guess, that was part of what was eating at me, or what made my isolation keen, since now, with my troubles, that defiance, that memory haunted me. When I remembered the laughing squeeze, the touch of her lips when she wanted to breathe into me, the raspberry color of nipples, I realized how those memories protected me at bad moments.

Years ago when Pauline came to my office and sat outside, beyond the reception desk on the cracked leather sofa there, her hair spiked, her legs in torn fishnet stockings, her eye shadow dark and brooding, the other assistant prosecutors came in and went down the hall, one saying to another, "Who's the bimbo in the waiting room?"

"Someone I'm seeing," I said.

"No kidding, Frank. Is she a witness?"

"No," I said.

"Not yet," said another assistant prosecutor. "Hey, Frank, only kidding. You don't have to get that way. Jesus."

The bar Pauline liked was not only dark but subterranean, at the bottom of some steps that curved toward the depths, a yakuza joint where we got a table after going through the bar which was surrounded by fishnets, dark webs that smelled of the ocean: not a prop, but the real thing. We were the only people in the place who weren't Japanese, and as we sat in the shadows, she leaned against me and whispered, her blue eyes now inky (as those hieroglyphics on the blotter), "When you touch me, I can feel it for days. Reach under my skirt for a moment and put your hand on my thigh. I'll have something to remember you by for hours. It is a miracle it doesn't leave blisters . . . "

We stopped, our heads filled with the star-like clarity of the sake, in front of a jewelry store next to the Ritz. The window was filled with satin pedestals shaped like a woman's neck, and on these things there were diamond necklaces, the sparkle of them like starlight, too, doubly so because of the sake. Pauline put her hand on the glass and said, "I want one of those, not because of the diamonds, but because it is so improbable, like us, that you would knock right through everything that is between us, education, money, experience, and give me that. It's like acknowledging what happens to us in my apartment. Will you get it for me?"

"I don't know," I said.

"You're chicken," she said. "Aren't you? You haven't listened to a word I said. You think I'm kidding, don't you?"

"No," I said.

"I'm going to give you a week," she said. "Then I'll take care of it."

Her apartment in Cambridge had a porch at the back where we'd sit in the evening in the summertime, Pauline naked on a chair back in the shadows, her heels on the edge of the chair, her elbows on her knees, the light falling over her skin like a piece of silk: that was her all over, that she could wear light like a piece of lingerie. At the back of the house on the other side of the yard, a man, a postman, who was on vacation, washed out his underwear, fourteen pairs of jockeys, and hung them up on a line like a child's drawing of the domestic. He got up in the morning and drank his first beer and listened to his Louis Armstrong records ("Hello, Dolly, Hello, Dolly . . . "), and then the next day there was one less pair of jockey shorts, as though he was measuring out his life this way. Pauline looked at him and said to me, glowing in the shadows, "You know, I think I should go over there some afternoon. But it might kill him."

"Or break his heart," I said.

"But Frank," she said, "that's what hearts are for. What else are you going to do with it?"

"You could protect it," I said.

"Oh, Frank, you're so old fashioned," she said. "You've got to live as though someone is going to dynamite your heart. Any fool can see that."

But in the middle of the night, she breathed into my ear and said, "Yes, darling, I want to be protected. I can't tell you how much I want that. Will you do that for me? Would you? That's why I want the diamonds. It's a sign. Will you just give me a sign? Tomorrow you'll have six days."

At the beach we stood as the water made a susurrus, like wind in the trees, as the last part of a wave washed over our feet. For an instant it looked as if we were wearing liquid socks. We stretched out on the sand, the sun beating down, our skin salty, and sometimes we swam and floated out there, the rise and fall of the ocean at once soothing and ominous. She said, "Feel that. You can't stop it, Frank." Then we went home and took off our bathing suits, which clung to us, and I tasted the salt on her skin. "Look. There's another pair of jockey shorts gone. It's like a calendar. You've got five pairs left."

We went for a picnic in the evening in western Massachusetts, for which I had made a basket. We had a blanket, too, which we spread out near a beaver pond. The clouds drifted by, the shapes of which we tried to name, a knight, a horse, figures engaged in the most intimate embraces, she said, that's what that one looks like. See what she's doing to him? And when we were home, she said, "Tell me about love, Frank. Is it real? Can you die of it? Can you tremble just thinking about the man you love? Can you have an orgasm, just thinking about a man? Sit still. I'm going to try right now."

"Who are you going to think of?"

"Richard Nixon, you ninny," she said. "That's what you get for asking."

The last pair of jockey shorts disappeared.

"Well," she said. "Where are the diamonds?"

"You're kidding," I said. "Aren't you?"

"I never kid," she said. "You haven't got them?"

"No," I said.

We sat on the porch of her apartment, and over the warm air of that space between the buildings, where gardens had been planted, Louis Armstrong's voice floated in our direction, a memory of the past itself, some perfume of another age. Pauline took off her clothes and then sat back where only I could see her, and the sunlight, or the glow of the last of the day, made her skin white.

The next night, or so the police report said, she went to the sake bar and talked to a man who had lost a finger. She asked if it hurt, and he said that it wasn't anything to speak of. There were other things that were more important, like loyalty. Did loyalty hurt? she asked. Yes, the man said. That was what hurt the most. Then she got up, perfectly steady on her feet, and stood in that bar's underworld light. A thin, tall woman in fishnet stockings, a short skirt, a tight-fitting black top, and spiky hair, her blue eyes absolutely piercing, even in the dim light, as though she could see, in the most profound way possible, just how things really were.

If someone was in her way on the avenue, she walked right through them, not apologizing, not even noticing that she had just pushed someone aside. Her entire aspect, some people told the police, was one of exquisite resolve.

She kneeled on the sidewalk and pried out a brick that lined the edge of the square of dirt around a tree. She spent a little time, picking up one brick, turning it one way and another, and then picking up another. She chose one, in the end, that sparkled like broken glass. It was shown at the trial, and it was obvious that it had a lot of mica in it, which sparkled even under the fluorescent light of the courtroom.

The jewelry store was closed. Still, the lights were on and the diamonds were displayed on that black stand that so looked like a woman's neck. The gold letters on the window were sedate and elegant, as on the invitation for a polite wedding.

Pauline wound up, just like those pitchers we had seen when I took her to a baseball game at Fenway Park, and threw the brick. It made a perfect shape, and even though the window was safety grade, the brick smashed right through it, the shreds of glass, all in the shape of a million triangles, fell to the sidewalk. Pauline came up to the hole, reached in, and lifted a necklace, which she let hang from her hand like a dead snake.

The police had their guns drawn when they got out of their car. She held the diamonds, the spectral colors of them in the lights of the police car showing as a million points against her black clothes, as though she was part of the most clear and star-marked sky. The cops pointed their guns. She held the diamonds. A crowd appeared, as though they simply emerged from the stone of the buildings.

The police had a video camera in the car. She didn't run, didn't flinch, and she didn't even really look at the guns. Instead, she said, "See, Frank. That's the way you do it. No hesitation. Either you have it or you don't."

Then she said to the cops.

"You tell Frank Mackinnon I want to see him," she said.

"The assistant DA?" said one of the cops.

"That's right," said Pauline. "That's the one. I can have an orgasm thinking about him."

"No shit?" said one of the cops. "Can you do it now?"

"You want to see?" she said.

"Put down the diamonds," said the other cop.

"You're going to have to take them from me," she said.

"Come on," said the cop. "Don't kid around."

"I never kid around," she said.

So, they took them from her. When they were done her nose was bleeding onto her clothes, and she turned toward the camera in the police car, her hands cuffed behind her as she said, "Frank, didn't you understand love? You're breaking my heart. Can't you see?"

The next day they showed the tape to Maxwell Jenkins, a tight-assed man if there ever was one, who had caught this case, and he was in my office in an instant. As fast as he could get there without running. I told him that Pauline and I had been involved, and that she thought I had made a promise.

"Did you?" he said.

"What?" I said.

"Did you promise her diamonds in exchange for sexual favors?"

A film of sweat appeared on his forehead and on his upper lip, which showed he thought maybe he was really onto something.

In the hall, the sound of a woman's high-heeled shoes sunk into the first migraine headache I have ever had, a spike into a jellyfish. It was up to Jenkins how she was going to be charged. I sat down.

"Cat got your tongue, Frank?" said Jenkins.

"No," I said. "Of course not. I didn't offer her diamonds for anything." He polished his shoes on the back of his pant legs. It was a way of hiding his disappointment. "But," I said. "I want to ask you something."

"You mean like a favor?" he said.

"That's right," I said.

"I bet I can guess. Oh, I bet I can. You want me to go easy. Isn't that right, Frank? What are you doing hanging around with these cheap sluts?"

"Max . . . ," I said. I got out of the chair.

He stepped back, just like that.

"You don't have to get that way, Frank," said Jenkins. "Take it easy. Take it easy."

He went into the hall, his shoes squeaking where the woman's high heels had made that tapping, and even from my office, it was possible to hear Jenkins say, into each door he passed, "Get this. Mackinnon wants us to go easy on his squeeze." Then he came into my office and showed me the previous charges that had been entered on Pauline's sheet. Resisting arrest, sale of marijuana, possession of stolen property, fraud, trafficking in stolen credit cards. Her father and mother had been arrested, too, many times, since they had a chop shop, a place that reduced stolen cars to auto parts, which they sold around New England. Pauline had grown up in the business and had been arrested for transporting just about everything: carburetors, alternators, computers, air bags, all packed up in boxes that looked brand new. She had moved up in the business, too, and had been involved as an organizer of the distribution of parts as far as Miami. The Cubans had been great customers. But then she had quit all of that, at least for a while.

"I'm asking you for a favor," I said.

"Well, Frank," said Jenkins. "I can only do that if she buys a plea."

Of course, she insisted on a trial, and when at the end I went to see her in the courtroom, she faced me, her eyes at once as attractive as they had ever been, as though this trouble was the kind of thing that made her so desirable. "That man," she said. She pointed at me. "Right there. He failed me. Don't you see?

Frank, I'm sorry for you. I could have made you so happy," the judge hammering the gavel all along and then called to the bailiff to turn her around and to make her shut up. I went out of the room, hearing her call, "Frank, Frank, Frank. No one can love you the way I did. And you threw it away. Don't you remember? You were supposed to protect me."

She was sentenced to a year and a half.

About ten years ago I was in court. The halls were marbled and appeared like a mausoleum. There is nothing like the hall of a courtroom: the indifferent formality of the floors and walls perfectly confront the troubled if not desperate nature of the people who wait there, their expression one of hoping for the best, but knowing the worst is probably going to come. Mixed in with that is the endless waiting for an attorney, for a new schedule, for a delay, as though you could get somewhere by putting something off, when in fact you were just making the anxious moment last forever.

Jeremiah Gordon, another district attorney, stood in the hall with his British suits, his shirts with the white collars and white cuffs and colored sleeves and fronts, the bow tie perfectly tied. He said, "Hey, Frank. You remember your squeeze from a while back?"

"Who?" I said.

"You know," he said. "The one who broke the window and took those diamonds."

High-heeled shoes and cops' brogans echoed in the hall, the sound at once chaotic and familiar.

"Step in here for a moment. You remember her name?"

Pauline stood with her same posture, perfectly straight, but coiled, still defiant. She was in her thirties now, hair with a little less sheen, but somehow her vitality, her kill-the-world-for-pleasure quality, was stronger than ever, as if she had had time to stand at more dangerous cliffs than I could imagine. She turned her head and tossed her hair just the way she used to years before. She smiled and said, "Frank, why how nice to see you. I bet you don't feel bad yet, do you?" Then she faced the judge, who asked if she understood the charges against her, the details of trafficking in stolen car parts, which she had gone back to as though by gravity, and the fact that she had been arrested while she was carrying a specific amount of cocaine. The pickup truck she drove had been loaded with stolen air bags and a transmission for a Porsche. She nodded, but then she turned back to me.

"Frank," she said. "You should be charged here, too. If you just had the courage to love, I wouldn't be here at all."

He sentenced her to five years. She was led out by two bailiffs, one on each arm, and as she looked over her shoulder she said, "Frank, I'll bet you'll end up in trouble, you know that? It will sneak up you. And you know why it will happen? Because you try to be careful. Because you think feelings can be hidden."

[CHAPTER TWENTY-ONE]

THE NEWSSTAND IN Harvard Square is, by comparison with the people who surround it, a sort of temple of the serene. The sidewalk is filled with the jugglers, the three-card monte boys, one woman with a piercing in her nose who held a sign that said FORTUNES TOLD. FINANCE: $6. LOVE: $9. Next to her were the tie-dye shirt sellers (the one product that seems as constant as toilet paper), competing guitarists, each with a battery-powered amplifier, one singing "I Want to Be Sedated," one more retro, all hammering away for a dollar or two or to maintain some ever-receding dream. There, in the middle, stood the kiosk with the newspapers laid out on overturned milk crates. The *Globe* said, in large type, CITY COUNCILMAN INDICTED. KICKBACK SCHEME WITH ORGANIZED CRIME FIGURE, MANNY VERRAZANO, FOR SUBSTANDARD CONCRETE.

"Hey," said the news vendor with a change apron on his fat belly. "Are you going to pay for that or just walk away?"

"Oh," I said. "Sorry."

The dollar disappeared into his hand like a rat devoured by a snake.

"They're going to fry that guy, I'll tell you that," said the vendor. He tapped the story. "He can just bend over and kiss his ass good bye."

"You think so?" I said.

"Does a bear do it in the woods?" he said.

"I guess," I said.

"No guessing, Jack," he said. He put a finger onto the front of the *Globe*. "This character is roadkill."

He arranged the girly magazines, one just covering the front of another. The store window behind me, where I read the newspaper, smelled of the donuts the place sold. The news vendor was probably right: Boston loved a scandal, as though it was a way of knowledge, a morality play, the same pattern shown again and again, like something from the Middle Ages. The accusation, the denials, the outrage, the fight to the death.

The Raver moved sideways, along the newly cleaned window, his hair in the wind that carried the scent of a recent shampoo.

"Remember . . . ," he said to me, his hand picking at my sleeve, then turning the paper so he could see the front page. "The good and just and beautiful, which generates and holds together all things . . . And thou wilt give thyself relief, if thou doest every act of thy life as if it were the last."

In the fourth paragraph the story said that they had the councilman on tape, soliciting a bribe and giving his guarantees that the thickness of the concrete, poured for a new road, and the depth of the gravel beneath it, would never be checked. After the jump, next to an ad for Feline's, was a picture from the tape. Grainy, but all the more damning for that.

"Listen to me," said the Raver. "Listen. You are worried. Did you pour the lousy cement?"

"No," I said.

"Hey," said the Raver to a man who stood behind a card table covered with neatly folded tie-dye shirts. "Where's your contribution? Didn't I tell you this spot costs? Pony up or move on . . . "

One of the musicians started in on "I Want to Be Sedated" again, and the woman with the piercing and the three-card monte boys all looked hungrily at the ten dollars I dropped into the musician's cigar box. The opened lid had a painting of a woman with dark hair in a gold burst. My father had used cigars, sent to him in a Red Cross care package from his father, to trade for blood sausage in Poland.

• • •

The barbed wire was bright at the top of the fence, and the piles of cars still stood with that modern solidity, as stern as those faces on Easter Island. I had gotten this far, but the coming scandal and the loss of Pia's trust (if it looked as if I had lied to her) were right there, as definite as those piles of broken automobiles and as tragic, too.

Yana was at the computer, as always, her white hands on the white keys. But every now and then a woman walked behind Yana's chair, her gait familiar and pleasant, a mature woman but still oddly sultry. Her hair was dyed red and her freckles showed when she turned and made the short walk, about fifteen feet, before she turned again. Then she came up to the window, her eyes set on mine: it had been a long time, but even so we stood there, mesmerized, unblinking, surprised.

The samovar gave off a wisp of steam, like a thin beard on an old man, but the tea, with that exotic scent, was just waiting.

A couple of clean cups sat on the plywood counter, although only one had a handle. Stas's chair was empty. Outside the wind moaned between those stacks of cars, which seemed like evidence of sudden and yet hidden violence.

"Here, Frank," said Pauline. "Let me get you some tea."

The samovar made a trickling sound as she filled the cup with the handle.

"You want a cookie?" she said. "Chocolate chip. From that upscale bakery in town. I remember you had a sweet tooth."

The tea was the temperature of a kiss. Yana typed, then scrolled through a page of photos and Pauline said, "No. Those are twice what they should be."

The samovar made that trickling sound. Pauline offered a cookie, holding it out as though it was a way of reaching across those years. It was sweet and buttery.

"So, Frank?" said Pauline. She was still thin, more knowledgeable, it seemed, than ever. "How have you been?"

"I came to see Stas," I said. "Do you know where he is?"

"And what about me, Frank," she said. "Aren't you glad to see me?"

"Of course," I said.

"Just listen to him," she said to Yana. "Butter wouldn't melt in his mouth, would it? What a cool one you are, Frank."

"Why are you here?" I said.

"Business. I was born and bred to the trade. My father taught me. Didn't you read my sheet all those years ago, or were you too busy trying to pretend you didn't know me?"

"I tried to help," I said.

"Tried to help," she said. "Now isn't that something?" She turned to Yana. "You hear that?"

Yana scrolled down the page.

"There," said Pauline. "We can do something with those air

bags. Are they genuine Mannhausers? At that price they may be phony. How many have they got?"

"Three hundred," said Yana.

"Maybe we can knock them down a little?" said Pauline. And as she looked at the screen, she said, "It's funny how things work out, Frank. I was in Florida, you know, looking for a deal on parts and I make an offer to Yana, and we get to talking and she says she knows you. How about that? So I thought I might come up and see how things are doing in my old stomping grounds."

She turned, her eyes that same blue, at once furious and filled with grief or regret. As though it was stronger after simmering for twenty-five years. She seemed youthful, although she was tired, and dropped her eyes, as though showing them to me was hard work.

"You two were close?" said Yana.

"It seemed that way," said Pauline. "Didn't it, Frank?"

"We were close," I said.

"Ah," said Pauline. "But not close enough."

"That's right," I said. "I didn't understand."

She stepped closer, her nose just inches away from mine.

"And what would you have done if you had understood?" she said.

"I don't know," I said. "It was a long time ago."

"Some people, they just move on. They get married. They have a kid. Like Frank here. He's got a daughter, don't you, Frank? Is she beautiful?"

"What are you crying for?" said Yana. "I don't want a kid. That's for sure."

"Wait until you're a little older," said Pauline.

Yana shrugged. She scrolled another page of air bags.

"Those look good, too," said Pauline.

"I'm sorry," I said. "We were young. What did we know?"

"You were young," she said. "Not me. No, sir. I didn't get to grow up that way. In the auto parts business, you have to learn the ropes pretty fast."

"I guess," I said.

"There's no guessing about it," said Pauline. She wiped her eyes with a handkerchief, which she put back in the pocket of her black jeans. "I guess you went around and broke a lot of other hearts, just for the hell of it, huh?"

"No," I said. "It did something to me, too. You think it didn't?"

"Can I believe that?" she said.

"Why not?" I said. "Why would I lie now?"

She shrugged.

"I don't know," she said.

"Well," I said to Yana. "Tell Stas I came by to see him."

"Sure," said Yana. "Have you got a message for him?"

"Just tell him I came by," I said.

Yana shrugged.

The door came open with a squeak, like something caught in a trap, and then the air, tinted with oil and plastic seats that have been out in the sun, blew into the room. Keys clicked. Then Pauline followed me outside. The wind moved through those piles of cars.

"It was good to see you," I said.

"Fuck that," she said. "Don't be so polite. You don't want to see me."

We listened to the wind.

"Did it really do something to you?" she said.

"Yeah," I said. "Why do you ask?"

"It might make a difference," she said.

The stink of oil, the earthy scent, a few sad blades of grass, the icy triangles of glass.

"You look worried, Frank," she said. "I wonder why that is?"

I shrugged.

"Nothing special," I said. "Work. Time. Nothing special."

"You never were a good liar," she said.

"No," I said. "I never was. I just tried not to feel certain things. But that catches up with you. One day, well, you make a hash of things, like a case, and you did it because you had so much under wraps."

"I warned you," she said. "Don't you remember?"

She cried, leaned against me, trembled there: in that touch the years took on a new weight, as though a hundred times more heavy now, in confronting them, than in just looking the other way.

"So, Frank," she said. "I want you to ask me something."

"What's that?" I said.

"Ask for my help," she said.

"What kind of help is that?" I said.

"Don't be stupid," she said. "It's clear enough. You can do it or not."

"OK," I said.

"That's not asking," she said.

"All right," I said. "Will you help?"

"I'll think about it. Maybe I'd like to watch you twist in the wind," she said. Then she put her hands on my chest and shoved me away. "Get out of here. Go on. Leave me alone. That's what you were good at."

I drove away but still glanced up, from time to time, to the rearview mirror. She stood with her arms crossed beneath her breasts, the wind moving her hair, her eyes set on the car. A blimp floated overhead, silver and swollen as it towed a sign that said LOWEST MORTGAGE LOANS. MANCHESTER BANK. COME IN TODAY.

[CHAPTER TWENTY-TWO]

AT THE END of June the box for a pregnancy test sat in the wastebasket in the upstairs bathroom in my house, the one next to Pia's room, although she had her own apartment in Cambridge now. Robert probably lived there, too. Here, in her bathroom at home, the wallpaper was the same as when she had been a child: sail boats on little waves, with sailors, in blue hats, hiking out over blue water, their teeth as white as whale bone. And, for a moment, the question was why she had brought the pregnancy test here, to her old bathroom. So, I put the pregnancy box back in the trash, although now I buried it under the used Kleenex and tissue that had been on the bottom. Then I sat on the turned-down toilet seat, with a little sort of blue rug on it, and considered the facts.

The little stick was blue.

Pia sat downstairs in my study. Robert was about to arrive. I had invited him for the weekend on that land along the Delaware River. We'd spend some time in the woods, along the water, maybe gather some watercress at the top of a seep where the bear appeared from time to time. And, of course, I thought we would have a picnic where the cress grew.

Pia and Robert hadn't yet enrolled, but they both had their first-year law books and were already reading them.

We'd stay in that stone house that had meant so much to my father and had hurt him in a precisely equal amount. It was a way of appeasing the dead of the previous generation. And, in fact, I had come up here, to this bathroom, to get some Band-Aids, since I have noticed that this is a critical item to have on a trip to this land. Someone was always bleeding, sometimes worse than others.

Alexandra left this trip to me, since, she said, the land had always left her feeling like something was lying in wait. No, she said, if she got moody, she'd go into the small graveyard behind our house and spend some time with Juduthan and Polly Wainwright, or at least their fading stones and the stones of their children.

So, you can't say I hadn't been warned about intensity. Pia stared into the distance, as though she could see the greatest of all mysteries: the arms of DNA combining like the collision of galaxies. I packed a picnic in a basket, and I carried it and a bag with some clothes and a sweater in it, one I always took to the farm, a leather one that had belonged to my grandfather and father. Sort of stinky like a cigar.

I put the basket and bag on the floor in the study. Pia was on the couch. I sat down next to her.

"What's in the picnic?" she said, although she kept staring into the distance.

"Pâté, raspberry tarts, white wine," I said.

"Sounds good," she said as though I were describing a method of execution or the details of a hanging.

"I've got something to tell you," she said.

"Oh?" I said.

"Yes," she said. "I've got something to tell you and I have made up my mind about it."

"All right," I said.

"All right?" she said. "Just like that? No questions, no chess games, no gambling, no bets, no deals?"

"I saw the box upstairs," I said.

She shrugged.

"I'm pregnant," she said. "Is Jerry going to be up there, when we have that picnic? It's going to be down by the river, right?" she said.

"Well, I don't know," I said.

"It will be by the river," she said. "And we'll ask Jerry. Do you know if he's taking his phenobarbital?

"I guess," I said.

"I guess he isn't," she said.

The water dripped in the kitchen, a small, harsh *tip*, *tip*, *tip*. A breeze made the leaves hiss, one against another, a susurrus that filled the room with an intermittent pressure. Pia put her hands together, as though praying, and then put them between her knees.

"Well, there's Robert," she said.

We put his bag into the Gray Ghost, and Pia got in the back, where her eyes had that same distant gaze, that same expression of seeing into another life or another galaxy. Robert got in next to me and we sat in Pia's silence, the sensation of it like a weight in the car.

"A penny for your thoughts," said Robert.

"Contracts," said Pia.

"Are you going to take that this year?" I said.

"Yes," she said. "I'm doing the reading beforehand. Serious stuff."

So, we went the same way I had driven my father's ashes, carrying this time not what was left of him, but what might be part of him, one generation folding into another, although Pia had decided not to have the child.

The prison on Route 2, with its perfectly gray walls, seemed different in the way it accused. Now the place seemed to have some special knowledge, some understanding, if only by association, of the damned. And as it went by in the gray blur, like everything I wanted to avoid, I was left with a sense of fatalism, and a certain awe, too, as though the mysterious side of things had been codified here, not our errors so much as the deepest fears we have about ourselves. The place had gravity, a tug or a suggestion of a scale that was beyond my understanding. You'd think a prosecutor would understand this gray concrete, but some essence, in its illusiveness, left me desperate.

The Delaware Valley, from the top of the ridge, was a smoky blue, and the hawks were up in the thermals, wings stiff, alert to a mouse or squirrel that didn't notice the moving shadows. We went along the river, the long straight glides marked by eel traps, shaped like the Vs of migrating geese. And here and there, close to the land my grandfather had owned, the trout made rings where they took a mayfly. Cream variants, I thought. White as apple blossoms.

We went up the road to the farm, as always, the dirt track a little worse every year, and then we came to the stone house road and turned on it and went down to the house itself, the enormous cobbles of its walls seeming brutal, to be used for a stoning.

We unloaded our things, but Pia stopped me when I took the picnic out of the car.

"I don't think we want to have that down by the watercress," she said. "That's what you were thinking, right?"

"Maybe we'll see the bear," I said.

"Too hot," said Pia. "He's got the sense to stay away right now, don't you think?"

"Probably," I said. "Maybe he knows the Girls Club wants us to get rid of him."

"If it's the same one," she said.

"It doesn't matter about that. He's getting in the way, isn't he? Or maybe he's a little suicidal."

Down below, about a hundred yards away, the seep where the watercress grew was a brighter green on the green of the ferns.

"So, you want to have the picnic down by the river?" I said.

"By Jerry's," she said with an air of sadness. "He'll come along."

"Who's Jerry?" said Robert.

"My cousin," said Pia.

"Good. I'd like to meet him," said Robert.

"OK," said Pia.

Jerry's house was as always: it suggested the disorder if not the violence of a junkyard, and the car hoods and pieces of metal picked up at wrecks along the river mixed perfectly with pieces of plywood he had found at fire sales to give the place the air of one of those small shrines that people make along the side of the road where someone has died, a warning and insufficient memorial to the trouble that had really taken place.

Jerry sat on a broken lawn chair in his blue jeans and blue work shirt, a hat that said I WENT OVER THE FALLS AT NIAGARA, his hair gray now, sticking out from the sides of his hat. The river, on the other side of the road, was a silvery sheet, but here and there, around large rocks, it broke into foam.

"Well, Cousin Frank. And Pia. How-how—," Jerry said.

Pia waited. I did, too.

"How, how, how . . . "

Robert didn't move. His expression the same as when he faced the garbage man in Boston.

"How are you?" said Jerry.

"Fine," said Pia. "Good to see you, Jerry. I want you to meet a friend of mine. This is Robert."

"Nice to meet you," said Jerry.

He took Robert's hand.

"Sorry we're going to have some lousy weather," said Jerry.

"Looks pretty clear to me," said Robert.

"Maybe," said Jerry. "That blue starts slow, but it builds, you know?"

"We're having a picnic," I said. "We'd like you to come."

"Isn't that sweet," said Jerry. "Sure. Over there by the river is nice."

Pia and Robert took the basket and went across the road, the cars making a sort of hush and tear as they went by on the two-lane highway between us and the river. Jerry took off his hat and brushed back his hair.

"Are you taking that stuff they give you?" I said.

"You mean the phee-pheee—," he said.

"Phenobarbital," I said.

"Don't, don't, don't," said Jerry. "Phenobarbital."

"Are you taking it?" I said.

"Sure, sure," said Jerry. "Just like clockwork."

We stood opposite each other.

"You haven't forgotten?" I said. "You could take one now, if you did."

"I told you," he said. "Goddamn storm. Let's eat before it starts."

The road had been resurfaced with glassphalt, and when we

went across it, the sun made the flecks of glass look like the track of an enormous snail, although it was more ominous than that, as though the flecks of light were tokens of ill will. Jerry put his head down and ran, just in front of a car, a black SUV. Robert stood up and watched and then Pia put her hand on Robert's arm, and they took the tablecloth and spread it out, one of them on one end, one on the other, as though they were making a bed. The tablecloth settled with that gentleness of a hot air balloon as it landed.

"Maybe it will hold off," said Jerry. "But that blue is always a sure sign."

It was clear on the horizon, and yet, in the air, the scent of moisture hung. Maybe it was from the river. A mass of blue butterflies rose from the bank, the shudder of them like visible anxiety.

The pâté had the hint of pepper and pork and fat, and the cheese was so sharp the blue veins, like marble, seemed to sting. I opened the wine.

"Maybe it's just the butterflies," said Pia.

"I don't know," said Jerry. "What's that poem, Cousin Frank? I think of it when that storm comes."

"Hopkins?" I said.

" . . . li . . . li . . . the ooze of oil crushed . . . dappled dawn drawn . . . "

"This pâté is wonderful," said Robert. "Jerry, would you like some?"

Jerry put out his hand but he was looking into the distance.

"What's the blue like?" said Pia.

"Like outer space, or something. A haunting sort of blue," said Jerry. "Maybe like a pregnancy test. I saw a show on the Nature Channel about how fast the tests are."

Jerry took another piece of pâté.

A drop of rain and then another fell out of a blue sky, a small tap, cool and lovely but mysterious.

"I told you," said Jerry.

"Yes," I said.

Pia poured more wine.

"It's really coming up now," said Jerry.

"Where?" said Robert.

"Over there," said Jerry. "It comes from the other side of the river and then it gets closer and closer and before long you have it wrap around you . . . "

We sat while the river made that rumble, bumble, humble. Jerry stiffened, legs out, just like a board, as though he had been in some kind of experiment and they had turned on the current, and, of course, he made that noise, that *ah*, *ah*, *ah*, and then thumped the ground with the back of his head, but Pia had come around, or was trying to, but Robert was already there.

"He's got bridgework," said Pia.

Robert reached in, took it and put it in his pocket, just as Pia had, and I looked for a stick, but used the handle of the knife, made of wood, to get into Jerry's mouth, although this was dangerous, since he could fall or roll or somehow get to the blade. Then Robert, with a gentle caress, put his hand under Jerry's head and held him to keep the pounding from getting worse. But Jerry went on, legs kicking, spitting pâté, slobbering, the saliva as silver as the river, and Pia was already calling the ambulance, and the seizure became repetitive but different, as though begging for mercy, and Pia came to hold his head, too, after making the call.

I held Jerry's legs, not to restrain him, but just to make sure he didn't turn over or bounce away. The slobber from his mouth started to bubble. Pia looked down at it and then directly into Robert's eyes.

She cried now, the sobs as deep, almost, as the heaving of Jerry's chest.

"How did he know about the blue?"

"He sees it. Like something from the underworld," I said. "Like a storm. He told me he could see it on TV, on the Weather Channel. Something coming his way."

Jerry kicked harder and that begging for mercy continued. It was so constant as to be like a man who is filing a bar in a prison with a dull saw blade.

"Blue like the pregnancy test," she said.

Pia went on crying. Robert stared into her eyes.

"Are you pregnant?" he said.

"Yes," she said.

He held Jerry, and did what he could to comfort him, which was just to keep that banging from hitting anything hard. Overhead, in the air that really was blue, but perfectly clear, the most beautiful sky I had ever seen, a hawk turned with a precision that was so keen, so precise as to be like mathematics. Dapple dawn drawn . . . Jerry was right. The river broke up around those stones, and the butterflies arrived again in a blue, shuddering mass that hung in the air around the twitching, begging man.

"Goddamn," said Mary Drucker. "I don't know what we're going to do."

Her assistant gave Jerry a shot and the convulsions slowed down and then faded away.

"Hit him with a two-by-four?" said Mary.

"He's stubborn," I said.

"Well, I guess it runs in the family," said Mary.

"That's possible," I said.

"Here's his bridgework," said Robert.

Mary put it in a little bag she had and then they brought

down the gurney. The ambulance went away, toward Port Jervis, and then we sat down at what was left of the picnic.

We splashed ourselves with the green water of the river, which seemed forgiving or maybe it was just soothing. Robert washed the blood and drool off his hands and some had even gotten on his face. He splashed some water on me, and then we sat on the bank.

I tore a piece of bread. Had some pâté. Robert took a sip of wine, then a piece of cheese. The river went along with its sound, as though it was so indifferent to us as to leave us a little lonelier than before.

"I didn't want to tell you like that," said Pia. "I'm sorry."

"It doesn't matter," said Robert. "The question is, what are we going to do?"

• • •

Upstream the water was calm and it showed the fish had begun to rise: the rings formed with a gentleness, a precision of mathematics. And there, in that almost impossible delicacy, the mayflies like flecks of some god that decided to reveal itself for a moment, in that cool, oddly grassy perfume of the river, I thought, What is she going to do about the baby, related to the future of the Mackinnon family? But, of course, I already knew.

The grass made that *whip, whip, whip* on my pants as I went up to the car. Robert just walked, head up, shoulders square, Pia next to him, her hair so bright in the sun and in the glare of the river that I was left with a sense of mystery again, as though I had glimpsed things as uncanny as that blue light Jerry saw.

I put the picnic in the trunk. Robert got into the front seat. Pia in the back. No one said a word.

So we went up the road through what had been my grandfather's land, a deer going through the woods with an almost bouncing gait. Graceful and harsh. Neither Pia nor Robert looked at the deer. It just ran away and left them to their own thoughts.

Then we turned down the road to the stone house, which needed to be graded, and I had to keep one wheel of the car on the hump in the middle. Pia's silence was like a gas, or a hiss, or a physical presence, and I guess we were all afraid that if we started, if we spoke what was on our minds, we'd never stop. Or worse. We would say about five words and stop forever. Silence hiding the possibility of more silence: the worst there is. She didn't want the baby, or she wanted it but thought she couldn't have it. This only made the silence worse, or the worst silence is that one right after finality makes itself apparent.

The car went over a rock that was pushing up out of the road a little more every year and now seemed to be like the crown of some enormous head that was coming up out of the dirt. The Audi's undercarriage scraped as it went over it.

"That rock gets worse every year," I said.

"I'll help you get rid of it," said Robert. "We'll drill some holes and put in a couple of charges of dynamite. Nothing but chunks to take away."

"You need to wash your face," said Pia. She said this to Robert and then to me, and both of us went into the bathroom, one behind the other, using the pink bar of soap and the towel, which I threw in the hamper when we were done, a way to make all of this disappear, but as the lid of the hamper fell shut, that silence was there again.

I sat at the table with a drink and Pia sat there opposite me. Robert sat down, too.

"We're done," said Pia to Robert. "You and me. I'm not having the child. You know that."

Robert stiffened now, as he had with the garbage man.

"Do you think I'm to be discarded, just like that?"

She shook her head.

"You heard me," she said.

I closed my eyes: if I could reach my father, my grandfather, my grandmother. What would they say? What advice? What wisdom had eluded me that I should be able to produce right here? In the midst of that sense of exclusion, as though time was darkness, Jerry's cry hung, that surprise and profound need.

"Please," I said. "Please . . . "

"Please what?" she said.

"Let's sleep on it," I said. "We're tired."

"That's all you've got to say?" said Pia.

"Maybe he's right," said Robert.

"I just don't know," Pia said. "I just don't know."

She cried with a frank, easy motion.

They read their law books until late. Then we all sat at the table under the yellow light, the shape of an enormous creature, like a five-foot bat, swept around us as a moth fluttered up to the fixture. It was like someone dragging silk across our shoulders. A moth in the house.

"Good night," said Pia. She put her damp face next to mine as she gave me that small, daughterly kiss, so soft, so much an expression of everything I wanted to protect.

"Good night," said Robert.

Their voices came through the door of the downstairs bedroom, the one that had a door and a double bed, a vibrant buzz like a fly against a window. Did they talk about the law, lectures they'd have when school started, the river as shiny as foil? Still, I knew and they did, too, that not talking about some things is a way of really saying the most about them.

In the yellow light the moth came to rest: it landed on the

outside of the fixture, and in the lack of movement, in the disappearance of those enormous wings, the room was that much more silent.

That silence, or the not talking about it, made me realize, with a certainty like the one you feel when the sun rises, that I had missed something in the attic of the farmhouse. My grandmother would never have left a silence like that, not for the panicked descendents who needed to reach her.

[CHAPTER TWENTY-THREE]

IN THE MOONLIGHT, as I ran to the farmhouse attic, thea dust in the road was as white as flour, and the woods went by like a black wall, smeared by my own locomotion. I went up to the main road but thought, No, no, that will take too long. I don't have the time. Then I went into the swamp, which was not completely dry at this time of the year. Were the copperheads on those hassocks, those rises where scrub grew? Or were they in the water? I knew for sure that they were pit vipers and that they sensed heat. Well, I was hot, sweating, the moisture under my clothes even at night making me as wet as though I had been in the rain. And then my shoes filled with water, since it seemed more likely that the snakes would be on the semidry land, rather than in the brackish part of the swamp. The splash of the water, the glistening of it, silver as the moon, was like amniotic fluid. I pushed through the brush, came up to the road and into the scent of the pines, then went across the field, the pond, the moon sliding across the still surface like a small round boat pulled by a child. Then up the stairs of the house, the creak of one step louder now than ever, the dust exploding as I opened the trunk and threw the notebooks on the floor, the check registers, the letters in that ribbon from a piece of lingerie.

My grandmother, dead these many years, was testing me. Or was it that she wanted me to be desperate enough to refuse to give up? Is that how she saw the world: desperation used as a tool, as a motivation?

My pocket knife was jaundiced in the light, yellow steel, and I held it in one hand and opened her trunk and then ran my hand along the one place I hadn't touched before, the underside of the lid, that cloth lining which appeared to be just covering the leather of the top. But now, under my fingers, the shapes were hard and had been disguised only because they had been packed in, above the lining, so tightly as to seem like a solid piece, but were really just pieces of a puzzle that hung together.

My knife ran along the inside of the top of the trunk. The lining came away like the gentlest shroud, and under that gray cloth and held in place by tape that was yellowing, too, were three notebooks. She wrote on the first page:

> So, you found them. Of course, I am curious about whatever relations would take the time to look for these books or to be interested. And there is something else here, too, whoever you are. Now that you have these notebooks, it means I am speaking to you across a darkness of infinite scale. And what does it feel like for you to be at the edge of the infinity that separates us? Or for an instant, to sweep that dark curtain aside?
>
> I can say that this moment is what makes us human, and the very darkness you confront will make you burn with a

light so heartbreakingly short, just a breath on the coals, but which (if you are like me) will be distinguished by caring for others. That is the best. The darkness you face is cunning and it knows that time is its ally, its devious, vicious compatriot, and that the two together can get people to do all kinds of things out of fear, out of terror, which, let me tell you, is not something to be sneered at. So, this is the moment of dark illumination, where all love is dark (because it is gone) and all fear is white (because it has been proved out). And as to who you are, if you are one of mine, you probably have the illusion of the strength of solitude, and I'd like to say that I want to embrace that hard, hard joy of being alone and making a decision. What you know in solitude can allow you to endure moments like this one, a combination of the wonderful and the horrifying.

But I wonder how you knew where the notebooks were? What hint, what clue? Or did you just go through the box, top to bottom? Are you one of those people who are methodical, or one like me, one who looks for the hint of a pattern in the way creatures live? That's my mystery, or the one I will not be able to resolve, not unless things are far more surprising than I believe. Here is what I believe: one day you will stand in front of this box alone. And the abyss will be between us.

Outside, an owl hunted with a rush of wings that instantly stopped, only to be replaced by a perfectly grieving shriek. A field mouse out too late. Then the wings, the rush of silence.

• • •

I have hidden these out of shame as I know they could cause someone grief, but after a while, when I knew what had happened, I thought that perhaps the truth, that dangerous substance, will want to emerge, no matter what, and that it might one day be of some use. That is my hope.

We decided not to talk about it, Pop and me. That was best. After the paperwork for Chip and our grandchildren, if we had any, after Pop had tried to instill order into the chaos I had let into our house, we stopped the clock. It was as though nothing had happened. Still, I thought, while I was willing, at times, to say that what had happened to me was chaotic, in fact I thought and had to realize that it was not chaotic at all, but the item that keeps human beings flowing from generation to generation.

The boys were away at school. Chip and Jack, who died in the war. So, it was just me, alone at the farm, and Pop, who came for the weekends, although every now and then he brought the boys, too, but soon he stopped that altogether, especially when he told them that I had gone to Europe, and that women in their late thirties sometimes had the urge to culture. Of course he helped me, came up with the money, helped arrange for an apartment in Paris through his connections, and for a doctor, too. The doctor had such brisk, touching manners, and he treated me with an attitude that, I guess, would have been more suited to dealing with an American girl, a teenager, who had managed to get herself into this condition.

At first I thought it was some odd, physical missing of McGill. The first thing was a soreness and swelling of my nipples, but then I thought this was some physical ache, and that it always happened anyway, before I got my period, but the period didn't come. Not for two weeks, then three, then a month. I sat at the farm, in the fall, and watched the leaves of the maples appear as though they were filling with blood, just as my breasts began to swell and become warmer to the touch.

I was sick in the morning, but only Charlotte knew about that, but she was polite and restrained, although she left for me a light lunch afterwards.

Pop came to the farm and we sat in our coats on the porch. The wild turkeys walked across the grass. The hawks as they found the thermals. I worked in these books, as you can see in another one, included here: I tried my hand at drawing, too, and if you look at the pictures of raccoons, bears, deer, even copperheads and timber rattlers, which I saw as they looked for a den, they have, in their eyes, a longing, confused look, as though they realized that life is so brutal it cares for not one individual, but only all of them, and this means a lot of misery, if you are one that is not looked after in the pack.

• • •

My grandmother wanted to know if Pop could really go through with it, pretending to be the father of the child, but while he said he could, he had a faraway look in his eyes, something my grandmother thought was just the beginning, and while he was a man of tremendous perseverance, she wondered if this look and the impulse behind it wouldn't fester and make matters worse, especially if, after a couple of stiff bourbons, close to the top of a water glass these days, he might make a mistake . . . in front of the boys.

So, Paris.

• • •

Pop had rented an apartment on rue Buci. And he had been considerate, too, since it was on the ground floor, at the back, quiet and not one that I would have to climb five flights of stairs, when heavy, to get the apartment at the top. The apartment had a room for a maid, a woman who was silent, dark, like a figure made of smoke, who drifted in and out. My French was sufficient, and we could talk about what we were going to have for dinner or lunch. I did the shopping at the open-air market on rue Buci, and across the street, where the butcher had his stall next to the one for the cheese seller, but when I brought these things home, the maid, who doubled as a cook, prepared what I had bought, although she set the table in the dining room for one and then ate her own dinner, a miniature version of what she made for me, in the kitchen, sometimes standing at the sink, sometimes at the small table there, with her glass of red wine and her constant, almost mechanical eating. I sat before the plate she left for me.

People passed by the window in the dining room, and I saw the men in their dark clothes, the women in their stylish coats, their gaits so proud, so elegant, as though they had practiced all their life to walk past the window of a thirty-eight-year-old woman who was pregnant by a man not her husband. It was here, when the clink of the silver against the plate was so loud as to sound like a small automobile accident, I went through the details of how I had come to be living on rue Buci with that silent woman who seemed to be a cloud of smoke from a sooty fire.

The eating alone, like this, seemed like part of the punishment. I ate slowly, as a matter of defiance, sometimes putting my hand on the swelling stomach, and while I waited, which I knew was coming, for the first kick, I kept brooding.

Still, what I know about love, or a large part of love between men and women, comes from the time I had to consider the matter as I ate the rack of lamb with spinach, the salmon with morels, the steak tartare with fried potatoes. It was a variety of liturgy, I suppose, and something I did to keep myself company. After all, when you are most lonely you think of when you were most joined to someone else, to the point of feeling that you were not one person, but two combined. This matter of codifying what I knew about McGill, about my feelings, left me knowing that the sensation of this variety of love (of which, of course, we have many) was one that left me not only whole, but warm, and somehow correct, not in the right and wrong sense, but in the sense that I fit with the stars, or that because of what was happening between me and another human being, the night sky didn't seem so mysterious, or its mystery was at that time reassuring. It made me feel as though the scale of what I felt was honored by the worlds, the distance of the stars that I saw with my own eyes. With that intensity, with that certainty, this experience, this sensation, which we all love, is as nearly as I can tell one of the most demanding, exquisite, and dangerous (not a sufficient word, really) of all the items that human beings go through.

This is what I missed, at those meals set for one and with those elegant women going by in the street: the warm certainty, the conviction that I could communicate by a touch, the warmth of a hand, just that. And so, I was left with a constant longing, a tug for something gone. That was the bitter lesson: even though it was all illusion, all hope and bizarre behavior, I still felt the tug of what had happened. On some occasions I stopped the fork, my hand on my stomach, and remembered a touch or a look, a kiss, a throb in some intimate place, all hitting me with that mixture of regret and desire. This condition, this suspended, protracted longing, which could never be forgotten, is right at the heart of what I taught myself at that dinner for one. That longing, that unbreakable isolation, which couldn't be soothed by the lover (who had proven to be untrustworthy), is at the center of the regret when human love goes wrong. And the amazing quality, the item that left me woolgathering in that apartment in Paris, or when I went for a walk by those restaurants that put off the most wonderful aroma of roasts, of potatoes with garlic and rosemary, of tartes framboise in the oven, is that this desire for what would never have worked doesn't make humans less, or diminished, but more, or larger, and that somehow the pain of this makes us wiser.

Of course, the loyalty from Pop was so unexpected. He reached to me from the depths, from all humiliation, all sense of self-loathing, all sense of betrayal simply pushed aside. He had something to do, and he was going to do it. I had a bank account. The maid. A doctor. The doctor had made arrangements for the hospital and a nurse. The baby kicked.

The telegrams came on Monday and Friday: Catherine stop report weight and health stop any needs stop love Pop.

Love? It left me shaking and added to my sense of what I know about this substance, which is so necessary, so hard to obtain, more difficult to keep, so easy to lose, and which leaves such a violent, vicious wake, sometimes, when it goes.

A telegram said: Practical considerations stop letter to follow stop Pop.

I should have known that the lawyer in Pop would take over at a certain point, since, after all, if you are a pilot, after twenty-five years, you think like a pilot, and if you are a lawyer, after twenty-five years, you think like a lawyer.

The letter was in the little box in the hall, and I put what is called a skeleton key into the lock on the door and took it out and read it at that plate for one. At least it was some company. Pop, in his letter, explained that he could not, in thinking about it, accept the child as his son, since that meant that the will he had made, the trust he had set up, and all the other benefits to his offspring would flow to this child, too. And while Pop could do this for himself, he could not, in all honesty, cheat his sons out of what was theirs because of, as he put it to be polite, "what had happened." What ideas did I have?

We had one solution, which I sent to Pop: we would say to the boys, when I came home, that this was the child of a relative of mine who had lived in Europe and who had died in childbirth. Pop and I would take this "cousin" in. We would bring him up in our house, but he would not have the benefits of a son, in terms of inheritance and other advantages, since he would already have the generosity of our taking him in.

He wrote again to say that he would have the French birth certificate translated and that he had contacted the doctor in Paris to enter the name of the mother as not being Catherine Mackinnon but my sister Celeste Muriro. He would work out the details of citizenship. Everything could be arranged.

I was at the outdoor market, very heavy, reaching for a banana, when the man there, François, of course, said, "*Madame, il a commencé. Voici de l'eau.*" Or "Madame, it has begun. Here is the water."

So, I stood with the bananas, which François had put in the string bag I used to go shopping, as though this, the gift of the bananas, would help. Then he went across the street to use the telephone. I felt the cold air and knew that I should walk to my apartment and get the bag I had prepared and go to the hospital, just as the doctor had told me to do, just as he had told me to have the hospital call him, but for a minute, maybe two, I wanted to feel the cold breeze on my wet stockings, if only to be reminded of just how alone I was and how, if there was ever a time when I should take pleasure or at least strength from the solitude I had learned to live with, this was it.

The shadow, the whiff of black smoke, stood at the door, the small bag in her hand, which she gave to me as though she knew what it had taken for me to pack it alone, the thing open on the bed, and then I went to the bureau to take out clothes that would fit after the birth, the touch of them enough to blister my fingers, or, worse, that caused me to stop, as though frozen, to think of those moments when McGill and I had been alone or when he had come into the house with the scent of pine sap and sweat. I took the bag and thanked her.

"It is nothing," the maid said and shrugged.

I had been in labor before, but not like this, in that French room with the gray walls and the nuns in their starched habits, not one of them ever really looking at me, and this, of course, left me to my own devices as the contractions came closer and closer. And much to my amazement, I thought of those moments of McGill's when he said that he could see a blue storm coming, all blue as a bruise in the sky, and then he would go stiff. I often thought, and surely thought when I was in labor, that this was a price he paid for being in love, or at least not able to control himself with me, because he said that the sky got that blue when he had been excited or upset and when he was with me he had never been more excited and more upset, because, he had said, he had always wanted to be a decent man, but somehow it had come to this. I tried to remember how smooth his skin was, just as the scent of pine seemed to be in the room as the worst of the birth came, the transition, and then I saw that the nun mopped the hall with a bottle that said *L'odeur du pin*. And so I came up against the hard fact that it wasn't just love remembered or used as some defense against the birth, at which I finally screamed louder than I have ever screamed before. The scream came from the fact that I was alone, that

McGill had been insufficient, and from a paradoxical but profound love for what Pop had done. Stood by me. And not out of vanity, or because he wanted to avoid a scandal, but from his belief that it is what he should do and what he wanted to do. Stand by me.

• • •

My grandmother and the baby went to the apartment on rue Buci, and my grandfather had arranged for a nurse. My grandmother walked endless miles, to the Luxembourg Gardens, to the Tuileries, since, as she wrote to Pop, "No matter what, I must never, under any circumstances, look as though I have given birth. I must look five years younger."

And not only did she exercise, she went to those perfume shops and cosmetics shops on the right bank, and spent a small fortune, she said, like the French women who went there to soften their skin, to make it clear, and when she came home, pulling up to the house in a Buick driven by my grandfather's chauffeur, Wade, she had Jerry with her, in a small bassinet, and she looked more than five years younger. Jack and Chip looked at each other and then hugged her and said how wonderful she looked. I imagine she didn't look old, although she began to age almost instantly, if the photographs from this time are accurate.

So, the baby was brought into the house, and Jack and Chip didn't really pay him much mind, since he was twelve or fourteen years younger than them, and soon they went to Yale, and then the war started, and by the time they came back, Jerry was away at school himself, although it was a special school. And finally, after Chip had come home, gotten married, and started work as an academic and a spook, Jerry lived in a town along the Delaware, Lackawaxen, and worked odd jobs, getting by, odd, having seizures, and finally when my father was in his thirties and moving up as an academic-spook, Jerry built that house out of spare parts and junk he picked up along the side of the road and at the scene of accidents. This, of course, was about the time I was born.

These extra books, the ones I had found under the lining of the trunk, had been tied with what I supposed to be French ribbons, pink, or maybe a just now faded red, and I tied the diaries shut with this ribbon, although my bows were not as neat and precise as I wanted, and so I did it again, as though by making it perfect, like something on a gown made in Paris, I could communicate with my grandmother.

Then the trunk lid closed like a bear trap. Bang. The dust rose in a cloud again.

The boxes, the trunks, the old lamps with shades that were covered with dust, so as to have the color of some old, intimate stain, the broken-down rockers and children's toys, all washed up here as though time was a force like the wind or tides or something that liked to push things around. Then the stairs creaked under my feet, and outside, on the front porch, the moonlight was brighter now. And then I went along the pond, where a fish stirred at an insect, or along the road to the stone house, where I stopped with only my breathing for company.

It was getting light, and the road had only a grayish luminescence in the dawn, but as I came to the stone house road and turned down it, that dark shape appeared as though it had been waiting.

The bear stood sideways, against the hillside. Its head seemed as heavy as a bowling ball, or, at least he seemed to have trouble holding it up, since as he stood there, against the gray stone that emerged from the hillside, like the remains of something that was no longer useful, he kept lifting his head, as though it took effort. Dark fur against the hillside. The living evidence of how things that seemed so right could so easily go wrong.

We faced one another. His eyes were that same oil-colored hue, although even more opaque, or something darker than dark, a color that not only had no light but actually absorbed it, that vacuumed it up from the landscape in which we both stood.

The bear swayed from side to side, or at least its head moved back and forth. It was otherwise silent, although its claws made a scraping sound as it came uphill, toward me, as though it had been a guardian all along of those diaries and was now called upon to protect them as he had always wanted. Or perhaps under the circumstances, with the light changing, I thought such a thing. The bear stood on two feet and clawed at the air. Then it stepped toward me so that I could smell that rotten salmon odor, or something like a skunk smell that has almost worn off, and I stepped closer and said, "Get out of my way."

The bear swayed from side to side. Yes, it seemed to say, we will settle this later.

It turned and walked into the brush, its blackness dissolving into the blackness of the undergrowth, which, for a moment, made everything look not like brush but a mass of bears, but then I shook my head and went down that road toward the house. The books were under my arm, and I seemed like an old schoolboy who was late for an exam.

The light was on. Pia sat with her hair in a mass at the table in the stone house, a cup of coffee in front of her. Robert sat in a pair of sweatpants and a fleece jacket that had a North Face logo. He held his coffee cup in both hands, but even through the window they were obviously shaking. Pia spoke and put her head down. At the window, where I stood like some phantom, their voices vibrated in the glass of the window, where I put the tips of my fingers. Could I make sense from just the touch? As though by a variety of Braille?

She was proud, I suppose, or more like me than I had given her credit for. She had made a decision to get rid of the child. She was going to stick to it, and even though she loved Robert, she had made a decision, although it was desperate and in an odd way made her close to Jerry. It was almost as though Jerry's cry, his almost religious plea, the garbling of God's grandeur lingered there in the room.

She stared at Robert, and for a moment I thought she was going to give him the précis of the scientific reports she had so causally reeled off for me.

She bit her lip.

He stiffened, sat right up.

"All right," he said. "What are we going to do?"

She put a hand into the mass of her hair.

I tried to answer, as I reached for the window, that question my grandmother had asked, or implied. Just who the hell was I and did I know any more about this, who I was, by standing at the chasm that was deeper than I had ever imagined, and I thought, yes, yes, I know. I'm not so different from her.

She hadn't burned those books because the truths in them had come at a cost so high as to leave her lonelier than ever, but yet she couldn't destroy what she knew to be true. She'd just have to hide it. And after all, I had spent a life hiding certain truths, like how I felt about things, only to have them blow up in my face. I didn't keep notebooks about animals. I read Tacitus and Xenophon. What was so different? Not much.

The sky was the gray of a woman's stockings, and the air had something else, too, like a faint scent of powder. The trees appeared as always at this hour, not ominous so much as though they had been witness to a nightly secret. The stone house emerged from the shadow.

Robert stood in the living room, his bag open, the methodical way he went about packing it not precise so much as just playing for more time. Pia sat at the table, head on her arms, crying now with long, slow heaves, as though she was so exhausted that this was all she could do, that even this took almost all the effort she could muster.

My shoes were filled with swamp water, and for a moment I wondered if I had been bitten and not noticed it. What would the first signs be? A puncture wound that wouldn't stop bleeding? I came up to the door, my feet making a *squish, squish* just as I imagine my father's had when he walked to the Wursthaus for a drink after flipping his car into the river. The stink of the swamp mixed with the sweat on my shirt, and a trickle of blood, as though this wouldn't be complete without that, ran along the side of my face and into the sweat and dampness of my shirt.

I pushed the door open.

"My god," said Pia.

"Here," I said. I pushed the notebooks across the table.

"Robert's leaving," said Pia.

"No, he isn't," I said. "Not just yet."

"I think I am," said Robert.

"You and I are going outside," I said. "Pia has some reading to do."

I opened the first page of the first book and pushed it across the table, into that golden light.

"Right here," I said. My finger trembled and the blood, as I leaned over, dripped onto the table. The paper towels were by the sink, and I used one of them to make a sanguine smear across the table.

"Come on," I said to Robert. "We're going to watch the sun rise."

I took a bottle of scotch that I kept for emergencies, and we went outside, through the grass, and sat on a log, a piece of gray deadwood. Like two bums on a park bench. The sky was like a gold coin just stamped in the mint.

"Jesus," said Robert. "Is this what marriage is like?"

I took a long, hot pull of whiskey.

"As nearly as I can tell," I said.

"Well," he said after the fourth drink. "It takes more balls than you'd think."

The chickadees flitted from one branch to another, and a deer browsed along the wood road, flicking its white tail from time to time. The rays of sunlight came through the mist in lines and the scent of the earth was at once damp and mulchy. Eventually, the door of the stone house opened and Pia came out. Robert and I stared straight ahead, and she put her hand on his shoulder and said, "Hey."

"You've got something to say?" he said.

"As a matter of fact," she said. "I do. Are you ready to be a father?"

He took a drink and turned to me.

"Life is full of surprises," I said.

[CHAPTER TWENTY-FOUR]

A MONTH BEFORE the wedding I took down a book from my shelf and read: "He who falls obstinate in his courage, if he has fallen, he fights on his knees. He who relaxes none of his assurance, no matter how great the danger of imminent death; who, giving up his soul, still looks firmly and scornfully at his enemy—he is beaten not by us, but by fortune; he is killed, not conquered."

The threat (or was it a warning?) from Stas was coming. Just a matter of time. I guessed it would be a note to the office, a short one that suggested a district attorney was involved in corruption. The writer of the note wondered, without giving a return address or anything like that, whether the district attorney's office would be interested in the details. Maybe it would be sent to more than one person, and I would get a copy, too. That, of course, was one way to do it. But then the difficulty is that no matter what you think, you always come across a surprise. Sometimes I sat in my study and felt that slippery grasp of Cal's hand as the trash blew under the bridge and the gulls hung in the breeze, like fate personified.

Or maybe I should say that I had two versions of time running in tandem, the wedding, and the other course that started out there with those piles of smashed cars, so much like icons of the age, the stolen parts, and, of course, the man from Russia.

Pia and Robert set up a website for the wedding with pictures of the farm, of animals that my grandmother had written about, of the farmhouse, of them holding hands, and, of course, it gave directions to the wedding, which would be at the farm. Or what was left of it. I had asked the director of the Girls Club if we could use the farmhouse for the reception (more attempt, on my part, to address ancestors, just like any primitive tribesman), and she had said yes, although something in her voice, a sort of mild threat or reticence or something, gave me a little pause. I knew she was up to something, but what? What did a woman with a crew cut and glasses like Buddy Holly's want? Money? Well, I guessed we could arrange that. But I didn't think it was money.

We interviewed two women who did calligraphy and hired one. She had blond hair that was so pale as to seem almost white, and she wore a blouse that showed an edge of the tattoo of an eagle that was on her back. She arrived in the morning with her small snakeskin case, which held her pens and ink, and she sat at my desk, where she addressed the envelopes for the invitations with a slow, patient writing, the ink, which came from Japan, she said, filling the air with a scent of the ocean and a musky perfume, like the aroma of an unpredictable god. I brought her tea. She drank it with the same beautiful precision.

"So, are you an etymologist, too?" I said. "Do you know about words?"

"Try me," she said.

She went on writing, the tip of her pen, which probably came from Japan, too, moving across the heavy paper with the same intensity as the emperor writing a haiku.

"What's the difference between a threat and a warning?" I said.

"Hmmmm," she said. She reached for another envelope. "A warning is someone telling you not to do something. A threat is what happens after you've done it. Sort of like crime and punishment."

The invitations were printed on paper I picked out myself, cream-colored stock, heavy, so that you felt it was something important when you picked it up. We sent them to more people than we thought would come, but then Alexandra and I gathered up the little envelopes that came in the brass slot of the door in the house in Cambridge, like a slot machine that was paying off after a long, dry spell. We picked up the little envelopes, each one seeming ominous to me, now, since each one didn't appear so much as just an invitation but a ticket to a spectacle where someone might get killed, or even a wedding where the bride gets left at the door. But, of course, this was just me brooding: trying to see the details that were too opaque, too much of the future to get my hooks into. But isn't the future the most important part of being alive?

Alexandra and I sat at the kitchen table with two shoeboxes, both from New Balance, one for regrets and one for acceptances. None in the regrets box. A full house.

"Jesus," said Alexandra. "That's a lot of people."

One of the envelopes was a little cheaper than the ones I had ordered, more yellow, lighter, and it hadn't been addressed by the calligrapher, but in the hand of someone who didn't write English very well. I imagined it on the fiberboard table next to the Mac where those auto parts were displayed. I put the small envelope into my pocket, and when we had done the tally for the day, and Alexandra said it was time to take a bath, I went to the small graveyard in the backyard near Juduthan Wainwright's stone. The slip of paper inside had been torn from a spiral notebook, and there in Stas's hand a note said, "Have I got the date for the wedding right? I looked it up on the web. And, like I said, the only threats you have to worry about are the short ones. Maybe I'll come to see you there. Bring some friends."

In the backyard, in that small cemetery, I sat opposite Juduthan's stone, the scrap of paper in my hand. So, Juduthan, I thought, what would be the worst? Violence at the wedding or the beginning of a scandal a week before it? Which threat was he going to make good on? Both? What do you recommend? Did you ever come clean, no matter what? Then I thought of Pia's promise that I would regret it if I had lied to her about Aurlon, which lie, of course, would be elevated to a matter of principle that spread, like a poison, through all things between us. When you have acted as though principles are important, and if you have been pleased to see that your child has absorbed this belief, you can bet, as though it were law, that one day you will find yourself asking a child to put a principle, and an important one, aside. At some profound cost.

In the morning, I dressed for work in a new gray suit, a blue tie, and shined my shoes. Then I drove back to Boston and parked near the Ritz hotel, where I walked up and down the block, by those trees in their small holes in the sidewalk and from which Pauline had taken a stone, dressed in her fishnet stockings and dyed hair and tight-fitting black top, and had stood in front of the jewelry store and thrown the thing, just like a pitcher at Fenway Park.

I, too, stood in front of the window, where the diamond necklaces were displayed like starlight, and then I went in and stood next to the man in his dark suit as he took out the diamond necklace I had pointed out and put it in a little box, which he wrapped in tissue paper and put in a little bag (something like the one I had used to carry my father's ashes) and handed it over, even before he had run my credit card through the little slot: it was his way of saying that he could tell that a man like me understood all aspects of love, and there was never a doubt about the payment.

[CHAPTER TWENTY-FIVE]

THE CATERER, BLACK'S as it was known, and Mr. Black, always Mr. Black, showed up at our house in his white van with BLACK's written on the side in wedding-invitation script, got out of the driver's seat, his bald head silvery in the last light of the afternoon, his fat fingers touching the hair at the side of his head. Then he directed his assistants, who lugged in some boxes filled with samples. Pia and Robert and Alexandra and I began to taste them. We started with hors d'oeuvres, small triangles of salmon with a caper paste, not bad when you got down to cases, stuffed mushrooms, a little greasy, and puff pastry with some ridiculous hot dogs inside, which I have always detested as a sort of rank attempt to be cute.

But as I wiped my fingers on a caterer's napkin, which had the texture of an expensive hotel sheet, and somehow the atmosphere of a sheet, too (as though everything had to do with a subdued eroticism), a shape moved along the sidewalk, on Brattle Street, at the entrance to the drive. A shadow that I knew not so much by the details of what it looked like, but how it moved, which was with a definite menace.

"So," said Mr. Black, "the stuffed mushroom recipe has come down in my family for generations. From Budapest. It has paprika, and not the junk you get here. I obtain it from Hungary. I go each spring."

"Yes," said Alexandra with a sort of wall of falseness. "Very good."

"Mr. Mackinnon?" he said.

"The salmon is good, too," I said.

"None of that farm-grown stuff," he said. "Have you ever been salmon fishing?"

The shape went by the end of the drive, not limping, but with a staccato quality, like the wing of a bat, and as dark, too, the color of black crepe.

"Excuse me for a moment," I said.

"Oh, no, Frank," said Alexandra. "You aren't going to punt to me on this. Don't even think about it."

"I'll be right back," I said.

"You don't like them?" said Mr. Black. The disbelief ran back, through generations, to Budapest.

"Lovely. Just a moment."

One figure walked on the black stones of Brattle Street. It went about a hundred yards and turned and walked back, haunting in its unpredictability. It was like a stain on the air.

"I thought I'd pay a courtesy call, Frank," said Stas. "You know, we were getting to be pretty good friends, but now . . . " He shrugged. "I don't know. Don't you want to be friends, like before? You never had to see the rough side of me. That's something a friend doesn't like to show."

Stas wore a black jacket and a black shirt and his hair was cut short. He hadn't shaved, and the sun left his close-cropped hair and beard like the grit of sandpaper.

He looked into my neighbor's mailbox. Bills, fliers from Wal-Mart, a hardware store, Stop and Shop, an ice cream store with a coupon for a real gelato, a pitch for some gutters around the roof. The truth was, I needed new gutters.

Stas waited in the fall heat: it was as though he was thinking it over. Why was I being so difficult? Is there something I had missed? Was I dim? Sort of like a Russian coal miner who thought the safety rules and regulations were going to be observed.

"You know, Frank," said Stas. "You need new gutters. Maintenance is everything. You want to make sure you take care of something before it happens. It's so much easier that way."

"What are you doing in front of my house?" I said.

"I just wanted to see Harvard Square. Go to the bookstores. Here. Look."

He took a book out of a plastic sack from Booksmith and flipped open the pages to the photographs in the middle: a shot of Kolyma, one of the camps in the Gulag. He said, as he looked at the picture, that the prisoners ate the glue from books. He guessed they must have been pretty hungry to do that. And, he said, here's the really messed up thing: the political prisoners were pushed around by the ordinary murderers and rapists.

"I noticed a prison in Walpole," said Stas. "A lot of barbed wire around it. We had a lot of barbed wire in the Ukraine. In Russia. Siberia. Like here in this book."

"Don't even think about it."

"Frank," he said. "I came to tell you that I don't have a lot of time."

"Get away from me," I said.

"Don't kid yourself, Frank," said Stas. "Where are you going to go for help?"

I took a step over one of those gravestone-like blocks of slate pavement that is the Brattle Street sidewalk.

"I want to tell you something," said Stas. "Rumors in prison get started, you know that? Say a guy is in for some corruption charge. But the rumor gets going that he is actually a child molester. You know what happens to those guys? A priest was convicted recently and you know how he died? In that prison in Concord?"

"I heard," I said.

"Like I say," said Stas. "I'm thinking it over. But it can't go on forever. There are two guys who are being railroaded for some misunderstanding about auto parts. Something to do with some guy who came from Florida and got into trouble up here. I'm just mentioning this and saying I haven't got a lot of time."

"Go away," I said.

"A lot of balls," said Stas. "Well, I hope your daughter has a nice wedding."

The pigeons went up and down those stones of the sidewalk, anxious, hunting for a crumb, their feathers smooth as skin.

"Get those gutters fixed," said Stas. "It's the smart thing."

He glanced at my house and then walked down that uneven sidewalk, his shape seeming to rise into the hot air.

• • •

"Well," said Alexandra. "Try this."

She held out a small round of dark bread. It had a layer of butter and a layer of caviar, the taste of it at once fishy and mysterious.

"Real Iranian," said Mr. Black. "I have a connection with a pilot who flies to the Middle East. He brings it back for me."

"Pretty good," said Robert.

"All right," I said.

"The main course," said Alexandra. "Venison. Wouldn't that be right?"

The assistant opened an aluminum case. Venison in juniper berry sauce, morels.

"The key to serving venison," said Mr. Black. "Is that it must be warm. To serve venison, we will need extra servers."

"Some of my friends are vegetarians," said Pia.

"For vegetarians, I can do a nice squash and walnut risotto," said Mr. Black.

Outside, the street was empty, and somehow the lack of movement, the lack of that phantom shape, seemed more ominous than its presence. Then we tried other things, guinea hens, hard to eat, chicken, ghastly, but as the assistants produced these things by a sort of culinary legerdemain, I thought of McGill, about the smell of sweat and sawdust from those soft woods, or of my grandmother and how she had looked out the window while her bare feet touched, with a thrill, with a tickle, the carpet beneath her feet. And how Pop had done what was required of a decent man. The open-air market on rue Buci, the table set for one.

So, we kept at it, Robert and Pia and Alexandra tasting the main course, and then the varieties of cake and the icing and then we got through a discussion of what should be served and who was a drunk and did the bartender have insurance, because none of us, the lawyer I was and the lawyers my daughter and Robert were going to be, wanted to be on the wrong end of a lawsuit that came from someone getting tanked up and driving down the main road from the farm and right into the Delaware.

Pia said, "And it's all set with the Girls Club, right?"

"Sure, sure," I said.

But that woman with the butch haircut and those glasses with the heavy rims left a message for me. Of course, she did this after the invitations been mailed, with map included, and the address of the website, which also had directions to the farmhouse where the tent would be set up and where we would eat that caviar, salmon, venison, with the risotto for the vegetarians, and where we would drink champagne, as though the world was new.

Buddy Hollyette said that same bear from my land had not only gotten into the garbage again but had stalked a girl, a thirteen-year-old who had just gotten her period. Buddy Hollyette was convinced that this was a dangerous thing, not saying whether she meant the period or the bear, but given her dislike of life, she probably meant both, and that the bear was obviously going after young girls when they were having a period. Surely, this couldn't go on.

She had complained to my father and what had he done? Nothing.

She said that while she hated to interfere with the plans that had been made, if that bear followed another Girls Club member around or got into the garbage one more time, she would have to withhold the right to use the farm for the wedding.

Now, I put down the phone and thought about going to court to get an order forbidding her to do just that, but then that meant bringing up the deed, which was written in a way that was not as clear as my father should have written it, since he liked, in a legal document, a little "wiggle room," just in case it became convenient for him to no longer have the rights he had fought so hard to obtain. So, there I was, in my study, surrounded by the lingering aroma of venison and morels, guinea hen and chicken and puff pastry with those ridiculous hot dogs in them.

I called Robert.

"You and I have an errand to do. Next weekend. Will you help me?"

"Does a bear do it in the woods?" he said.

"Yes," I said. "I guess he does."

Then I opened the gun case in my study, took out the Mannlicher my father had given me, saw that it still had a thin sheen of Hoppe's oil on it, and that, on the shelf at the top of the cabinet, a box of 6.5 mm ammunition sat like fate itself.

Then Alexandra and I went through the other things: tent, bridesmaids' dresses, groomsmen's jackets and pants, flowers, transportation from the church to the farm, serving help, champagne, a bar, and then, of course, there was the matter of music: a band. Pia had always liked music, and she had gone around the house with her headphones on and then those little things that stick in the ears, moving this way and that, so that I had the physical sense of the music but not the sound.

She and Robert wanted a popular band, and two days later the members of the band came into my study, heads shaved, tattoos here and there, spiderwebs and such. The men wore earrings and the woman who sang came too, her pale skin deep in a habit of black hair, and we all sat there for a while, looking at each other, a district attorney, his wife, and this collection of drug addicts who had come together to talk about money.

So, we started in, one way and another, how many hours, how much money, a guarantee, what happens if it rains, and other matters, and while we went through it, the manager of the band nodding in a certain way to let me know we had solved another problem, the singer stared off into space and then said, at the end, when all was settled, in Latin, "Peace be with you." Then they all got up and went out, leaving a scent of perfume, musk, incense, and something else, which could have been a smoky residue of a drug they smoked, opium or something like that, an alluring scent, a musky perfume of desire so perfect as to have a kind of mathematical certainty. I guessed that's what opium was: the math of desire.

"All right," said Robert. "That leaves the bear."

Before bed, with the list of things we had decided about on the sofa next to Alexandra, she said, with a sort of wistfulness, as though remembering a restaurant in Rome where she had eaten sautéed zucchini flowers, "Maybe I need something to look forward to. Don't you think we should get away, too?"

"Sure," I said. "What do you have in mind?"

"Rome," she said.

"Again?" I said.

"Yes," she said.

"If we get out of this in one piece, I'll take you to Rome."

"Oh, Frank," she said. "Wouldn't that be nice?"

[CHAPTER TWENTY-SIX]

THE MOTEL WAS on Route 2, next to an Italian restaurant that looked like one of a kind but was part of a midlevel chain, more like a knockoff of a restaurant than an actual place. Pauline's truck sat in the parking lot of the motel. The truck bed was filled with cardboard boxes, all neatly taped and stamped with logos, Genuine Moon racing parts, Magaw cams, Flash-Tech tachometers, BST Safety Textiles (manufacturers of air bags), and Newco Autoline (transmissions). The cardboard squares fit together as neatly as the wooden blocks in a child's puzzle. Only one other car, a Nissan with fenders so rusted as to look like red lace, sat in the parking lot, and these two made the lot forlorn. It was two in the afternoon and all the lovers and drunks had left earlier. The parking lot was covered with broken glass, just dust, really, as a sort of monument to the endless hard nights that had been experienced here.

Pauline stepped out of the truck. I got out of the Gray Ghost. She wore a blue dress and the scent from years before, or maybe it was a powder, but I recognized it the way you instantly recall the scent of honeysuckle and where you were and what music was playing when you last smelled it. She took a step and stopped, one hip at a sultry angle, just as she had done years ago. Her hair had been done and she was wearing a little makeup. Her smile was the same as when I had come to her apartment with a bottle of wine, which we drank while her neighbor hung out his underwear to dry.

"Thanks for coming, Frank," she said. "I didn't think you'd show up on such short notice."

"Well," I said. "I'm alone. My wife is at the farm, getting ready for the wedding. I just came from the last fitting for my daughter's dress."

"Oh, Frank," she said. "You went to see the dress?"

"Yes," I said.

"Isn't that sweet. I guess the wedding is coming up pretty fast. Just days, right?"

"Yes," I said.

She held up the motel key with that little plastic paddle suspended from it.

"I've already got the room," she said.

She held the key and swung the plastic paddle of it one way and then the other, as though thinking it over. The plastic disappeared into a circle, like one made by a propeller. She shifted her weight from one foot to the other.

"We never went to a motel, did we?" she said. "That was too tawdry for us, wasn't it?"

"No," I said. "There wasn't any need. We weren't hiding anything."

"And we didn't travel together either, did we? You know, on the road together and hearing the trucks rumble along as you felt how wet I was . . . never wore underwear when we were in the car," she said. "But we never went anyplace. Not far away. No chance for escape, right?"

"Should we go in?" I said.

"I'm thinking about it," she said. "What is it about old boyfriends? You hate their guts for awhile, but then, you know, you get all confused about being young." She tapped the key against her teeth. "But Frank, you don't stay confused for long if you're one bitter bitch."

A truck shifted down on the highway and made the asphalt we stood on tremble.

"So, I wanted to show you just how good I could make you feel. If I was in the mood."

The concrete path went along the fronts of the empty motel rooms, all the same, the plastic curtains behind the dusty glass, the aluminum frames of the window, the doors with the thin veneer of wood, the doorknobs that looked as if they had come from Wal-Mart, and yet in the empty rooms I felt the valence left by fatigue or a desperate passion that had been there and gone. These things left a kind of vacuum behind. The trucks went by on Route 2, shifting down with a rumble and a cloud of smoke. Pauline put the key in the door with one hand and held my arm with the other.

"Oh, Frank," she said. "I get trembly. After all this time. That's what I'm so bitter about. Why won't it just go away? Do you think it would go away if I helped you?"

"I don't know," I said.

"Maybe it would make me feel superior. And not so fucking bitter."

She pushed the door open. The place smelled of air-conditioned cigarette smoke, cheap perfume, antibacterial soap, and ozone from the professional-grade vacuum cleaner. A small desk had been against one wall, but it had been swung around so that one person could sit on one side and another could sit opposite. A chessboard had been set up there, white pieces on one side, black on the other. Pauline stood next to me.

"It wasn't easy, Frank," she said.

His hair was shorter, but his skin was the same snake belly white, improved by the acne scars that, in an odd way, suggested dueling scars. His hands were white, too, the fingers still long and delicate, like a pickpocket's. He wore a Don't Tread on Me tee shirt with a snake on it, a pair of blue jeans, and some Timberland boots. A leather jacket lay on the bed next to him.

"Sit down, Frank," he said.

The chair had a black plastic seat, a veneer back, little gold tabs on the end of the legs. Aurlon Miller lit a cigarette and blew a cloud of smoke into the air.

"I thought we'd play chess," he said.

He picked up a black pawn and a white one and put them behind his back.

"Pick," he said.

I drew white.

Pauline sat down on the bed, crossed her legs, put her laced fingers together over her knee.

"Aurlon and I go way back," said Pauline.

He opened with a king's pawn. I answered, doing so by rote, although I kept my eyes on that pale skin. He moved a pawn. I knew he was going to bring a bishop out and then a knight. A basic opening. But I wondered if he had learned anything new since we had last played. Trade for pieces, concentrate on endgame? Simplify things to the point where it was easy to see. Pauline squirmed on the bed. Ran one hand along her leg, down to her ankle, where she undid the buckle of her shoe and let it fall to the carpet. She smiled.

He traded when he could. I castled. He looked across the board and said, "I bet you're surprised to see me."

"Yes," I said. "I thought you were gone."

"You mean dead, don't you?" said Aurlon.

"Yes," I said.

He castled, too.

Aurlon looked at me. "You thought you were pretty hot with that Aron Nimzowitsch stuff. Took me a while to catch up, but you were always one jump ahead of me."

"I played a lot of chess," I said, "when I was in school."

"Uh-huh," said Aurlon. "And you couldn't resist it, could you? You had to rub it in, right?"

"I don't know," I said.

"Sure you did," said Aurlon. "You rock-ribbed snob. You turned up your nose at me. You had to beat me. You had to show Pia that I wasn't up to your standards, right?"

"Yes," I said.

"Hmpf," he said. "That's what I thought."

He traded, bishop for bishop, set up a trade for queens. Did he really want to do that?

"So, you wanted to beat me down. Make me feel like something from a gutter, like something that climbed out from under a rock," he said. "You know what I thought about that?"

"We were just playing chess," I said.

"Fuck you," said Aurlon. "We're here to settle things. You wanted to beat me down. And you know what? I don't take that easily. Everybody does that. They underestimate me, you know that?"

"Tell me where you've been," I said.

"Ask her," he said. He pointed at Pauline.

"Here and there. Up and down the coast. Florida to Maine," said Pauline. "Yana told me they were going to sell you up and down the coast like an air bag."

"Too bad," said Aurlon. "We were going to fuck this guy up." He lifted his chin toward me. "You thought you could somehow humiliate me, and that I won't play for higher stakes. That's what I do, see? I play for higher stakes. You may think I was just after your daughter, but after a while, when you started in with that Aron Nimzowitsch bullshit, I thought I'd show you what high stakes are."

I moved a pawn. He answered. Outside the trucks rumbled when they shifted down.

"How much cash have you got on you?" said Aurlon.

"Three hundred dollars," I said.

"There's an ATM in the lobby of the motel. Let's play for five hundred," he said.

"Why?" I said.

He shrugged.

"When I saw how you were trying to bust my chops, I went to see Stas. And then when you needed a car part, I sent you out there, and he charmed you. So I went back to Stas and Stas said, 'The guy wants to get rid of you.' And, I said, 'So what if I go?' Stas said that would make for some interesting possibilities. Like I'm gone, and Frank Mackinnon here asked to make me disappear."

"How could you make sure I'd go out to see him?"

"Oh, Frank," he said. "I could see you hated paying those prices for Audi parts. And you know what? I kept putting a little pinhole in the hydraulics. It was just a matter of time until you said, Hey, I'm not paying that kind of money at the Audi dealership. You were just a sitting duck."

He ran a finger over a pawn.

"Ain't that the truth?" he said to the wall. Then he turned to me and said, "So, let's make it for five hundred."

"How did you get him to come here?" I said to Pauline.

"I wanted to show you I could make you feel good," she said. "If I was in the mood."

"How?" I said.

"Aurlon is wanted here and there. Theft in Florida, rape in Orlando, some other things. Yana told me."

"Ukrainians. Jesus," said Aurlon.

"So, I used the rape charge in Florida. And some other things. I told him I'd call Orlando, some other places where people would like to talk to him. And he knows I don't lie."

"She doesn't lie," said Aurlon.

"So I told him he better meet me here," said Pauline.

"And if you were gone," I said to Aurlon. "Why, then Stas could try to get me to help him with a case, right?"

"Make your move," said Aurlon. "Five hundred, right?"

I set up two castles, one behind the other, power right down the middle of the board.

"That was the idea," said Aurlon. "Yeah, we almost had you. That's what I call stakes."

He countered, brought out a knight.

"So, five hundred?" he said.

"But you'd have to stay gone," I said. "For this to work."

"Check," said Aurlon. "Just two moves."

"But you'd have to stay gone," I repeated. "Otherwise I wouldn't be so cooperative."

"Make your move," said Aurlon.

I moved a bishop.

"You're such an innocent, Frank," said Aurlon. "I'd only have to be gone long enough for you to help Stas and his friends *once*. Just once. Then they'd have you. I could come back and they'd have the goods. How would you explain helping them? They'd have you good and proper. Check."

One move. Mate.

"That's five hundred you owe me," said Aurlon.

That institutional smell seemed to grow in intensity. The scent of exhaust from Route 2 came into the room.

"I could make a list," I said. "Of the things I could charge you with. Conspiracy to obstruct justice, conspiracy to blackmail, and, you know, some other matters that would be pretty easy to hatch up . . . "

"That's five hundred dollars . . . ," he said. "But look, you don't want me. You want Stas. He's the bad character here, right?"

I knocked my king over. Pauline put her hand in her dress to adjust a strap.

"If it hadn't been for her, I'd never have come here. But when she makes promises, you got to watch yourself . . . "

The drawer of the desk opened with a squeak, and the heavy motel paper (as though good stationery would make the stink and desperation of this place go away) made a little rumble as I pushed it across the table. I put three hundred dollars on the table, too. And a pen.

"Write Pia a letter. Tell her you are sorry that you disappeared. You just had to go. A rambling man, right?"

"And you'll get the other two hundred from the ATM?"

"Start writing," I said.

The ATM was in a glass booth with an oily film of handprints on the sides, and these obscured the parking lot and the highway. The machine made an ominous clicking, and then the twenties came out. Heavy, new, and as crisp as if they had just been ironed. Then I went back to the room.

He held out the blank paper. Not a word.

"See, we've got to work this out delicate like," Aurlon said. "We've got to solve some problems here. You're a smart guy. So the first problem is Pauline."

"I just wanted you to know I could help, if I wanted," Pauline said. "And then, you know, say I don't help you. I let Aurlon slip away into the shadows. It might be fun to watch a scandal with you at the center and for you to know that I could have stopped it. You see what 'bitter' means?"

"I'm getting the idea," I said.

The building shook as another truck came down that grade outside.

"But say I go see Stas," I said. "I tell him I've seen you. I guess he'd have you at the bottom of the harbor in about twenty minutes."

"That's a risk," said Aurlon. "But I don't think he's there yet. I think he'd help me get away."

"That's a pretty thin reed," I said. "That thought."

"It's a risk," said Aurlon. "I have to say that."

"So what are we going to do?" I said.

"Give me the two hundred," said Aurlon.

I passed it over.

"Now I could write to Pia and say I had to leave town because you hired a thug to come after me," said Aurlon. "She kept after me, you know, to tell her if anyone threatened me. A cop, she thought. But cops, thugs, it all sort of runs together sometimes."

"Don't you see, Frank," said Pauline. "It all depends on me. If I want to help, we'll feed Stas to the wolves. We'll get Aurlon here to testify against him. And, you know, we'll work out a deal where we forget those charges in Florida."

"It could be done," I said.

"Just listen to him," said Pauline.

"Sounds good to me," said Aurlon. "So?"

Pauline closed her eyes. Then she said to Aurlon. "All right. Get the fuck out of here. I'll let you know what I decide."

Aurlon stood up, put two hundred dollars in one shoe, two hundred in the other. A hundred in his pocket.

"I could just grab you right now," I said.

"You haven't got a legal right to do that. You'd have to get a warrant. Or you'd have to call a cop. And I'd be willing to bet that Pauline would help me get out the door. So, just forget it. And what would it look like anyway, if it comes out that you were trying to grab some guy who was blackmailing you? Where's there's smoke, there's fire. This is Boston, remember? Its lifeblood is scandal."

"Get out of here," said Pauline.

"Too bad, Frank," said Aurlon. "We almost had you. And we might yet, if this one"—he pointed at Pauline—"helps out."

He went out the door. The trucks went by on the highway and then a cop car shrieked. Outside the maid pushed her cart along the concrete, the wheels squeaking. Pauline undid the first button on her dress. She turned back the sheets on the bed.

I took her hand.

"You didn't believe me," she said. "All you had to do was ask for my help."

We sat at the end of the bed. Pauline undid another button. The familiar scent of powder rose from her chest. The sheets smelled not clean so much as disinfected.

"I think we should just sit here," I said.

"Don't you want to thank me," she said. She touched the turned-back sheets.

"I think we should just sit here," I said.

"I've been waiting a long time, Frank," she said. She undid anther button.

"You smell wonderful," I said.

"For old time's sake, Frank."

She took my hand and put it inside her dress.

"Let's just sit here," I said.

"And then?" she said.

I shook my head.

"We've got something else to talk about," I said.

"I guess we do," she said. "Just to prove to you that I'm not so dumb. Aurlon is in real danger now."

"Un-huh," I said.

"If I let Stas know he was around and that you knew about it, I guess Aurlon would have a half-life of about twenty minutes. Then it's out in the harbor for him . . . I could do it on general principles. He doesn't have a clue what he's talking about."

"But you wouldn't say anything, would you?"

"I don't know, Frank," she said. She took my hand and put it inside her blouse. "Are you sure?"

"It would just make us sad."

"Maybe that's not the way I'd feel about it," she said.

We sat there, our faces close together as though we were about to kiss.

I reached into my pocket and took out the velvet case with the gold at the edge where it opened. Pauline kept her eyes on mine. I put it into her hands, and when she opened it, she sat on the edge of the bed, the case in her lap, the diamonds there like a collection of stars that had been reduced and strung together: blue sparkle, red sparkle, hard, white flash. She let them dangle from her palm, as years ago when they hung like a small, dead snake, and then she ran the diamonds across her lips, across her neck, in her hair.

She stood.

In the bathroom, the strand in her hand, she opened the toilet seat. She looked at me and let them slip, one at a time, the color of them the same as the water, which was bright with the overhead light, the reflection of the mirror, and something else, a kind of brightness that came from Pauline's own trembling, as though her feelings had their own energy, their own sidereal radiation. The diamonds disappeared, one at a time.

She put her hand on the lever, then she turned to me.

"I didn't want the diamonds," she said. "I wanted to know that you cared enough to get them."

She pushed the lever. The water came with a rush, a sort of diminished roar.

We sat in that motel. The trucks went by and their long trail of exhaust leaked into the room. After a while she stood up, put on her shoes, and said, "Well, Frank, didn't I keep my promise? Couldn't I make you feel so good? Just so good?"

She leaned forward. I kissed her on the neck.

"Yes," I said. "You did."

She hesitated in that motel scent.

"The address," I said.

"What?" she said.

"Aurlon's address," I said. "I'll probably need it."

"No, Frank," she said. "No."

On the motel's little pad I wrote Tim Marshall's numbers, landline and cell, and told her she should call him with the address.

She held the small, cheap slip of paper in her hand, the thing trembling with her regret and fury, and then she put it in the pocket of her blouse.

"Don't hold your breath," she said.

"All right," I said.

"Thanks for the diamonds," she said.

"Sure," I said.

Then she went out the door.

I sat on the end of the bed again as the trucks rumbled, and I was left with the memory of the light on Pauline's skin, those rows of jockey shorts, one clothespin holding the end of two of them, and as they dried, and as Pauline whispered from the shadows, Louis Armstrong played, "Hello, Dolly, how nice to have you back where you belong . . . " How could I have known, years ago, that I would end up in a motel on Route 2, humming that song and thinking of revenge: the gears and pulleys, the flywheels and pushrods, of time in action?

I opened my cell phone and called Tim Marshall. When he picked up he said, "Frank Mackinnon. You remember that dumb Bulgarian at the gun club? You know what he did?"

"He did a Dutch job on himself," I said.

"How did you know?" said Tim. "Did someone in the office tell you?"

"Just a guess," I said.

[CHAPTER TWENTY-SEVEN]

THE WEDDING WAS on Sunday. A week away. When I called Alexandra, she said the caterer had started to bring tables and tablecloths, chairs and silverware, and members of the band had been around to see about the power, and so we were going to have to hire an auxiliary, but quiet, generator.

At home, I got out a suit bag and put in a morning coat and striped trousers, a new suit for the rehearsal dinner, shirts, ties, studs, shoes, shined for the occasion, and then some rough clothes for the other job.

Robert answered his phone.

"Are you ready?" I said.

"Sure, Frank," he said. "I'm ready."

The scotch was warm and soothing, and I went along the shelf, where I stopped at Marcus Aurelius.

The Mannlicher felt light in my hands: just the weight to carry it all day, as I had years ago when I had hunted deer with my father and when he had used it to hunt deer with his father, who had used it to hunt alone, before his sons were old enough. Now, I removed the bolt, cleaned the barrel with a push rod and a brush, and then changed the attachment so I could run a rag, soaked in Hoppe's 9. Then I wiped the barrel and receiver, put the bolt back in, slipped the rifle into its canvas case. The box of 6.5 mm ammunition went in, too. Then I put it in the car, with the rest of my things.

On the way out of town the prison guards looked down from those lofty gray walls, and yet, while the place was as stern and unforgiving as ever, the prison had another quality. It seemed amazed by the possibility of surprise, which places like this didn't take into account. After all, this place seemed to say, everything is decided.

The road up from the Delaware was one that I had taken with my father and one that he had taken with his father: just a dirt road with fieldstone walls on both sides, the construction of a ruin, just stones piled up with a geometric precision, as though people were sacrificed here as in ancient civilizations. Gray stones, covered with green and white lichen, and behind the walls red and white oak stood along with stands of spruce and pine, the green seeming oddly hopeful in spite of everything. It was a dry September, and the Audi left a trail of dust, which even in the air showed a bit of sparkling pyrite, bits of gold. A deer, its white tail flagging, ran alongside of us for a while.

"What if we can't find it?" said Robert.

"I don't know," I said. "My father should have shot the thing when he had the chance."

"Why didn't he?"

"He left the job to me," I said. "He loved to get someone else to do something he didn't want to do."

"But why didn't he want to?" said Robert.

"It's hard to say," I said.

We turned toward the farmhouse and went along the road, which was lined with pines, big ones that two men couldn't reach around. Then we came up to the two stone pillars that marked the entrance to the farm, square prisms of stone my grandfather had put up and which now looked like some marker of an ancient grade.

• • •

The tent appeared achingly white on the brownish grass of September. The sides were rolled up, and long tables with tablecloths had been arranged with white folding chairs. Soon the silver and napkins and glasses would be laid out, too, with a sort of mathematical precision. Back in the woods, just out of sight, the auxiliary generator, set up for the opium-smoking musicians, made a slight throbbing, as of an anxious heart, and in front of it a technician, in a tie-dye tee shirt that probably came from Harvard Square, waved to someone out of sight. The generator stopped. Everything was working.

Robert and I stood in that cloud of dust.

"I sure hope the heat breaks by Sunday," said Robert.

The woman from the Girls Club, Buddy Hollyette, drove up to the farmhouse, too, in her ancient Willys, double-clutching as she came up the drive, and then she came out and stood in the heat, her shape shimmering there, and said, "I could accept a promise from you that you would get rid of the thing, the mangy creature, but I did that with your father."

"I know," I said.

"And what did it get me?" she said. Her glasses had a layer of dust, and she took them off, wiped them with a Girls Club handkerchief, and put them back on. Then she leaned closer.

"If I let you go ahead with this," she said—she gestured to the tent, the generator, and toward something else, too, the general air in the field and the house that seemed somehow essentially nuptial, which, of course, she was naturally suspicious of—"you'd do the same damn thing. Why is it that men turn into their fathers? Just like clockwork. So, here's the way things are. Get rid of that monster. If you don't, this isn't going to fly. I've talked to my lawyer. But then you're a lawyer, too."

She said this as though announcing a nationality, as though I was a Bulgarian.

"That's right," I said.

"Then it's just between us," she said. "Your word and mine. How's that?"

Robert stepped up.

"Fine," he said.

"Who's this?" said Buddy Hollyette.

"The groom," I said.

"Great," she said. "A groom."

"What did you say," said Robert. He stiffened. "Do you have something to say to me?"

"You heard me, Frank," she said.

She got back into her Willys, cranked the engine, and drove out, leaving a cloud of dust. With the grit in my mouth, I wanted to say, Listen, I'm not my father. Not by a long shot. My father would have let the air out of your tires and then put a hornets' nest in your spare. He would have found a way to make you profoundly uncomfortable in some intimate way. He was full of tricks, and not all benign. That's what a spook is. He would have gotten two thugs to throw you through a window because you were causing trouble. He would have found a way to appear blameless, a victim, innocent, generous, and abused. When he was through with you, you'd be begging for mercy from a jail cell where you would be sitting for having been charged with perversions you haven't even heard of. Maybe you'd end up with a lobotomy. All the dead Yale men knew some tricks, right out of Skull and Bones. And you know, as well as I do, that they are gone forever.

We went out the drive and up the road to the stone house, which, at least, was clear. The trees on the sides were slowly forming a bower, but you could see beyond those stone walls an understory of mountain laurel and shadbushes. Then we went over that stone in the middle of the road, came around a turn, and pulled up on the brown grass where Alexandra's car was parked.

She came into the heat of the afternoon, her clipboard to keep track of details in one hand, the other touching the sweat on her forehead.

"So, you poor mutt," she said. "You're going to do it. Isn't that the deal?"

I gave her a kiss on the cheek. The Mannlicher was in its case, and when I reached in we all listened to the zipper as I opened it up. The Mannlicher slipped out of the case. Then I pushed the brass hulls into the open port, the magazine being circular and taking one shell and then turning to take another. Five plus one in the chamber. I closed the bolt and put the safety on, a little tab that stood straight up.

"Did you see the generator?" said Alexandra. She kept her eyes on the rifle. "Those opium-smoking musicians are happy as can be."

It was late afternoon.

"Yes," said Robert.

"Well," said Alexandra.

"That woman with the butch haircut should watch the way she talks," said Robert. "You have to face up to being sassed. You know that?"

"Not now," I said.

Alexandra leaned close, kissed me on the cheek, and said, "I'll see you later."

In this heat, I supposed, the bear was down by Trout Cabin, someplace in those green shadows, which he would take like a verdant and cool blanket. Maybe he would even get into the stream and emerge, dripping long lines of water and gasping in the heat.

The woods were that same mixture of eastern oak and pine, blueberries and cane, raspberries in the clearings. From time to time, if you were alert, you saw a deer or a fox, a grouse, or a snake, just as my grandmother had.

Robert and I went to the top of the land, or the highest elevation, which was the swamp at the top of Trout Cabin, or at least where it originated. We stood by a spring there, where, in the gray clay bottom, the clear water bubbled up, spilled over the lip of the small pool, and made a silvery start downhill.

"We'll do it in an orderly way, from top to bottom, with stops at wet places. But he's down there," I said.

"Fine by me," said Robert.

We went through the swamp until we came to the top of the stream. At the top of Trout Cabin the water flowed in long spouts from pool to pool, but even water had a metallic shimmer where the sun broke through the canopy. Then the landscape became steeper and we came to the V of the gorge, to the shadows, where I thought the animal might be waiting. And what would we do at that moment, face to face, as my father had left him to me?

Of course, my father had known this moment was coming. How many times could this be avoided? Was it just a chore or something else?

"You don't want to do this, do you?" said Robert.

"What do you think?" I said.

We went along that stream, the noise of it not reassuring and bubbling but more penetrating than that, as though the repetitive sound made words and if I was just smart enough, I could understand them; but it was all opaque, a noise like *arber-arber-arber*, endlessly repeated until it sounded like a plea made at the end of fatigue, when something deeper than words was being employed.

"But don't you see?" said Robert. "The bear is eating garbage now. It isn't afraid of people. You know that. And you know, too, that it's just a matter of time before it mauls or kills a Girls Club girl. You know it."

"Does that make it right?" I said. "This thing was part of my father's world, this land, this animal. It was how he grew up. Me, too."

"Listen," said Robert. "You know that the majority of random attacks on people are made by black bears."

"I know," I said.

"So getting rid of it is the right thing," said Robert. "Would you shoot a rabid dog?"

Halfway down, in the hot shadows of the afternoon, in the lines of light and the scent of spruce, a hump moved. The bear traveled in the heat, his sides fat and glistening from the summer diet of raspberries and blueberries and god knows what, pancakes and sausages and the remains of Cheerios and hamburger that had been in the Girls Club's garbage. His oily coat had a natural sheen. His fat sides swayed as he moved away from the relative coolness of the stream. The sweat ran down my sides and it tickled, too, where it ran out of my hair. Robert took a blue handkerchief out of his pocket and rubbed his face. Then the mosquitoes started in with that insane buzzing, as though they had to make you nuts before taking your blood.

The bear was going to another spring, not so far up, a wet place where my father and I had seen him: a seep where the watercress grew, and where it was cool because the moisture made a sort of wallow. I should have known that's where our appointment was going to be. That's it: appointment. How could I ever have thought otherwise?

So we went around the stones that stuck out of the hillside, scaled with lichen the color of old copper, and through the leaves, where a diamondback rattler would be so perfectly camouflaged. Some snakes were still in the gorge and this, of course, is the way that fate or chance found a delight in pursuing you in more ways than one. Today was a likely day to find the last timber rattler. So we climbed and went up the shelves of broken stone, putting my hands into places I couldn't see and then coming into the abandoned and overtopped apple orchard, where the barkless and dead trees were as white as bones. The old wood road up to the stone house was overtopped by oak, and cool, and the grass grew there as though it had been mowed.

The bear came to that wet place, dug at the watercress, tore at a piece of deadwood to get the white grubs, which, when disturbed, seemed to fall out in a mass of anxious movement. Then he turned, his face scarred, his eyes small and black, his expression one of constant consideration. So, it seemed to say, you've come back. What happened to the old man who was with you before? Where is he? Do I have to deal with you now? The bear dug in the grubs and looked up from time to time. Do you have what it takes? he seemed to say. Do you? The other one couldn't.

The bear seemed to me a perfect expression of everything that could go wrong mixed with everything that was beautiful and right. And it was that crack, that abyss between the two where uncertainty found a natural place to exist. An ordinary human being craves only a little clarity, just a touch of certainty in these matters. No, not craves. It's more than that. We have a wild longing for it. So, as I looked at him, the creature seemed like a perfect example of the problem of being alive: why couldn't I make a deal, or come to some understanding? Why couldn't I say: Stay away from those girls, from the garbage, just stay away and I will protect you.

The creature's dismissal was a perfect expression of how, in our despair and longing, we made our appeals to every mystery there is, and yet we are ignored. And then something else lurked around in all this, which was the passage of time and the fact that this land, whatever it had been for my father, wasn't the same anymore. Time had done its worst here, too. My father had the luxury of letting this creature go because he ignored the house trailers and ranch-style houses being built, each year, all with garbage cans out back. And somehow, in the bear's constantly hungry presence, he was a reminder of what time had done and how it ground everything into dust. The creature stood there like mortality itself, like everything I couldn't control, and that left me with the sense of approaching loss. And how close had I come to the abyss, which is the loss of love, all for some sleazy racket?

And yet, it was still beautiful and a part of the world of my father and his father before him. Somehow, I just wanted to be a son of a man who had been a son, with all the attendant troubles. Killing this thing, because it had become dangerous, was a matter of killing part of my father's world.

Now the bear looked me in the eyes, and seemed to say, It's

endless, endless, you will never get away from the difficulty of being human, never. I'm here, causing trouble, to remind you. What did your father do? Why, he couldn't face up to it, could he? Didn't he cheat you? Wasn't he a spook? Didn't he lie?

So, my father had said, when we had been here together before, when he was broke and worried and ashamed, at the bottom of the cesspool of despair, here—he's yours. You figure it out. It's yours now. How do you like it? Trapped, huh, Frank, between what you know and what you hope for? Between the complications of ugliness and the possibility for beauty.

I sat down, put my elbows on my knees, held the rifle steady that way, flipped the safety off.

"Head or heart?" I said.

"Head," said Robert.

Here and there a bird, a chickadee or a crow or even a dove, flitted from place to place, and even though they didn't make any noise, the movement suggested sound. All I could really hear was some interior hissing that I couldn't shake, of being trapped by who and what I was and that no matter how hard I tried I was still found wanting.

To do the right thing, I had to kill off the last of my father's world. I was already imperfect, damaged, flawed, but still capable of love, I thought, and didn't that count for something? What about the years with Alexandra and Pia? And even Pauline, for that matter, as messed up as it was. Maybe that is what my father meant when he passed this creature over to me: the sheer number of possibilities in being human will leave you feeling that you weren't enough.

The creature waited. It had its head down, eyes on me, his pink tongue lapping that scented water. And even so, with all the thinking, all the justification, all the attempts to explain myself,

I was still left with that sense of self-accusation, of somehow wanting to hang on to what was going to have to go.

The bear stood sideways, swaying a little above that trickle of water, its head turned toward me. The shadows of the woods fell over him like a cape, a shadow that he needed now that the moment had come. Then he looked uphill, perhaps to walk up to the stone house or maybe over to the swamp between here and the farm. That's all I needed: for him to appear near the ponds before the night's dinner.

"Give me that," said Robert. "I'll do it."

"No," I said.

"The thing is going to get away."

He put his hand out.

The bead in the rear sight was just behind the bear's shoulder: a heart shot. Wasn't this what my father and I had discussed, when we had been here before, when the three of us had met only to put this moment off? Then I swung to those lines that crossed, one drawn from the ear to the eye on the opposite side, and another line drawn the same way from the other ear, crossing just above the nose. The safety went off with a little click, Germanic, certain, final.

The sound was as though the engine room of the world had been opened for just an instant. Then the steel door slammed shut. The bear sat back on its haunches, just like it had found a bag of garbage and wanted to go through it at its leisure, and then it looked at me, its eyes dark, penetrating. Then it lay down in the watercress, made a sort of rattling sigh, and stopped moving. The gout of blood flowed into the wet spot, through that scented watercress and then down with the silver flow into Trout Cabin.

"The coons will get it," I said.

"Yes," said Robert.

"The ribs will look like a musical instrument. A xylophone."

I unloaded the rifle, the brass hulls collecting in my hand. Then, with the action open, the way it should be done, I gave him the Mannlicher. "Here," I said. "This is yours."

"Why?" he said.

"You'll have to do the right thing one day," I said. "Maybe it will feel all wrong. The reasons will seem right. But somehow you'll still feel bad. One world ends. Another begins."

"I don't know what you're talking about," he said.

"Give it a little time," I said.

I passed it over and he picked it up as though he had been carrying it all his life. We went away from the wet place that, when I turned back, showed a stain, a mound, that looked as though someone had dumped a load of asphalt here to be used to pave a road. And, of course, I thought, Yes, that's what will probably happen after all. Pia and Robert and their kids will want an apartment in Paris or Rome. The foxes and bears, the snakes and turkeys, they will have to move further west.

We went side by side up that bowered path, and while I considered going through the swamp, I came to my senses, since while it was one thing to climb out of Trout Cabin in a hurry where there were a lot of snakes, it was another to go through a swamp at this time of the year. So we went by the stone house, where I waved to Alexandra, who knew the problem was gone because there was only one shot.

We started up that road, which was hotter here than down below, the dirt looking like a mirage, that silver that shimmers in the road, although here there was an island in the middle, the high point between the ruts, so that it looked like a long island in a silver sea. The dust rose around our feet and we went through the shade of the pines. I wouldn't want to say we had killed the bear. In the silvery dust, it seemed to be an expression of the godhead, of the complications of being human, which, or so it seems to me, are what the gods delight in. No generation can hang on to the past: its time comes and its time goes: the alternatives are all so dark.

[CHAPTER TWENTY-EIGHT]

ROBERT'S BEST MAN had a stutter and at the rehearsal dinner, held at the farm house, he got stuck, like a car in a mud hole, the tires spinning. Robert stiffened, waited, his eyes moving over the rest of us as though we better not try to help. We sat at a table that was in the shape of a T, the bride and groom at the head of the table, the parents on each side, the other guests along the T. White tablecloth, crystal glasses, good silver, venison and morels, a broccoli soufflé, and a chocolate soufflé for dessert. Light and cheerful in that room with white walls, the large fireplace next to which my grandfather used to brood and drink, and where my father had come home from the war, and where I came, too, for summer vacations and swore I would never be like them. The scent of a million cigars from my grandfather was just noticeable, as though he still existed, although his presence had obviously been disguised, or someone had tried to disguise him under a layer of latex paint. He hated latex.

Then I took Alexandra and Pia down to the stone house, Pia on my arm, as I escorted her from the party as a good father should.

The golden light in the stone house fell over us with all the haunting possibility of the passage of time, and the stories, too, that seem to have a life of their own: the time Pia got lost in the well, outside this house, and how I had used a tractor to drag a stone over the opening so she could never get in again.

I poured myself a drink in that golden light.

"You always made sure nothing went wrong," she said.

"Well, there's always a chance," I said.

"What do you mean?" she said.

"Anxiety," said Alexandra. "That's all it is. Right?"

The scotch burned.

"Yeah," I said. "Guess that's right."

"Then how come you seem worried?" said Pia.

"Can't fool you, hmpf?" I said. "Well, you have to remember this is one of those portals people go through. A daughter marries. Something changes. Not a thing you can do."

The stone house had a particular silence that came from the stone walls, which not only kept the sound out, but seemed to have distilled time, as though it was embedded in the centuries or millions of years it took to make the rock in these walls. We sat in that almost infinite silence, aware, at least for a moment, how our love for each other was strong and up against that hard infinity. Then I kissed Pia good night, took a drink upstairs, and got into bed. For a while, in the dark, Alexandra spoke to Pia in the downstairs bedroom, which came through the floor of the loft where it was as a buzz and stop, a buzz and stop, the advice of a mother to a daughter on the eve of a wedding, the hum, the vibration of it seeming to come not just through a wooden floor (which came from the white pine on this land) but through time as well. I tried to calculate this, back to the land between the Tigris and Euphrates, to Egypt, and just as I could see the muddy, broad Nile and the reeds at the side, which was a sign I was about to fall asleep, Alexandra pulled back the sheets and slid in next to me, sighed, took my hand, and said, "Well, what about that asshole Russian? The one who was threatening you?"

In the morning the bridesmaids came in the door with their dresses, hair driers, combs, cases of makeup, bottles of perfume, new stockings for the ceremony. Then they went to work, taking showers, shaving legs and underarms, working on Pia's hair, powdering themselves, using safety pins in more ways than I could count, and as they wiggled into their pantyhose, their clothes, they used the mirror in the kitchen where I tried to shave and then gave it up. They looked over my shoulder and said, "Sorry, Mr. Mackinnon. Tight squeeze."

My suit hung by the door, like a scarecrow at Buckingham Palace. Tie, shoes, vest, jacket.

"You know, Frank," Alexandra said. "This isn't a place for a man. At least right now."

"Uh-huh," I said. "I think I better take a walk."

So, outside, beyond that cloud of perfume and lemon soap, shampoo and powder, cosmetics and delicate clothes, I turned downhill on the wood road that leads to the stream. There, next to one pool that poured a silver spout into the next, I went downhill toward the Delaware. Surely, this was a good time to stand next to a river and be there as the power of it, the liquid force, the delicate meniscus of the surface tension all floated by as though it always had been there and always would be. A poor man's mysticism, I guess, but none the less necessary for all that.

At the bottom of the stream the land opened up, or flattened out, and here the heat was more silver and more shimmering than in the woods. Well, it was the marriage not the wedding, I guessed, and maybe a little heat was a good thing, if only to remind Pia and Robert that nothing worked precisely the way you wanted it to.

Still, the heat flowed along the river in layers, each packed against another, some layers hotter than others, but the entire mass of hot air moved above the Delaware's serpentine path.

At the mouth of Trout Cabin, just opposite the Delaware, I splashed a little water onto my face. Jerry's house, that collection of the leavings of car wrecks, fires, construction debris, hubcaps, with a high-tech solar collector on top, was just behind me, a shrine to the dead.

The river was on the other side of the road, a silver like mercury, something or someone moved with the same swaying motion of the heat. And as I stood and walked closer, as I came down to the road and put a hand over the glare, the shape there resolved itself into a woman, still attractive after all these years, ten years younger than me, still perfectly correct in that heat and the motion of the glare. Pauline wore a thin dress and high-heeled shoes. She came across the heat of the blacktop and said, "Frank, there you are. I've been looking all over."

The swaying of the heat from the pavement matched the swaying of her thin, almost transparent dress. The ten years she was younger than me were critical ones: she emerged from the hot, moist shimmer and took my hands, both of them, and looked into my eyes and then she embraced me. She wore nothing but that thin dress, and in the heat there was the press of the mons, the soft crush of a breast, the hard touch of a nipple, the aroma of perfume and sweat that rose from her neck, the scent of her hair, the tug of her arms on my shoulders, the light, tender, even loving touch of her fingers on my neck.

"It's hot," I said.

"You're telling me," she said.

"Come back in the shade," I said.

"What's this house here?" she said. She pointed to the hoods and plywood.

"It's a long story," I said.

"It's so green back here," she said. "Can you count the different shades? Look, there's one, and two. There are five shades, one on another, like pieces of cloth . . . "

The air by the stream was cooler, and maybe it was just the movement of water that made it seem cooler, although the touch of her fingers against mine seemed hotter than ever, and my palms were moist, too. She put her lips against my neck and ear and whispered, "It's good to see you, Frank. Although it breaks my heart." She closed her eyes and swallowed. "What times we had."

The water rushed in that constant way: as though nothing could stop it. A perfect reminder of how once something got started, like those moments when Pauline sat on top of me and laughed, the tightening of her grip like love itself, it doesn't stop, at least not in memory; it lingers and grows, it seeps into who and what you are and never leaves you alone. And this, with the accusation of failure, and not knowing what to do or when doing the right thing comes at such a price, or a price so ridiculous, left me dizzy with the possibilities for trouble.

"And what do you think, when you think of me?" she said.

I splashed a little cool water on my face, and Pauline looked at me as though I was trying to hide the fact that I was crying.

"The impossibility of it," I said. "You realize it at a certain point, and that's it."

She looked down at her feet. Then she stepped out of her shoes and into the stream and said, "Oh, Frank. That feels good. You can't imagine."

Then she stepped out of the water, her calves slick with the wetness, her eyes on mine.

The two stones by the side of the stream were like small stools and we sat on them, although here the heat of them was exactly the opposite of those stones in that small graveyard in my backyard, and so we sat, her fingers on my knees, as the water flowed from one pool to another, a drop of about five feet, and from there another five feet: a sort of cascade of silver, tinted green, and a number of shades of green. We stared across the water: it was as though the heat made the time that had passed palpable, that we were sitting in the passage of it, that it pressed against us, made us feel it, the rank shove of it.

"I've made mistakes," I said.

"Well, who hasn't?" she said. "Although you sure fucked up the Citron case. I followed that in the papers. Boy, what a mess."

She leaned her head against my shoulder so that I came back into her scent, her light touch, and then she stretched her legs into the water, where it washed over them, like the surf when it slides back into the ocean.

"But I fucked up, too," she said. "Bitterness is a mistake. It's sort of like being greedy, like being a miser."

She stepped into the stream and got her dress wet to cool off, and the material clung to her youthful figure. She said, "Don't I still look nice?"

"Yes," I said. "You are beautiful."

Then she moved against me again, put her hands on the back of my neck, kissed my cheeks and turned, back into the heat, into that swaying mirage, those silver pools in the road along the Delaware. Her figure seemed not to disappear into it so much as to sink, to get deeper into that lake of mercury, swaying, leaving a trail of fragrance, and, of course, defiance, too. The river flowed, the rocks looking like the prows of ships, and overhead the hawks flew, looking to see if something was stupid enough to show itself in the heat.

Just as she approached the swaying curtain, that hot air, I said, or called out, "Pauline! Pauline!"

She turned to me with the undulant, silvery wall behind her.

"Thanks," I said.

She nodded and then disappeared into the heat.

I went uphill, through the woods, the spruce and pine, to get dressed.

[CHAPTER TWENTY-NINE]

THE BRIDESMAIDS WENT out in a cloud of perfume and cosmetics. I dressed in that cloud, my shoes shined, my striped pants pressed, my shirt with the tab collar at my neck with a reassuring crispness. Pia primped in the bedroom. It was just us now, since I was going to drive her to the chapel, where my father's funeral had been, and then walk her up the aisle.

As I made a white cream of soap with my brush and worked it into my beard (gray here and there, more salt than pepper), I went through the wedding guests who had been arriving over the last twenty-four hours. Robert's parents showed up in sedate, precise clothes and kept in the shadows, aside from a shaky moment at the rehearsal dinner, and then Robert's friends from school in California, all of them distinguished by a certain gait, a sort of bobbing walk, and even the ones who didn't have sun-bleached hair seemed to have it anyway through a process of attitude that was so profound as to leave me a little intimidated. And then, of course, Pia's friends, some of whom I had known from the time they rode bikes together in Cambridge, with training wheels, and whom I had taken along when Pia wanted to go for pizza or a hamburger, these women and a couple of men all grown up now, and when I recognized them, in their adult incarnation, I still felt them with us as we had gone to a hamburger stand, their arms out the window to feel the wind. And then a man who had built boats at the Cambridge boat club, dignified, upright, polite, and precise with his Australian accent, and who had nodded to me when he had arrived. I had the feeling that he was looking around at the stands of ash on the land, as though he wouldn't mind having one of the trees to use in his boats. My friends from work, even Jimmy Blaine, who had betrayed Cal and had come out to the Tobin Bridge to show sympathy to the man he had exposed and put in the position where the only solution was a Dutch job. I had learned, the hard way, that in an office like the one I worked in, you had to go along to get along, even when it meant inviting people like this, careerists and schemers, to a wedding.

Tim Marshall arrived, as upright and harsh as ever. Marshall had with him two men I had seen from time to time, detectives who had worked in Boston for so long they seemed to carry a perfume of the city with them, not quite the air of corruption as the atmosphere of fighting against it or living in it, like a shark in the ocean. They were in their late thirties, had short hair, and one, who worked undercover, had a gold ring in his ear, although his hands, or his right hand, was disfigured from having been broken in an arrest long ago. The two detectives, dressed in dark clothes, were carrying guns, or so it seemed by the cut of their jackets, and one had a lump around his right ankle, which was probably another holster. Tim once told me that he didn't feel dressed without a pistol. Along with them the local constable arrived, his jacket bright green, and he stood with a certain pride of association when he had been introduced to Tim and the two men from Boston.

Of course, Alexandra's friends from her job, from school, from the neighborhood all arrived, too, all in dresses that were silk or at least slinky, and they formed a posse of grown-up, elegant women, who drifted along as a competition with the bridesmaids, who surely had youth and beauty but at least here they had to face elegance and womanliness, perfectly realized. Jerry was there, too, and while I hadn't seen him in the church yet, he had been up at the farm, pointing out to the guests who were killing time a deer that had died in the woods and how the vultures were circling like black flags. He wore a jacket, moth-eaten and with patched elbows, that had belonged to my grandfather and which Jerry must have stored in a Styrofoam chest filled with mothballs: you could smell it a hundred yards away. Then, finally, I had invited Charlotte, and the few people who had worked for my father and some even my grandfather, but they were old now and must have come up to the church with a walker.

I dried my face, put on my shirt, tied my tie. And now, after that cloud of feminine power had gone out the door, and Pia and I were there alone, the essence of what the place had been reasserted itself for a moment: rough and manlike, a place where men had come to hunt deer and drink and play cards, which I had been part of but which was now gone for good. The men who had been here with my father and grandfather were mostly dead and gone, and all that was left was that lingering, odd, lonely atmosphere of a place where something had come to an end.

"You look beautiful," I said.

"Do you think so?" she said.

"Just lovely," I said. "I'm proud to be with you."

"Oh," she said, "you say that to all the brides. I just hope this goes smoothly."

"Me, too," I said.

She looked at her watch.

"How long does it take to get there?" she said.

"Five minutes," I said. "We pull up in front of the chapel. I come around and open the door for you. You take my arm. We walk in."

"I know, I know," she said. "We've got six minutes. Let's go."

The landscape slid by, the pines still green, the sky in the distance a pale blue. Those vultures still turned in the air over the kill in the woods. On the way, I said, "You're sure about this?"

"Yes," she said.

"No second thoughts?" I said.

"No," she said.

The approach to the chapel is along the river, and from a distance it appeared as a white, clean building, a sugar cube on a brown tablecloth, and as we got closer, as it grew in size, as the cars around it appeared as individual objects, not just clutter, she took my hand. Then we pulled up to the church: the white siding, black shutters, the black fence around the churchyard, although in front, where two pillars stood, bouquets of delphinium had been tied with a white ribbon. Pia held her flowers, the ones she was going to carry, in her lap.

We stopped in front of the door. Three men walked toward us, out of the heat, their shapes momentarily obscured by that shimmering blacktop. I went around and opened the passenger side door, and Pia stepped out, her presence, her dress so white it made an afterimage in the sunlight. Stas, Seymon, and Timofei walked along the cars, their swagger different from the boys from California, as though they meant it not for fun, but another matter all together. The scars on Stas's face were the color of the fieldstone that was visible in the cliffs along the river, and Seymon and Timofei looked as before, like hired help for the spooks my father had worked with. They were dressed in gray jackets and black shirts, a sort of gangster chic.

"Psssst," said Stas. "Frank."

"Get away from me," I said.

"You keep saying that," said Stas. "And what good does it get you?"

"So this is your daughter?" said Timofei.

"What's going on?" said Pia.

"I'll talk to you," I said to Stas.

"Where are you going to talk to us?" said Stas.

"Right over there," I said. "There."

A large gravestone stood in the middle of the cemetery, the color of it the same as the old scars on Stas's face. Around it the sanded paths were yellow and clean.

"Just as soon as this is over," I said.

"All right," said Stas. "We've got a date."

They walked through the gate of the cemetery, the hinge of it making a long, low moan.

An usher, one of the grooms from California, opened the door with a bounce and swagger as though he was taking his surfboard down to the beach. The organ began to play and Pia and I stood for a moment in the foyer of the chapel. Then we began, one step at a time, all of the faces turned toward us, including Tim and the two men from Boston and the local constable.

"That's them?" said Tim.

"Yes," I said.

"Come on," said Tim to the men from Boston.

The local constable stood up, too, in his green jacket and his wrinkled pants, although he was wearing an obvious holster where he carried, I knew from long association, a .357 magnum.

They went by us, as though they were getting off a subway and we were getting on. Then Pia and I slowly worked our way down the aisle, where, at the end, Robert and his best man, the one with the stutter, waited, although they glanced now not only at us, but at Tim and the men from Boston as they went out the door, not slamming it but going fast to that squeaky gate of the cemetery. Stas, Seymon, and Timofei smoked by the large headstone, their eyes now set on Tim and the others. The smoke seemed to drift away over the stones like ghosts.

The faces in the crowd stayed on us, but every now and then one turned toward the men outside, the two groups getting closer. The organ played. Pia had her arm through mine, but she gave me a tug, a loving, warm pull.

Outside, Stas, Seymon, and Timofei spoke, and while I couldn't hear the words, it looked like "Hey, fuck you." Then Tim spoke and the detectives and the local constable said something, too. Timofei put a hand in the middle of Tim's chest, and Tim, like an old bartender opening a bottle of beer with a quick snap, put his palm on the back of Timofei's hand and leaned forward. Timofei's mouth opened in an O, as though a pain he had only heard about was now here. He stepped back, one hand cradled in another. Tim spoke again, and while I couldn't hear what he said, the expression suggested, the shape of his lips seemed to say, Am I making myself clear? Timofei nodded, as though he had some things to say, too, that would clarify matters. He reached under his jacket, to the left side, under his armpit. Tim shook his head and spoke, just once, which looked like "No." Stas said, or his lips seemed to say, "What? What? You've got that shithead Aurlon?"

Then we came up to the altar, and the minister said, "Who gives this woman in matrimony?"

"Her mother and I do," I said.

Alexandra glanced at me and then I sat next to her.

Outside Timofei still had his hand under his coat, but as he began to bring it out, with something the size of a small brick in it, or just a lump under his jacket, one of those men from Boston, who glanced in our direction first, as though timing his action with the ceremony, made a quick movement, part with his elbow and then part with the palm of heel of hand. Timofei sat down on the clean yellow sand, not far from where my father was buried. The blood appeared between his fingers, the color of it like a Christmas ball, and as shiny, too.

The congregation strained with the effort not to look, but half-turned to the churchyard for a glance, the faces of these witnesses to the wedding at once solemn and horrified, but intrigued, too, and blinking with surprise, if not something like enjoyment. At least they were that way until Seymon reached under his coat and took out a revolver the color of those tombstones. Then, as though they could make this go away by pretending it wasn't happening, they turned back to the altar. There, at least, they found something they could depend on.

"And do you, Robert . . . ?" said the minister. But he glanced, too. Silence seeped into the church with such intensity that even the ordinary human sounds, breathing, shifting, sighing, the bubbling of indigestion, the creak of an old joint stopped, too.

One of the detectives with short hair and the earring put his hand on Seymon's wrist, moved to one side, and then, with his back to the congregation, as though breaking someone's arm could be done in a manner that was at once discreet and polite, brought his weight to bear. The pistol, as blue as fieldstone, dropped onto that sandy path. Seymon looked up and screamed, a harsh, guttural sound, which seemed to come from the steppes, from the Ukraine, or from someplace a long way from here, came into the church.

The congregation stared straight ahead.

"Go on," said Robert to the minister. "Finish. I'll take care of that later."

He stood up a little straighter. Pia held his hand.

That left Stas. He walked through the blood on the path, not bothering to put his hand under his coat, since he was too smart for that, and while Tim and one of the detectives leaned over the two men on the ground (do you put a handcuff on a man with a broken arm?), Stas came up to the window, directly opposite the altar. His eyes lingered on Robert, who turned once in his direction.

Stas's eyes came to the first row and then to me. Then he put one knuckle on the church window and tapped, once and then harder, his pale face with those scars against the glass, his breath making a cloud, but even so his expression was obvious, not exasperated but more profound than that, as though he had come up out of the ground to get what he had assumed was his only to find he had been cheated. He tapped the window.

"You," he said. He tapped the window, pointed at me. "You. You think I'll forget? Didn't we understand each other? Didn't we?"

• • •

"What did I tell you?" said Robert to the minister. "Are we having trouble understanding each other?"

Tim Marshall appeared behind Stas. I supposed Stas didn't even hear him coming. And, of course, like any good half-drunk cop who is ready to retire, he simply made Stas drop straight down, below the window, but we still heard against the side of the church a bone-hard *thump-thump*, where some part of Stas's anatomy, a knee, a hip, an elbow, hit the hard white siding twice and then stopped. The silence flowed back into the church.

Outside, Timofei kept his hands to his face, as though to hide what had happened, but the blood ran down his fingers and even his forearms, over his jacket, now dripping from his elbows onto the yellow sand.

"Do you, Robert, take this woman, Pia Mackinnon, to be your lawful wedded wife . . . "

Alexandra began to cry. Stas appeared again, like a figure in a jack-in-the-box, standing up now with some help from Tim, although he was wearing some silver cuffs, his shoulders broad, his posture bent forward as he went back to the center of the cemetery.

The minister continued, and as he came to "I now pronounce . . . ," Tim and the men from Boston pushed Stas and the others out of the cemetery, around the headstones and out to a car, where Tim now pushed them in, and the local constable and the two cops from Boston got in, too, a close fit, and drove down the river, toward the closest town. Tim stood in the dust. The river was in the distance, so calm and constant, its movement as always.

Robert and Pia came out the church door and got into Robert's car, both of them glowing. Then the guests came out, too, all of them pretending that nothing had happened, aside from the man with a walker, who said, "Jesus. And I thought a graveyard was a dull place. I wonder if anything like that will happen when I'm here?"

Then his wife helped him into a car, and everyone, minister included, drove up to the reception. That left just Tim, me, and Alexandra, and Tim said, "Well, I've got to tell you one thing. That Aurlon Miller? Boy, was he pissed off when we picked him up on a rape warrant from Florida. He said he had a deal with you."

"Well, not quite," I said.

"That old girlfriend of yours?" said Tim. "She was crying when she called me. So, maybe she isn't so bitter anymore."

"Maybe," I said. "Let's have a glass of champagne."

"You know, Frank," said Alexandra. "I think you're going to have to keep your word to me, though."

"And what's that?"

"You remember the trip to Rome?"

"Yes, I do," I said.

We went through the churchyard, and there, by the small stone that marked my father's ashes, I rubbed those crimson spots, some as big as a silver dollar, into the soil, and when I couldn't do it with the dirt that was there, Tim scraped some sandy loam, too, to cover it up.

"Let's have a little respect for the dead," he said. "Right, Frank?"

• • •

At the reception, at the farm, with that white tent in front of the trout ponds, with the guests in their cheerful clothes, with that band playing a schmaltzy version of an old song, "As Time Goes By," Pia and I had that dance that is required of all fathers and all brides. She put her palm in mine, and her hand on my shoulder. I was reminded of those hours we had spent on the river, with those chips of light, so much like an impressionist painting.

She said, "So, that little bastard was trying to blackmail you?"

"Let's not talk about it," I said.

"You're beginning to sound like your father," she said. "Why didn't you tell me?"

"They could make it look like I had gotten rid of Aurlon and because of that, I might lose you. And a lot of other things. But mostly you."

We swayed to that schmaltzy but still effecting sound of "Just remember this . . . "

"I see," said Pia. "Well. I think Robert is right."

"About what?" I said.

"You know what he said?" said Pia. "Loving someone takes a lot more balls than you'd think."

"He said the same thing to me about marriage," I said.

"It's the same thing," said Pia.

[CHAPTER THIRTY]

IN LOS ANGELES, before the trip to Rome, Alexandra and I went to a party for a classmate of mine from Yale, Jack Middleton, who had worked for the studios in public relations and was going to retire. The party was in his house off Mulholland Drive, and we stood where we could see the hillside, which was more like Greece than anything else. At least that's what it probably looked like before they built all those houses. Jack told me that when he first bought this house thirty years ago, deer had come into the backyard, but now the deer were gone although the coyotes were moving in. I asked him if he was going to miss working at the studio, and he glanced at that brown hillside, where the coyotes hunted, and he said, "You can't imagine what scandals we faced. Fatty Arbuckle seemed shocking a hundred years ago, but let me tell you, things have gone downhill from there. You can't believe." He shook his head. "You can't believe."

"Oh," I said. "Maybe I can."

So, we left for Rome from California. Since this was a sort of honeymoon for Alexandra and me (and she promised me, too, that we would have fried zucchini flowers, as a way of sharing some romance of Rome with me), we went first class. And to Rome from California the best way was over the North Pole.

Our flight left early, around noon. I drank that good scotch and sat by the window, while Alexandra slept in her leather seat. Well, I thought. We will go to the Borghese gardens. We will eat a gelato and go to the Marcus Aurelius monument. It will not be that we are young, but that we are wise.

I couldn't sleep.

When I go somewhere, I want to check my pockets to see that I have my passport, my tickets, my confirmation of a rented car, a hotel room, directions to a house I have rented. It is a sort of ceremony of anxiety, and even now that I am all grown up and know better, I still do it, and that is how I took the twenty-celon note from my pocket. It had that nude woman riding a spiral galaxy, lightning bolts coming from her fists, her expression somehow more relaxed than usual. Still, as I put it in the pouch for trash, I saw, on the back, the Raver's script: "Be content to seem what you really are."

I put my fingers to my neck and then looked at the second hand of my watch: the pulse was normal, as regular as it had been years before when I was rowing six miles a day. I'd have to send Dr. Stevenson a telegram: no toaster filament was going to be shoved into my heart after all.

This was early enough in the year so that the pole was still dimly lit when we got there. Everyone else in the plane was curled up with pillows or blankets and seemed to be sleeping deeply. I sat there with my scotch, trying to think of nothing at all, but I noticed the plane was losing altitude. Down below, the whiteness had a gray cast, a sort of dusty quality as though something had burned nearby. The plane got closer to the ice.

The intercom came on. For a while it amplified some quiet but still excited breathing. Then the breathing stopped.

"Is anyone awake back there?" said the voice, which I guessed belonged to the pilot.

But, of course, I had no way to answer. Everyone was asleep, and I couldn't very well shout, Yes, yes, I'm awake. What's going on? In fact, I thought of getting up and walking through the dim aisle to knock on the cockpit door. But these days, with the marshals here and there, all armed, I thought that maybe it was best just to nod my head, which made me feel stupid.

The plane lost more altitude.

The voice said, "Look out the window." The voice of the pilot was now intense, boy-like in its amazement, as though it had seen some previously forbidden thing but which was now visible for the first time.

Down below on the gray ice, which looked like the moon, something moved. It seemed gray, or gray-white, almost like the color of the ice, and yet it was brighter than that, more luminescent. And it seemed to move with a gait that was almost familiar.

The plane dropped a little more.

And then, as it lost even more altitude, the plane went into a long, slow turn, one wing dipped down. I was on the side of the airplane that was tipped down.

The thing on the ice kept moving. It seemed to be unconcerned with the texture of the ice cap: here and there cracked ice was pushed together into a kind of icy clutter, like a broken window that has been swept into a pile, and it appeared, too, that the wind had cut long gullies in the ice. It went forward in a straight line, only moving around a pile of ice that was almost vertical: mostly the creature wanted to get away from the enormous thing that could be circling in for the kill.

"Do you know what that is?" said the pilot.

I shook my head, although I was beginning to have my suspicions.

The plane made a wide circle, at an altitude that was pretty low. Perhaps I couldn't really see the texture of the fur or the flab of the thing as it ran in a way that suggested not haste, not hurry, but a perfect horror. It wanted to get away. The shadow of the airplane made a large black cross on the ice, slipping over the dry riverbeds like a piece of gray silk, its movement, at once so smooth and seemingly remote from the nature of the landscape, made the bear's terror all the greater: whatever was pursuing it did so with an ease that had almost no concern for the obstacles the bear faced. Then the bear began to bound, its legs reaching out, its entire aspect like a creature that is trying to jump over the things in its way. It didn't look over its shoulder, just straight ahead since nothing was to be gained by looking back. And in that headlong rush, I thought of the bear my father and I had faced, and that Robert and I had faced, and the moment of realizing one's own capacity for the worst. Is that what my father meant when he passed over the rifle? And just who was it for? What self-loathing did that animal inspire in me by its dignity and perfection? Or maybe it is better to say: the animal let me look into the dark, the entire gloom, where all one's fears reside. At least I had given Robert the Mannlicher that had come down from my grandfather to my father to me and now to him. What else can I call it but the cascade of being a man?

The plane gained altitude, and as it did, as it made a long, deeply banked turn over those broken sheets of ice, the rills all disappearing into the perspective of distance, I looked back at the creature that kept running. Then I went back to that drink and the gentle presence of Alexandra, who slept next to me.

Maybe, she had said, we'll get away from Rome. Let's rent a car and drive to Umbria. Hey, Frank, what do you say?

The plane landed. Since we were flying first class, we got off right away, right behind the pilots and the engineer, three of them altogether, dressed in blue jackets with gold buttons and gold strips on their sleeves. Two of them looked very sleepy, but one was wide awake.

"I saw the bear," I said to this man.

"Did you really?" he said.

"Yes," I said. "I saw the bear."